The Tree Farm

Seth Sjostrom

wolfprint**Media**

wolfprint, LLC
P.O. Box 801
Camas, WA, 98607

For information, contact wolfprintMedia.

The Tree Farm / by Seth Sjostrom. - 1st wolfprintMedia edition

Trade Paperback K

ISBN-13: 978-1-7350236-5-6

1. Aaron Shepherd (Fictitious character)-Fiction. 2. Cara Shepherd (Fictitious character)-Fiction 3. Romance-Holiday-General- Fiction.

First wolfprintMedia Digital edition 2020. wolfprintMedia is a

tademark of wolfprint, LLC.

For information regarding bulk purchases, please contact wolfprint, LLC at wolfprint@hotmail.com.

United States of America

Acknowledgements

Kathi Sjostom for helping me find the right path on my walk and doing her best to keep me on it. Battle on, we'll find a way. We always do.

Tom and Linda Sjostrom for their support and belief in me.

Hayden, my eternal inspiration.

One

Sweet giggles chorused throughout the Shepherd house, heralding the fact that it was Sunday afternoon. Once home from church, it was the one day in the week where the entire family could enjoy being together unburdened by work and chores.

Annie and her younger brother Chase sat on their bellies watching television. On the couch, their father glanced over his laptop to take in his children's laughter at what played out on the screen, occasionally sharing a chuckle himself.

From the kitchen, Cara Shepherd was elbow deep in pastry dough, enjoying the joyful sounds of her family. Each with their own activity, but they were all together under the same roof, just the same.

Aaron Shepherd also reveled in his Sundays with the family, even if he had a little workweek prep to complete. Just being together fueled him to tackle the hectic schedule to come. Hearing his children squeal in response to a commercial, he peered over his work.

The television showed a family huddled around a kitchen table, laughing and cheering as they maneuvered their pieces around a game board.

"Well, Christmas isn't *too* far away, why don't you two start making a list," Aaron suggested.

Annie and Chase's eyes went wide at the idea.

"You get the pencils, I'll get the paper!" eight-year-old Annie directed, sending her little brother streaking for the den where their homework supplies were kept.

Soon the children were busy scrawling their ideas on green sheets of paper, taking cues from commercials that played on the television. "I want *that* game, of course," Chase gleamed, scribbling on his paper.

"Me too!" Annie nodded. Her eyes widened, "And a Purrfect Pet kitten. They purr when you pet them, so cute!"

"I'm thinking the new game system, time for an upgrade," Chase grinned.

"How about you, honey?" Aaron called out to his wife, who had launched into full pre-holiday baking mode.

"I don't suppose a cruise or trip to Hawaii is in the budget..."

Aaron sang back, "Could be, if I get that promotion. It's looking good for the beginning of the year!"

"Well, I'll be happy with whatever, as long we are all together, and you have some time away from work and computers," Cara added.

"Fair enough, I think I can manage that. Not sure how I wrap such a thing...."

"You can wrap it in bows on our outside lights, how's that?" Cara suggested.

"I tell you what, once our bellies are full of turkey and stuffing this Thanksgiving, I'll tie up the bows, string the lights, the whole works," Aaron replied.

"Sounds good to me, just no kids on the ladders..."

Chase spun to his dad, "I want to go up the ladder!"

"I think you and Annie better be ground support. I'll need help keeping the bulbs off the ground."

"Oh, alright," Chase shrugged and returned to his Christmas wish list.

Cara came out and wrapped her arms around her husband, a kitchen towel draped over her shoulder. "How about you, what do *you* want for Christmas?"

Aaron looked thoughtful, "You know, if we got each other the same thing – time together, no distractions, I don't think I could ask for more."

"At least we're easy to shop for," Cara giggled, giving her husband a quick kiss.

"Are you ready for a family movie? I think the kids have been inspired by the wish list brainstorming. Too early for a holiday movie?"

"Pies are in the oven. I am all yours. I would *love* a holiday movie," Cara said, sinking on the couch. Annie and Chase joined them, each snuggling into the side of either parent. Cara gave Annie a squeeze and leaned her head on Aaron's shoulder.

"Sundays in the Shepherd household," Aaron whispered in his wife's ear.

"Doesn't get much better," she cooed, as the movie started.

Two

Mondays in the Shepherd household did not hold a lot in common with Sundays. Cara and Aaron scurried around in a pre-caffeinated fog. Annie and Chase rushed to eat their oatmeal and finish getting ready to catch the bus.

Cara saw to it that the coffee was brewing before swapping the master bathroom with Aaron. As much as she hurried to get the kids ready, it was herself that was usually pushing the clock. Ensuring the household was in order before seeing to her own readiness, typically left her scrambling as she readied to go to her substitute teacher slot, double-checking her phone to see which school she was going to that day.

Aaron slid into the room, placing a cup of coffee prepared to his wife's liking on the bathroom counter. Returning to the kitchen, he poured himself a cup coffee while reviewing the emails that poured in overnight.

One by one, he kissed his children on their heads as they wheeled through the kitchen to grab their lunches. Coffee in hand, Aaron pulled out a notebook and started sketching out his day.

Cara streaked through the kitchen, pouring the remainder of her coffee into a thermos and gave Aaron a kiss. "I've got kids to the bus, and then I'm off to Mountain View Elementary."

Picking up his coffee, he followed his family to the door, "Have a good day, guys. I'll see you after work."

"Bye, Dad!" Annie and Chase chorused as their Mom ushered them out.

"Love you guys!"

"Love you too!"

Smiling, Aaron closed the door and sauntered upstairs to finish getting ready himself.

Smearing shaving foam over his face and peering into the rapidly fogging mirror, he reignited the month-long battle he waged with himself. Work had overwhelmed them over the course of the year, and they were long overdue for a vacation. A trip to Hawaii in February when winter had worn out its welcome in the Pacific Northwest would be an enormous treat. He pictured the kids playfully being chased by the incoming surf, racing towards the beach while Cara quietly smiled over her book observing them.

He had promised Cara and the kids a vacation for so long, but like the kids in his vision being chased by waves, they always seemed to be chased by finances, never quite gaining enough ground. This year would be different as the promotion his boss had all but promised was his finally became official.

Smiling, he checked his blade work, smoothing his hand over his face. He nodded to himself, Hawaii vacation for sure. But then he thought of Cara. When they got married, all he could afford was a simple wedding band. Digging into his travel kit past his travel toothbrush and razor, he pulled out the deposit slip on a diamond ring. He mulled whether he would give it to Cara on Christmas or now that his mind was made up – in Hawaii.

Properly cleaned up and attired for the day, Aaron gathered his things for work. Picking up an envelope on top of his day planner, he studied it briefly. Recognizing the logo stamped on the back, he knew it as the bill for the brakes and tires on the family SUV. Setting it aside, he knew the next paycheck would cover it, he and Cara could use the following paycheck to tackle Christmas presents.

Sliding on his coat, Aaron grabbed his computer bag and thermos of coffee. Freeing his keys from their hook, he opened the door to leave the house. Just as he was shouldering the door shut, his phone began chiming in his jacket pocket.

Shouldering his computer bag, he hit the answer button and wedge it between his ear and shoulder as he made his way to his car. "Hey Dan, what's up? I was just heading to the office."

"You…you clearly have not heard," Dan, Aaron's co-worker and friend, stated, his voice an octave higher than usual and an accelerated pace.

"Heard what?" Aaron paused outside of his driver's door.

"It's over, Aaron. It's all over. The company is shuttered."

"What?" Aaron leaned against his car, moving his cellphone to his hand.

"Final paychecks will be issued to last Friday, and that's it. Oh, and that pension program that was "at-risk" …looks like it is gone too," Dan reported, his usually jovial voice drenched in despair.

Aaron furrowed his brows, trying to make sense of what he was hearing. "Tell me this is not a done deal. There has to be something we can do."

"I wish I could tell you I was kidding. Man, there are literally locks on the door."

"What do we do now?" Aaron asked, to himself as much as to his friend.

"Look, I gotta go. My wife is freaking out … we have a kid on the way. Let's catch up later and figure things out," Dan replied.

"Yeah, sure." Aaron hit the End Call button.

For several long moments, Aaron stood motionless in his driveway. When the late fall chill shocked his system back into action, he spun away from the car and retreated to the house.

Reeling from shock, he blankly sat his computer bag and thermos on the counter. Numbly, he added his keys to the pile.

Tossing off his coat, Aaron opened his laptop. Hitting the power button, he settled in as though this is how his day had been planned all along, if in an automaton fashion.

Selecting a job search site, he began scrolling through options near home. Slowly, as he picked through the disappointingly small list, he started widening his search geography. Next, he began stretching his scope of jobs to apply for.

Digging in, Aaron fired off a dozen resumes before his inbox alert captured his attention. Instinctively, he opened it. The travel agent sent him an itinerary and invoice for his approval. His eyes fell on the total.

With a sigh, Aaron rubbed his eyes. Inspired by his early search, he wondered if his plans could squeak through. Clicking into his online banking, Aaron pulled up his and Cara's combined account page. His heart sunk into his stomach, and when he saw their balance.

Aaron knew they were still paying off school loans and catching up with putting everything they had into the house. He didn't fully realize that they had been limping through with no savings at all. That meant not only could they not afford the trip to Hawaii, after paying the month's essential bills, they would barely have anything left, and that was before their mortgage payment.

Slumping in his seat, he stared at the bank statement. As hard and long as he tried, the numbers did not change.

Three

Aron had barely lifted his gaze off of his laptop screen all day. In between sending out resumes, he obsessively checked his work email, hoping there would be some change in the status. Aside from an email at precisely eight A.M. telling him and his coworkers what they had already heard by then, his inbox remained empty.

Curious, he sent his corporate email a test message from his personal account. In moments, his own email bounced back with a message explaining that the company was shut down and offered a public relations contact for inquiries. Knowing that is the message the world saw when his clients and network partners tried to reach out to him was disheartening and cemented the fact the company was indeed no more.

Rubbing his chin, he switched back to his job search when he heard a rattle at the door. Turning from his laptop, Aaron watched Cara, and the kids stream into the house.

Cara leaned back, startled to see a figure at their kitchen table. A smile swept across her face, "Hi, honey, I didn't know you'd be home."

"Yeah," Aaron laughed sheepishly, "I didn't either."

"Daddy!" Annie cried out and rushed to give him a hug with Chase close behind her.

Aaron quickly closed his laptop and offered his family a smile and widened his arms, pulling his children in close, "Hi guys."

"Since you're home, can you help me with my homework? I need to write a paragraph on what I want to be when I grow and find pictures that show that job," Annie asked.

"You bet," Aaron replied, "How about we get you and your brother a snack first."

Giving Cara a kiss as he walked into the kitchen, he pulled out two plates and started spreading peanut butter and strawberry jam on slices of bread. Getting the kids settled at the table with their snacks, Aaron caught the knowing look on his wife's face. Nodding, he walked into the kitchen. Grasping her by the hand, he led her around the corner.

"So, what *is* going on?" Cara asked in a hoarse whisper.

Aaron swallowed hard, looking past his wife to collect himself before squaring his eyes on hers,

"You know how there have been rumors about changes at work?"

"Yes, so you heard something today?"

"Oh, we heard something alright. I got a call right before I headed in this morning. They…they, uhm…they're shutting the company down."

Cara covered her mouth with her hand, "They what? When?"

"Effective immediately. Our last paycheck will go through last Friday," Aaron replied.

"What? How can they do that, don't they have to give you notice, offer some sort of severance?" Cara asked.

"No. No, they don't."

"Well, at least you have your retirement," Cara suggested, watching her husband's eyes, she cocked her head, and her eyes widened, "We *don't* have your retirement."

"Our type of plan was heavily based on the company value and futures. No value and clearly no future, means no retirement," Aaron answered.

Cara stared off down the hallway, her mind spinning. "You heard this morning? Why didn't you call me?"

Shrugging, Aaron replied, "I was going to, right after I got the call. I just…I just kept hoping a notice would come that it was all a misunderstanding. I didn't want to trouble you."

"Trouble me?" Cara asked, grabbing Aaron by the collar and pulling him close. "You can't bother me, honey. Ever." Planting a kiss on her husband's lips, she looked at him, smiling into his eyes.

"You're right. We'll get through this together."

"We'll pray on it. Work at it. We'll be alright."

Nodding, Aaron shared, "I've already sent out over a dozen resumes."

"See, you are already on it," Cara grinned. "And, we have been catching up on everything…it will be a little tight, because catching up took most of what we had."

"I know. That worries me. I checked the account today and…"

Cara's face twisted, "Not much but dust and cobwebs, huh?"

"Pretty much," Aaron nodded.

"You're good at what you do. I bet you have a new job by this time next week."

"We'll see. The whole industry is a bit rocky right now, and with the holidays coming, hiring tends to slow down until new budgets come out after the first of the year," Aaron cautioned.

"Maybe I can work more hours," Cara shrugged.

"But the kids need you," Aaron sighed, "I don't know."

Cara stared at her husband. Placing a hand on his cheek, "I can only imagine how today has been for you. Let it go, for now, you have done what you can. We're together, and we will forge ahead one day at a time."

"One day at a time."

"Come on. You know what we need?"

Aaron looked suspiciously at his wife.

"Cookies."

"Cookies?"

"Cookies. You, me, Annie and Chase. In the kitchen, stat!" Cara commanded.

Hearing the word cookies exclaimed, the kids came careening around the corner. "Did someone say cookies?"

"I sure did," Cara gleamed.

"Can we help?"

"We are all helping. Go wash up, meet in the kitchen ASAP!" Cara clapped her hands as the kids sped away.

"You're pretty amazing. You know that?" Aaron said to his wife, squeezing her close.

"*We* are pretty amazing," Cara corrected.

Four

"Brrr…it's cold in here," Annie said, rubbing her shoulders.

"Good morning, sweetheart. I guess it is chilly in here," Aaron nodded at his daughter. "Why don't you put a sweatshirt on, and I will build a fire?"

"Can't we just turn up the heat?" Annie asked.

"Well, we are trying to conserve a little."

"Conserve…we learned about that school. Like save stuff and not waste stuff," Annie pondered.

"Yes, that's right."

"Ok," Annie nodded. "I'll go get my sweatshirt."

Aaron went outside a grabbed a handful of wood. The early November air had indeed become crisp. The top logs had a light layer of frost on the top.

Heading inside, he made little paper balls and crisscrossed a few dry, smaller logs. Within minutes, he had a roaring fire as the patter of slipper-clad footsteps sounded behind him.

Annie snuggled up next to her Dad, feeling the warmth from the fireplace insert. "You know, I kind of like this conserve stuff. It's kind of cozy."

Aaron chuckled, "You know, you're right. It *is* cozy."

Snapping his fingers, he added, "How would you like some hot cocoa? I was just about to make coffee to make sure it was ready for when Mommy gets up."

Annie's eyes widened, "That would be great! With marshmallows?"

"Of course," Aaron grinned.

As the room warmed, the household woke to life. Chase joined Annie with a cup of cocoa, and Cara snuggled on the sofa next to her husband, each with a warm mug of coffee.

"This is kind of nice," Cara smiled.

"It is," Aaron admitted.

"Are you working today, Daddy?" Chase asked.

"I have some computer work to do, but I'm not going anywhere today," Aaron replied.

"Can we work on our Christmas lists again? It's almost Turkey Day!" Annie asked.

Aaron shot Cara a glance, "Sure, but...make sure to add an assortment of things, big and small that you would like this year."

"Great idea," Annie exclaimed, and the snapped her fingers, "Like for stockings!"

Aaron nodded, "Like for stockings."

"Are you guys done with your cocoa?" Cara asked.

"Almost," Chase answered, looking deep into his mug as he swirled it. Pulling the mug tight to his mouth, he lifted the mug as high as he could, helping gravity drain every last chocolately drop.

Pulling the cup away, revealing a brown mustache the ran along the entire length of his upper lip. "Now, I am. Thank you, Mommy. Thank you, Daddy, for making it."

Cara took his mug and collected Annie's as well.

Aaron followed his wife into the kitchen.

"This was a nice morning," Cara said. Her voice was chipper, but Aaron knew Cara well enough. Her smile was genuine, but somehow incomplete. It was a veil for a deeper emotion.

"It was a great way to start the day. The fire really makes most of the downstairs feel comfortable," Aaron replied. "Now, why don't you tell me what is bothering you beneath that beautiful smile."

Cara sighed. Pursing her lips, she shared, "I hated to stress you even more. The mortgage company called again. We are way past their grace period. They are going to start taking action against the loan."

"I see," Aaron said. Disappointed, but not hopeless. "Did you have a chance to talk to the realtor? What did she say?"

"It's a buyers' market. A terrible time of year for home sales, but she thinks she can sell it," Cara answered.

Aaron nodded as he listened, absorbing her news. "I'm not sure we have much of a choice."

"Where will we go? We won't be able to get another loan," Cara cautioned.

"We can't keep the one we have. We'll figure something out. First thing first, see if we can sell this house anyway and see how much we can get. Might be enough to float us until I have a paycheck coming in again," Aaron suggested.

"Ok," Cara's voice was resolute, "I'll let her know to list it."

Aaron hugged her tight.

"Any leads on jobs? How about that medical device company?"

Aaron furrowed his brow, "They weren't the right fit. They wanted someone who could withstand a long sales cycle and only get paid on contingency when I completed a sale. I did get a call back from the laboratory company. They sound interested. I have a follow-up interview with them after Thanksgiving."

"Well, that's good. When would you be able to start?"

"That's the thing with that job. It doesn't start until mid-January."

"I see."

"I have others I am following up with, too," Aaron replied. "I am looking at some filler jobs, too."

"Oh? Like what?"

"Well, you remember that tree farm up on Maple Hill?" Aaron asked.

Cara nodded, "Didn't we get a tree from there a few years ago?"

"Yes. It was nice up there. Trees were a bit rough, but had a genuine quality about them I guess. It would bring in some much-needed money. Probably not near enough, but it is not like sitting behind my computer is going to pay the bills," Aaron added.

"Yeah, it is something to consider if a job doesn't turn up that starts before the end of the year," Cara agreed. "I mean, you working at a tree farm?"

"I won't have to wear a tie," Dean shrugged.

"Just never pictured you the manual labor type," Cara giggled.

"I work hard, whether behind a desk or on my feet," Aaron looked cross.

"Like I said, something to consider."

Looking across the room at his laptop and back to his wife. "Yeah, something to consider."

Five

Aaron tiptoed through the house. Setting the coffee pot to brew and got a fire started while his family still slept. Digging through the pantry, he found the thermos that he took to work each morning. Filling it up, he was startled to hear a soft voice behind him.

Turning, he saw Chase rubbing tired eyes. "Where are you going, Daddy?"

"Good morning, Chase. You're up early, buddy."

Kneeling to give his son a hug, he looked at him, "You remember at dinner last night, I told you guys I was going to work this week."

"At the Christmas tree place?"

"That's right. At the tree farm on Maple Hill," Aaron said.

"Ok," Chase said sleepily. He shook himself and looked sternly at his father, "But I'm going to miss you."

Aaron chuckled and tussled his son's hair. "I'm going to miss you too, pal. You look after the girls for me while I'm gone?"

"Ok, Daddy."

"Good. I'll see you around dinner time. I love you, pal."

"I love you too, Daddy."

Aaron grabbed his key, slipped his jacket on and grabbed his thermos.

"Daddy?"

"Yeah, bud?"

"Can I watch cartoons?"

Aaron laughed. "You bet. Remember, we don't have cable anymore, but you can watch it on my laptop. Here, I'll get you set up, and then I have to run."

Driving to the farm, Aaron wound his way up the hills that overlooked town. His mind sifted through the unrequited resumes that he had sent out. The few interviews that had been accepted either weren't a fit for one reason or another or were delayed until after the holidays. As bills continued to pile up and the family's resources dwindling, the tree farm was at least a small contribution.

He had to admit, the further away from town that he drove, the more beautiful the scenery became. Soon the intermittent meadows and patches of forest gave way to rows of spruce, fir, and pine trees.

The peacefulness of the drive began to chip away at his nerves and stress. The further up the hill and away from town and traffic, the more at peace he began to feel. He could see why people lived out this way. If they worked from home or could stomach the commute, he imagined it would feel good to shed the worries of life away as you left town.

Coming to a driveway with a worn sign attached to an old pine arch that straddled the drive, Aaron pulled in. Following the winding gravel drive until it emptied into a parking lot that was encircled by several buildings. Directly at the end of the lane was a large home with a wide covered porch. To the right of the house was a large barn. On the opposite side parking lot was the tree farm store and tree staging area. Aaron pulled his car to a stop just outside of the store, which like the house, had a deep covered porch.

Putting the car in park, Aaron got out and looked around. Not seeing anyone to greet him, he stepped up onto the store's porch and leaned against a rail. The view from the porch allowed him to see the lower lot. The early morning sun peeking over the ridge bathed the farm in a soft, golden glow.

"Well, you're timely, I see. Good," a voice called from the side of the porch, near the tree staging area.

"Good morning sir, I'm Aaron Shepherd," holding out his hand, he received a sturdy shake from the grizzled man who approached.

"I'm Hal Jennings. Welcome to Maple Hill Tree Farm."

"Thank you, sir. My wife and I bought a tree from here a few years ago," Aaron shared.

"So, you said on the phone," Hal Jennings studied Aaron. "You don't mind me saying, you don't look much like the farm type."

"I'm a quick learner, and I work hard, sir."

"Well, this ain't rocket science, but it does require hard labor," Hal admitted. "You brought gloves?"

Aaron nodded, "Yes, sir."

"Good, you're gonna need them. But, drop the sir stuff. That worked for my granddad and my dad, who worked the farm before me, but I prefer Hal."

"Sounds good…Hal," Aaron replied. "I am ready to go if you are."

Aaron pulled out his gloves and slapped them in his hand.

"Well, let's say we give you the lay of the land first," Hal suggested and then paused. "You like a mug of coffee before we go?"

"I have a thermos in the car that I haven't quite finished."

"Very well. Grab it and meet at the barn over there. I'm gonna grab my own mug if you don't mind," Hal said and slipped away towards the house.

A few minutes later, the farmer reappeared with an enamel-coated mug, steam billowing out of it. Nodding towards the big barn door, he asked, "Give me a hand with this, will you?"

Together, they yanked on the big barn door and slid it open with their free hands.

Just inside, the barn was a four-wheel-drive utility vehicle. "Hop in," Hal said as he cranked the key on the farm vehicle. Sliding into the passenger seat, Aaron complied.

"Kind of like a four-by-four golf cart," Hal said, pressing the accelerator, launching the vehicle forward.

Careening through the rough trails of the farm, Hal pointed out the layout of the farm. He showed Aaron where the lots for each varietal were and how the growth stages for the future crops were cultivated. Passing several more outbuildings, Hal shared which had tools, water pumps, and other items needed out in the fields.

The tour took them to the top of the ridge, where rows of tall evergreens towered above them. Aaron looked at them, curiously, "Planted for the farm?"

"My grandfather's plantings. He had hoped to sell trees to the White House or Rockefeller

Center or something where a beautiful tall tree would be requested."

"Did you ever send one to the White House or Rockefeller?" Aaron asked.

"No," Hal shrugged. "Sent a few to the state capitol though, over the years."

Aaron nodded, taking in the sheer size and beauty of the trees.

Hal swung the Gator around a circle at the end of the trail. Pointing the vehicle back the way they had come.

"Wow," Aaron said, taking in the view from the top of the ridge. "You can see the whole town from up here."

"Laura…she was the love of my life until she was called by God a few years back…I loved it here. Used to say if she ever felt lonely, she would come up here look out over the valley. She was a country girl at heart, but as you can see, not too many neighbors up here," Hal shared.

"I can see why she loved it. It is amazing," Aaron offered.

"Well, that is about the run of it. We can head back. I'll get you set up with the day's chores. Got no shortage of them. I don't mind telling you, the farm has been harder and harder for me to keep up. I'm afraid I am running a bit behind schedule again this year," Hal admitted.

"No worries, Hal. I'll do what I can to see if we can't get Maple Hill Tree Farm back on schedule," Aaron said.

The farmer studied Aaron for a long moment. "It's good to have you here."

Aaron smiled and clapped his hands together, "So what's up first!"

Maple Hill Tree Farm was as alive with activity as it had been in years. Aaron took to the manual labor and fresh air work environment well. Cutting down and hauling away the trees that weren't healthy throughout the farm while Hal tagged trees by categories.

Aaron drug two trees that didn't pass inspection towards the trailer that Hal had driven to the field with a big green tractor. Tossing the trees in the back amidst others that failed to make the cut, he noticed Hal pull out a candy cane striped tag and string it on a particularly lovely tree.

"What are those tags for? It seems you picked out a special tree," he asked as he headed for another struggling tree on the other end of the field.

Hal looked up at Aaron. "Well, it never fails, that each year, right before the holiday, a single mom or military family comes up and all the best trees are picked over. So, I tag a few to be saved, so that those who deserve a nice tree the most, get a beautiful one."

"That's nice, Hal. I like that."

"You want to pick a few?" Hal handed Aaron some candy cane tags. "I like to sprinkle them among the varietals."

Aaron took the ribbons, "I would love to, Hal. It sounds like kind of an important job."

Hal let out a laugh, "You sound like you appreciate a good Christmas tree almost as much as I do."

"Well, I love Christmas…everything about it. The story of Jesus, the decorations, songs, family, the way the season transforms a community…," Aaron recounted.

"Laura would have liked you."

Aaron looked grateful, "Now, that is my *second* honor. I wish I had met her."

"Practically Mrs. Clause herself," Hal declared. "You know, it's just about lunchtime. Why don't we finish off with this field and head in for a bit."

"Lunch!" Aaron smacked himself in the head. "I didn't even think about that."

Hal smiled, "I'll make sure you get fed. We've got a full afternoon ahead of us. Can't have my star tree wrangler sapped of energy."

"That's kind…"

"I won't even hear no if that is what you were about to say," Hal snapped.

Aaron nodded, "Sounds good, thank you. I'll get this field cleared in no time."

The field had been completed, Hal and Aaron drove the tractor back down the hill to the house. The farmer made quick work in the kitchen, a clattering of pans and dishes later, Hal placed two heaping plates of food on the table. "Hope you like elk steak. Got a freezer full, and with just me, it's darn near a lifetime supply."

"Sounds great. It smells delicious," Aaron said.

As Hal sat and grabbed his fork, he watched as Aaron lowered his head in prayer. When he was finished, Hal asked, "You a Christian man, Aaron?"

"I am. How about you, Hal?"

Hal paused before he spoke, "I am. Haven't been to church since...since Laura's service."

"Oh. I'm sorry."

Hal shook him off, "It's alright. I probably would've skipped a few services back in the day if she would've let me. I suppose I've skipped a few too many since."

"I could understand how it would be tough," Aaron said. "At the same time, the church community can be a great source of support."

"I suppose so. Not sure I needed, well...maybe *needed*, but didn't want support. I just wanted to be out here on the farm. Keep my nose in enough work to keep me distracted, enough of Laura to keep her close. Without all those eyes staring and feeling sorry for me," Hal laughed at himself.

Aaron sat silently for a moment, taking in Hal's sentiment. "Well, you're always welcome to come with my family."

"Thank you, Aaron," Hal said and then changing the subject, "How's your steak?"

"It's fantastic! The sauce on it really seals it."

"Laura's huckleberry and jalapeno glaze. All of the ingredients come right here from the farm," Hal shared.

"Wow. This is an amazing life out here, Hal."

"I like it," Hal nodded. Pointing at Aaron's clean plate, "You want some more?"

Aaron shook his head, "No, I'm good. Thank you. That was perfect." Picking up his plate, he slid his chair out from the table.

"Tell you what, I'll clean up, if you want to get started on the lower hill that runs along the driveway," Hal suggested.

"Will do. Thank you again for lunch."

"Think nothing of it. Had to feed myself anyway."

"Alright, I'm back to work," Aaron said, grabbing his gloves and heading out the front door.

Standing on the porch, he drew a deep breath, taking in the mountain air and view of the valley. Other than getting paid a fraction of what he had been, he was beginning to enjoy his interim job.

Six

"Well, how was it?" Cara asked as she ushered her husband to the dinner table.

"You know, it was actually a lot of fun. After being behind an airplane seat, steering wheel or laptop for the last decade, it was kind of nice working outside," Aaron admitted. "I've got callouses too. I'm told it'd kind of like a badge of honor."

"What did you do, Daddy?" Chase asked.

"Well, I helped Hal, he owns the tree farm, clear unhealthy trees so the remaining ones can grow even better. I helped him mark trees, so it would be easier for shoppers to identify them. Some will be brought to town and sold at the hardware store too. The truck for them comes the day before Thanksgiving, so quite a lot of work to do before then."

Annie wrinkled her nose, "That was fun?"

"Well, yeah. It really was. Oh, and I got to drive a tractor, and this little four-wheel-drive vehicle called a Gator."

"Now, *that* sounds fun!" Annie grinned.

Chase looked confused. "A Gator?"

"It's green and tough. I guess the name Gator made sense to the manufacturer," Aaron shrugged.

"I see," Chase nodded.

Cara cocked her head, "The kids are out of school Friday, but I have to go in for a workshop. Any chance that maybe the kids could hang out at the farm for a few hours?"

"Could I drive a tractor?" Chase blurted out.

Aaron laughed, "We'll see about the tractor. I'll ask Hal if he minds. I'll have to put the kids to work. In fact, I have a special project in mind for them."

"I hope it involves tractors," Chase said.

"Are there animals at the farm? I want to look after the animals," Annie declared.

"It's a tree farm, not an animal farm. Though up in the hills, there is always a chance to see deer or elk. And bunnies. Lots of bunnies," Aaron replied.

"How many other workers are there?" Cara asked.

"Just me…and Hal."

"I remember that being a big farm. It seems like a lot of work."

"It is, he tries to do as much of it as he can himself, it has to be overwhelming," Aaron said.

"What about that charming store? How does he manage that?" Cara asked.

Aaron shrugged, "I guess the Women's Auxiliary from where he and his wife went to church helps out when they can."

"I see," Cara said thoughtfully. "I'm glad you enjoyed it out there. Thank you for doing it for the family."

Aaron shrugged, "It is something until I am able to crack the market and get a corporate job again."

Seven

The next day, Aaron returned to the farm. He opened up the barn and began gathering the tools that he would need for the day. He waited for Hal to come out to greet him, but after several minutes, he decided to get started on working the next field where they had left off the previous day.

Hauling his second load of cleared brush and trees past the house, he finally saw Hal Leaving the barn in the Gator. Waving, he stopped the tractor. "Good morning, Hal!"

"Morning, Aaron. I see you got going alright,"

"Yep. Just cleared the field next to where left off. About to unload this and move on to the next. I think we'll have them cleared around lunchtime," Aaron said, point to the load of brush over his shoulders.

"Excellent. How are you with a machete? I'll show you how to shape them a bit later," Hal said. Looking sheepish, he added, "Sorry I wasn't out when you got here. Some mornings, this old back just doesn't kick into gear until it wants to."

"No worries. Glad to help. Need anything else?"

"No. Keep up the good work. I'll see you at the house at noon. Got some elk stew simmering. I'll follow you with the tags," Hal replied.

"Sounds good," Aaron fired up the tractor and gave a wave as he continued with his duties.

Driving the tractor to the spot Hal had designated for the brush, Aaron emptied the load and headed on towards the final fields. Circling the back of the house, Aaron guided the tractor between the rows of spruce, firs, and pines.

It was peaceful out on the farm. The only noise was from the rustling wind or from Hal and Aaron themselves. It was a far cry from the bustling sounds in town.

Aaron loved how the throbbing drum of the tractor's engine cascaded into the stillness of the mountain when he cut the engine. Pressing on the parking brake, he hopped out to tackle the next field. Behind him, Hal steamed up in the utility vehicle and commenced with his tagging of this part of the farm.

In the center of this field, Aaron noticed a towering maple, its broad branches reaching out in a circle from its center. The Christmas trees in this field planted in a circle emanating from the farthest-reaching limbs. A handful of scarlet and yellow leaves clung desperately to their perch while their siblings had long seen fallen or blown into the wind.

"Laura's second favorite place on the farm. You should have seen it a few weeks ago. It was like a brilliant ball of fire against the sky," Hal said, watching Aaron admire the tree. "My grandfather planted that tree. It was the first tree he planted here. There used to be a little bench that sat under it. My grandmother would come out and read while my grandfather tended to the Christmas trees. My mother said she used to sit with me out here while my father worked the field. Laura visited with me out here as well. She would make picnics in the summer, and we would come out here and sit under the tree," Hal shared.

"Sounds amazing. I can imagine how it must look in its summer and fall glory. Something about it even now, lording among the evergreens," Aaron said.

"Yeah. It is kind of a sentry for the farm. Funny the things we get attached to," Hal laughed.

"It's a good thing. Especially how your entire family has enjoyed it. It's nice."

"Well, enough nostalgia, for now at least. We've got days before this place is supposed to open, and we have lots left to do," Hal said. His voice was cheery, but Aaron could detect the concern.

"You bet. I promised to get the farm back on schedule. We'll make it happen," Aaron assured.

Keeping up with his promise, Aaron worked hard throughout the day. He worked on shaping the trees and clearing the brush, maintaining the trails that wound from field to field. It was an exhausting day, but he felt as though he had accomplished a lot.

Returning the tractor to the barn, Aaron closed the doors for the night. Looking up, he saw Hal waiting for him on the porch.

"Well, another solid day in the books," Aaron smiled.

"Sure was. You are a hard worker. I like that," Hal nodded.

"So, I'm new to getting this farm ready for Christmas thing, where are we at and what is left to get done?"

"You've done a great job getting the fields prepped. Most of the shaping happens earlier in the year, but we'll finish whatever individual clean-up we need to do. Otherwise, tidy things up to get ready for guests. Next up is getting the trees earmarked for delivery to town cut down and ready for transport, but we'll wait until the days before the truck comes to do that. I have already marked them, but it is a good day's work or two to do that. Will you be able to be here the two days before Thanksgiving?" Hal asked.

Aaron nodded, and Hal continued, "The day after Thanksgiving, we have a route of tree deliveries, and the farm opens for business."

"What about the store?" Aaron asked.

"Since Laura passed, the Ladies Auxiliary usually comes out for a weekend and tidies up a bit. I'm not sure about this year. We'll have our hands full prepping the trees. We need to get the saws sharpened and ready and get the tree prepping area ready to go too," Hal looked a bit exasperated as he recounted all of the steps that still needed to be done.

Aaron smiled, "I think we can handle all of that. I'll be here every day to ensure we are ready for your guests."

"I like that. That is what Laura called our customers too- guests," Hal grinned. "Well, you should get back to your family. Thanks for your hard work, Aaron. It's been nice to have you around."

"My pleasure, Hal. I've enjoyed it. I'll see you bright and early tomorrow," Aaron replied.

Heading to his car, Aaron put the key in the ignition. He paused as he put the car in reverse to back out of his space, noticing Hal pulling a few pieces of wood from a severely dwindling pile and heading into the house.

Slipping the vehicle in park, Aaron snapped off the ignition. Recalling a rough cut pile of logs behind the barn, Aaron grabbed his gloves and got out of the car. Finding an axe, perched in the lean-to of the barn, he began placing logs on their end and swung the axe down to split them. Tossing the split pieces into a pile, he grabbed another chunk of wood and repeated the process.

As Aaron began working on his sixth log, a light bounced around the corner of the barn. The light came closer, and Hal called out, "I thought you were going home?"

"I noticed the split pile by the house was getting a bit lean. The nights are getting colder, figured I'd replenish it real quick," Aaron shrugged.

Hal looked a bit taken aback. "Well, I can't stand around and watch you, I'll grab the other axe."

Watching the surly farmer wince a bit as he lifted the other axe, Aaron called out, "Tell you what. I'm making pretty quick work of the pile, what do you say you grab the Gator and the small trailer from the barn, we'll have to get them from here to the house when I am done."

"Good point, I'll do that," Hal agreed.

Aaron lifted the axe high over his head and slammed it down on the next log.

An hour later, the dry rack by the house was replenished and the Gator was empty. "I'll add an hour to your pay," Hal said.

"No, you won't. This wasn't work, Hal."

Hal scowled, "Looked like work to me."

"Well, it was work, just not part of the farm work you are paying me for," Aaron laughed. "And I won't debate this with you."

Hal looked sincerely grateful, "You're a good man, Aaron."

"So are you, Hal," Aaron replied. "You good to put the Gator away?"

"I got it. You are already late to dinner with your family."

Nodding, Aaron admitted, "Yeah, I'll have to call Cara on the way down the hill."

Snapping his fingers, he suddenly looked sheepish, "Oh, I forgot to ask you, tomorrow is the end of the semester at my wife's school. The kids are out, and the teachers have a workday. She was hoping it might be okay if they worked with me for a few hours tomorrow. I'll make sure they don't cause any issues. They're good kids."

Hal laughed, "You don't have to sell me on them. Not much the kids can hurt around here, but plenty that can hurt them. Just keep them safe."

"I will. Thank you," Aaron replied.

"Thank you, Aaron. Now get out of here," Hal said, ushering Aaron towards his car.

Eight

Aaron arrived at the farm early. He wanted to get a quick start to provide Hal some assurance that they would get everything ready for the season. Pulling his collar up to fend off the morning chill, he opened the barn and prepped the Gator and the small trailer for the light-duty work he had that day.

Heading out, he set to start with the farthest field, high up on the ridge so that he could work his way back towards the house later in the day. Guiding the utility vehicle up to the upper crest, Aaron drove through the mist as the morning sun had yet to make enough of an appearance to burn it off.

Climbing to the turn-around at the very top so that he could orient the trailer to head down the trail, he paused at the overlook. Even through the chilly morning fog, the view was spectacular. The hills on the other side of the valley peeked through the mist, dotting the skyline as far as the eye could see.

Smiling to himself as he took a sip from his thermos, he started down the hill to kick off his day's work. As Aaron began trimming the most egregious of the odd branches on the Christmas trees in the high field, it wasn't long before he heard the tractor chugging up the hill.

As Hal headed up to the turn-around himself, he offered a quick wave as he spied Aaron amidst the trees. A few minutes and a few trimmed trees later, Hal parked the tractor alongside the Gator.

"Morning, Aaron!" Hal called.

"Good morning Hal. How's the back today?"

"Pretty good. Thought I was getting a good start of it, but I see you beat me nonetheless," Hal laughed.

Aaron nodded, "I wanted a good start to the day. Our to-do list doesn't daunt me, but by the same time, I know it isn't going to get done without a little time and effort."

"You remind me of me back in the day," Hal replied.

"I'll take that as a compliment."

"I think I meant it as one," Hal said, "You see a task, you complete the task. No excuses, just get the job done, whether it is behind a desk or out in the field in the middle of nowhere."

"Not a complicated philosophy, is it? I wish the corporate world agreed with our perspective," Aaron replied.

Hal furrowed his brow, "How did you land here on my farm, if you don't mind me asking. You certainly seem capable enough, just not exactly the farmhand type."

"Circumstances out of my control with the company I worked for. Our own success was our downfall. The faster we grew, the more our company leveraged itself against the future. They stretched beyond their means to the point where a marketplace pot hole sunk the hole ship...quickly. As employees, we pretty much lost everything. Not just our paychecks, but our retirements too," Aaron replied.

"I'm sorry. Right before the holidays, tough time to get hit with that."

"It is. No jobs like what we do available to start until after the first of the year, and even then, it's a pretty fierce market," Aaron shared.

Nodding, Hall acknowledged, "And that is how you end up on my farm. I'm sorry for your hardship, though I am grateful for your presence here."

"I think things happen for a reason. We don't always know what that plan is, we are just instructed to follow it," Aaron said.

"That's what Laura used to say. That's how I ended up taking over Dad's farm, too. I didn't set out to carry on the legacy of being a Christmas tree farmer. After a stint in the army, I expected to be an engineer. Dad got ill. Laura and I came back to see him and never left," Hal shared.

Aaron surveyed another tree and lopped off a stray branch. "There are worst ways to spend a lifetime and make a living."

"Certainly true. The living part can be a little rough. As in-town lots and big stores have been taking over the tree business for years, a tree farm is kind of relic of the past," Hal said thoughtfully.

"I suppose even the Christmas tree market has its cycles and changes with the times," Aaron said. "Still, there is something about nostalgia, especially with Christmas. That is why we came out and got a tree here a few years ago."

"And what about the last two years?" Hal questioned.

Aaron shrugged, "I guess with work and kids' schedules, we just grabbed one in town."

Hal raised his brows as if to put a stamp on his point.

"I get it. Well, let's control what we can control. Getting this farm ready for the season," Aaron said, waving his machete at the trees in the field behind him.

By lunchtime, Aaron had worked his way to the lower fields by the house. Hal had just parked the tractor alongside the house when a car came up the driveway.

Parking in front of the store, the car doors opened with two kids streaking out as they saw their father. Aaron put his machete in its sheath and knelt to receive full force hugs. Cara followed, her pace a bit more measured.

"Hal," Aaron called. "This is my family. My wife Cara and this is Annie and Chase - our two helpers for the afternoon."

"Fine looking family. Welcome to Maple Hill Tree Farm," Hal removed his glove and shook Cara's hand. "I was just about to scare something up for lunch..."

Cara smiled coyly, "I actually brought lunch with us, if that is okay. Probably not as amazing as the lunches you have prepared for you two, Aaron has urged me to add elk into our family menu."

"Sounds good, I'll set the table," Hal offered.

"I wish I could stay and eat with you, but I have to get to my end of semester workday, but I'll get the lunch out of the car. Annie, you want to help me?" Cara said, encouraging her daughter to follow.

Toting a casserole with Annie in tow with a pie for dessert, Cara walked the dishes to the table and bid her goodbyes.

Gathered at the table, the kids waited with their hands in their laps. Hal studied them briefly and understood what they were waiting for. "Dear father, thank you for the sustenance to nourish our bodies for this day as we are gathered to work...and play. We are grateful to be together at the farm and ask for your energy, wisdom, and grace as we get the farm ready for the holiday. Amen."

"Amen!" Annie and Chase said in unison.

Hal looked up and followed with his own quiet "Amen!"

As the kids dug into their plates, Hal studied them. "You two done much farm work before?"

Annie and Chase exchanged glances before shaking their heads and admitting they had not.

"We went to a pumpkin patch. They had animals," Chase said.

"Oh yeah? The one between here and town or out by Junction City?" Hal asked.

"By town, we went on a hayride," Chase said.

"They have the best Apple Cider donuts, have you had them?" Annie asked.

Hal smiled, "I have, in fact. They are quite delicious. That is the Jacobs' farm. Friends of mine."

"Do you guys remember coming up here? It was a few years ago," Aaron asked.

Chase looked confused, but Annie nodded her head, "I do. I remember you pulling us in a sled. Chase was in my lap. I rode the tree like a horse on the way back. It was fun."

"That's right. Chase was still pretty little. I think I carried him while I drug the sled," Aaron nodded.

Hal smiled, "That is the picture, the experience that we like to offer here at the Tree Farm."

"We should get back out there if we are going to get this place open in time to share that experience," Aaron suggested. "Let's put the leftover pie in the fridge and clean the dishes real quick for Hal."

Hal watched as the Annie and Chase hopped up and immediately carted dishes to the kitchen. Annie washed as Chase dried. Aaron put the pie away.

"Quite the crew. I expect this will be a productive afternoon," Hal grinned.

When the dishes were put away, Aaron gathered the kids to bring them to the field he was working.

"So, this is a Gator..." Annie said as they climbed into the small utility vehicle with Aaron.

Chase's eyes went wide, "Can we drive?"

Aaron studied his son for a moment and then scooting back in his seat, said, "Sure. Sit with me. I'll let you two take turns as we move from field to field today."

Chase climbed in his father's lap and grabbed the steering wheel, a huge grin spread across his face.

"Ready?" Aaron asked. Turning the key, he brought the Gator to life and slowly pressed the accelerator. With his hands lightly guiding the wheel while giving Chase most of the steering power, he instructed his son of which trail to follow.

Getting to the lower field just below the house, he had Chase park on the edge of the path.

"So, what do we do?" Annie asked.

"Well. I am going to trim any crazy branches. You guys can collect them and put them in the trailer behind the Gator. Then we go to the next field."

"And then I get to drive?" Annie asked.

"Yep, then it will be your turn," Aaron smiled. "It is going to take me a little bit to do the trimming, and I want to be able to use the machete. Why don't you guys play a bit, and then in about fifteen minutes or so, you can start collecting branches."

With that, the kids darted in and out the trees playing hide and seek. Aaron moved a few rows away from them and set to tackling his duty, cleaning up the rough branches. Aaron was warmed by hearing his children's giggles as he worked. It felt good to be able to focus on his job and have Annie and Chase near at the same time.

Hal leaned against the porch rail, blowing steam off of his coffee. From his perch, he watched as Aaron and the kids mixed work and play together. Every so often, Aaron would stop and love on his children before finding another tree to work.

The farmer didn't mean to gawk, but he was taken with the family and how they interacted. He and Laura had wanted children themselves, but they never were able to. Laura had set them with a fostering program with the church, and they had the opportunity to nurture several kids through that program.

He and Laura loved the kids that had stayed with them, and each year, he sends birthday and Christmas presents through the office that ran the program. Every once in a while he would receive a thank you card, photo or note. He enjoyed updates like graduations, weddings, and baby announcements. Direct interaction, however, was nearly non-existent.

Watching Aaron and the kids for a few more minutes, Hal returned to his own duties. It felt good to have Aaron and his family here, and he most definitely needed the help to get the farm ready for the upcoming holiday season.

Nine

Sunday was the first day of the week that Aaron hadn't gone to the farm. After enjoying a cup of coffee on the couch with Cara, they wrangled the kids to church.

Even after a hectic week, when all Aaron wanted to do was rest, he found Sunday service reinvigorating. It was like a weekly reset – focus on the family, a release of distractions, and reprioritization of what was truly important in his life.

While sitting in the pew, he prayed for provision and direction. He was lost in how to provide for his family, and the tree farm, while a blessing, was not enough for them to pay their bills, which were quickly spinning further out of control.

When the offering was a few rows ahead, Aaron squirmed in his seat. He felt his cheeks glow as he did not know what to do. He knew they barely had enough money that week for gas to get him to the farm and back. As the offering came by, Aaron shuffled in his pocket for his wallet. He had a ten and a twenty. It was all that he had for the week for gas to get to and from the farm. He felt guilty as he let it pass by.

Dipping his head, he prayed. He knew that faith was just that, faith. Fishing his wallet out, he pulled out the ten and reached into the row behind him to put it in the offering.

When worship was over, the Shepherd family mingled into the lobby, visiting with friends.

"Sorry to hear about the company shutting down, really affected a lot of people. How are you guys coping?" his friend John asked.

"Yeah, it's too bad. I invested a lot of myself into that company. A lot of people had," Aaron shared. "Didn't come at a great time, though not sure there is a great time for something like that. We'll be fine, I'm sure."

"Yeah, I figured as much. The financial rule, tithe ten, save ten and live on the remaining eighty percent. Comes in handy for times just like this, right?"

Aaron shuffled a bit, "Yep, exactly." He and Cara knew the rule, but got caught up chasing bills, keeping their cars running, squeezing financially into their home. They kept trying to get back to living in the margins, but had failed to do so.

"Well, let us know if there is anything we can do to help," John said. "Oh, the youth

Thanksgiving dinner is coming up. We are all pitching in, no more than $100 each family, and we should have the whole event covered."

"Sounds good. I'll make sure Cara knows," Aaron replied sheepishly.

"Hey, we are all going to lunch, why don't you guys come along?" John asked. "That new sandwich place is supposed to be great. A little expensive for sandwiches, but I guess they pile on the meat."

"Oh, I…we would really love to, but I think we have already have lunch in the slow cooker ready for us at home," Aaron said.

"No worries, have it for dinner and boom, you have your whole day ready to go. Come on, we'd love to have you guys join us," John urged.

Aaron shrugged, "Yeah, I'll see what the kids have going on and talk to Cara. I'll text you if we are coming."

"Alright, I hope we see you," John said and then saw his family and waved at them as they headed for the door.

Aaron let out a deep sigh. He was suddenly eager to collect his family and leave. Seeing Cara, he made a beeline for her. "You ready to go?"

"We have the Kitchen Mission today. We're supposed to pick a up a few cases of water on the way, don't let me forget, okay?" Cara said.

"Right, but…," Aaron started.

"Oh, there are the Pierce's. Will you grab the kids from their classrooms? Thanks, hon," Cara said and ran off to catch up to her friends.

Nodding, Aaron collected Chase first and then Annie. Walking hand and hand with both of them, he paused for a moment. Spinning to face them, he kneeled and pulled them in for a tight hug.

"I love you, Daddy," Chase said.

"I love you guys, too," Aaron said, collecting his emotions, he added, "It sounds like we have a big day ahead of us. You guys ready?"

"Yep, where are we going?" Annie asked.

"We are going to help people who need a little bit of help and maybe a bit of love," Aaron replied.

"Like what kind of people?" Chase asked.

"Well, people who don't have a place to call home or they lost their job...things like that."

Chase looked thoughtful, "You lost your job. Do you need help, Daddy?"

Aaron let out a laugh, "Maybe, buddy. Maybe."

Ten

Aaron recognized many of the families that had assembled for the afternoon's shift for the Mission Kitchen – a lodge-style community center with a commercial kitchen that served as a pop-up free restaurant for those in need. A small shop with essentials and grocery items was available as well, with the assistance of personal shoppers to guide them.

Aaron was happy to help, but he was also pleased to have an excuse to offer his friend John for not going out to lunch with his family.

Carrying in the cases of water stacked three high, he accepted the offer for the door to be opened and said hello to the families that were just settling into their duties. "Chase, you're with me. Annie, you're with your Mom," Aaron called over his shoulder.

Setting the water down at the end of a long row of tables, Aaron started opening the cases and had Chase line up the water bottles. Cara and Annie took over a station serving salad. They each donned matching aprons and slid on gloves, ready for the first guests of the day.

As they walked through, Chase bounced excitedly next to his dad. He already had a water bottle at the ready. When the first guest came through, Aaron looked up and smiled, "Hi, my name is Aaron."

The middle-aged man across the table looked up. Aaron had noticed it was the first time that the man looked up the length of the table. "I'm...I'm Teddy."

"Teddy, it is a pleasure to meet you. Are you from here, Maple Valley?"

"Uhm, I uh, no. Cartersville," the man said, looking a bit nervous.

"Cartersville...," Aaron thought to himself out loud and then snapped in recognition. "Honey. Cartersville has this honey farm and helps bee colonies through their non-profit program."

Teddy brightened, if just a bit. "Bees. Yes, the bee farm. A friend from school's family owns it."

"We went out there a couple of summers ago. Nice people," Aaron said.

Teddy looked thoughtful for a moment and then let out a little smile, "They are. They are good people."

"What brought you to Maple Valley, if you don't mind, that is."

Staring down at the floor and the glancing at Chase, Teddy was slow to speak, but Aaron was patient. "I made a mess at home. I had to leave, go somewhere."

"I can understand that. Starting over can be tough," Aaron admitted. Seeing the line build up, "Here's a bottle of water. If I get a chance, I'll stop by and say hello."

"Thanks...thank you," Teddy said.

As the next guest stepped, Aaron smiled, "Hi, my name's Aaron...."

The afternoon wore on, and the audience in the Mission Kitchen began to dwindle. The Shepherd family began helping clean up and put the Community Center lodge back into its standard form.

One of the guests that were funneling out abruptly turned and walked towards Aaron. "Excuse me."

Aaron looked up and smiled, "Teddy! What can I do for you?"

"I uh...I wanted to see if you needed help," Teddy responded.

Aaron hesitated for a moment. The brief conversation he had with Teddy as he made his way around to visit with as many guests as he could, he knew Teddy was searching for validation, for purpose.

"You know what, that would be great," Aaron said. "How are you with a broom?"

"I can do that," Teddy nodded.

"Here, you take this, I'll put the chairs up on the tables and Chase here can handle the dustpan," Aaron suggested.

Letting the work take the focus of a bit, Aaron asked, "What do you do for work, Teddy?"

Teddy stared down at the floor, hyper-focusing on the little line of dust he was compiling. "I uh, I get odd jobs here and there. Not easy finding anything that lasts too long," he admitted.

"You're telling me. I have been looking for work too," Aaron said, hoisting a chair and placing it on a table. "Shouldn't be as hard as it is. What do you want to do? What are you good at?"

Teddy shuffled a little. "Bees. I liked taking care of the bees. Not everyone likes them, but I do."

"Sounds like a special skill set. It's not always easy finding the job that fits your passion, but when you finally do...it can work out really well," Aaron said. With a quizzical expression, "How do you go about finding jobs taking care of bees?"

"I don't know. I only knew my friend's honey farm," Teddy replied. "I used to make the boxes that the hives go in. I liked that too."

"Like woodworking?" Aaron asked.

"Yeah," Teddy nodded.

Aaron laughed, "Another unique skillset. I am terrible with a hammer and nails."

Teddy paused for a moment and looked up at Aaron. A smile crept in the corners of his mouth,

"Yeah, they used to say I was the best at it. They had me make all the hives, said they were nicer than the ones they bought."

"Love to see them sometime. I'll have to check it out. Suppose the boxes you built are still out there?" Aaron asked.

"Yeah, I suppose. They're built pretty tough," Teddy replied.

"Ever think about going back?"

Teddy slumped, "I do. But...so much I can't take back. I don't know anyone would want me."

"I'm sure it's tough. With the holiday season coming, amazing things can happen. It can be a great chance to reconnect," Aaron said, putting the last chair on a table.

"Maybe," Teddy answered. The man's voice clearly conveyed that he was unconvinced that it would be a good idea, or he would be well received.

"Whatever the case, it's good to know you have skills to use whether going back or moving forward," Aaron said.

"Yeah," Teddy nodded, a bit absently. "Thanks for talking."

Teddy handed the broom back.

"Thank you for helping. It's a pleasure to get to know you, Teddy. Listen, if I happen to trip across a job for a beekeeper or a carpenter, how would I get a hold of you?" Aaron asked.

"You know those little one-room apartments by the bus station? I'm in the last one on the left," Teddy replied.

"If I see something, I'll come find you. I hope I see you here again, Teddy," Aaron shared.

Teddy nodded, "Yeah. Me too."

As Teddy left and the Shepherds put the last of the cleaning supplies away, Chase looked up at his father, "Where did all of those people come from?"

Aaron chuckled at the question, "There are people who need a little help all around us. Even in Maple Valley, which seems clean and everyone seems happy, there are those that struggle. Some have struggled most of their lives. Some just hit a rough patch and need a helping hand out of it."

"They seemed nice," Chase noted.

"They did, didn't they?" Aaron smiled. "Most of them likely are. Nice, good people can have tough times, too."

Chase nodded as he thought through the conversation.

"I'm glad we could help them. I hope they get better soon," Chase said.

"Yeah, I'm glad we could do what we could to help them, too," Aaron agreed.

Aaron looked thoughtfully at his son, "Sometimes they don't even need help."

"They don't?" Chase asked.

"No. Sometimes they just need to be listened to. Looked at in the eye like a person," Aaron shared.

"But they are people," Chase protested.

"Exactly," Aaron smiled and gave Chase's hair a playful tussle.

Eleven

"Well, we priced it to sell. We have hosted two open houses, and it is nearly Thanksgiving," Amy, the Shepherd's realtor recounted.

"So, what exactly are you saying?" Cara asked.

Amy looked at Cara and then Aaron. "I think the offer is the only one we are likely to get…until January. If you were able to hold out that long, I just don't see it."

Cara looked aghast, "But it is almost $30,000 under asking."

Amy nodded, "I know. The good news is it does just pay off your current mortgage."

"But that doesn't give us what we need to get by, find a more affordable home," Aaron said, looking concerned.

"I know. It is not ideal. But it sounds like you are up against the clock with the mortgage company. Getting out from under will at least take that burden off of your plate. I'm sorry, I just don't think we are going to get any other offers before action is taken on your house by your lender," Amy replied.

Cara looked at her husband, "What do we do?"

Aaron returned a grave look, "I don't know that we have much of choice. I guess we have to accept the offer and at least get out from under the mortgage."

"What do we do then? Where will we go?" Cara asked.

"I don't know. We will find a way," Aaron said softly.

Cara nodded solemnly, "We always do."

Twelve

Aaron's trips to the farm began feeling like a welcome escape. The beauty and solitude of the farm alone were welcome. But the work itself provided a mental break and outlet to relieve the stress of finances that were becoming increasingly challenging for the Shepherd household.

He smiled as he saw Hal waiting for him on the porch. He appreciated his time with the farmer, as well.

"Up early this morning," Aaron called.

Nodding, Hal answered, "Was wanting a strong start to the day. I was hoping you would help me on…sort of a different project."

"Sure," Aaron replied, "Whatever you need."

"Good. Hop in, we'll take the farm truck," Hal nodded towards the half-century-old red truck perpetually parked in front of the store.

Aaron was instantly looking forward to this new assignment as he had admired the truck each day he visited the farm. It's big rounded fenders and bright red paint job, the truck seemed as though it had leaped right out of a Norman Rockwell painting.

Climbing inside, Hal fired the up rebuilt engine and headed down the driveway. "This truck is amazing," Aaron said.

"1951 Ford F-1. It was my grandfather's. It was pretty well used and ultimately retired. My dad had moved onto more modern and frankly more usable farm trucks. This old thing was sitting collecting dust and rusting away in one of the outbuildings," Hal said as he guided them onto the main road down from the hill. "Laura had a painting in the store that had a truck just like It. She commented on it all the time. I started rebuilding it in secret one summer and gave it to her nearly as it is now for Christmas about fifteen years ago. Been a fixture outside the store ever since."

"It runs great," Aaron said.

"We loved it so much, we made it our primary vehicle," Hal nodded.

Aaron looked around at the immaculate interior of the truck, "Wow. I couldn't imagine. I am not exactly….mechanically inclined."

Hal laughed, "I wasn't either, until I was. It all seems complicated until you get beyond the shiny bits. Working the farm, when tractors or other things breakdown, not a lot of choice to but to figure things out."

"I suppose so," Aaron nodded.

"How are you with a hammer?" Hal asked.

"About as good as I am with a wrench, I suppose," Aaron shrugged.

"I have got to put better skillset requirements into my job descriptions," Hal winked at Aaron.

Pulling up to a building in Junction Pass, a neighboring town, Hal asked. "Mind grabbing the bag out of the back?"

Aaron went to the bed of the truck and reached over the gate to grab a large bag. Finding it cumbersome, Aaron had to use both hands to haul it up and out of the truck bed. Following Hal into the building, they made their way to a large room with stacks of plywood, lumber, and paint cans.

"What exactly are we doing?" Aaron asked.

"We," Hal said dramatically, "Are building the stage set for the Junction Pass Community School Christmas production."

Seeing the curious expression on Aaron's face, Hal added, "Most of the foster kids we had gone to this school. When we weren't able to take kids anymore, we started volunteering here. Well, Laura volunteered, I did as I was asked."

"I see," Aaron said, rubbing his hands together. "I am not sure how much help as a carpenter I will be, but I can lift heavy wooden things like a champ."

"That will be good enough to start," Hal grinned, and they began setting up saw horses and the tools that they would need for the day.

As the day grew long, Aaron and Hal admired the progress they had made, but realized they still had quite a bit left to do and with the farm closer to opening, this was the only day they had to get it done.

"Let me call in reinforcements," Aaron suggested.

Within an hour, Cara had arrived with the kids.

Giving his wife a kiss, Aaron smiled, "Thanks for coming, hon."

"Glad to help out. You caught me just as I was finishing with school and picking up the kids," Cara shared. Looking at the assortment of Christmas trees, gingerbread man and gingerbread house facades made out of plywood. "You two did all of this?"

"Well, Hal did. I was more of a shop hand, I think," Aaron admitted.

Hal put down his saw and walked over. "Don't let him sell himself short. He got the hang of it and began to resemble a craftsman himself."

"Yeah, just ignore the discard pile it took for me to get the hang of it," Aaron scoffed, noting the scrap wood leaned against the wall.

"I wouldn't have gotten this far without you," Hal pressed, "Unfortunately, we still have too much left to do."

"Well, where can we pitch in?" Cara asked.

Soon, Cara was busy with a paintbrush putting base coats on the set pieces and then following up with more detail work.

The kids followed their mom with trimming and decorations that Annie helped Chase glue and staple gun into place. Holding a piece of evergreen garland over a base of fabric snow they already fastened, they added a layer of detail.

Aaron and Hal were meanwhile connecting pieces with hinges so that they could fold into place but also be easily moved. For individual trees and candy canes, they made bases for them to stand on stage.

Soon, a little Christmas village of plywood was beginning to take shape. With a bit left to do, Hal asked Cara if she would order some pizzas, but he insisted on buying while they kept working.

Before long, they were all in a circle, eating pizza.

"I can't thank you all enough for coming and helping," Hal said.

"It's fun," Annie replied in between bites of pizza.

"I'm impressed. I don't know that I have ever seen my husband with power tools," Cara teased.

"I use power tools," Aaron defended himself, "Not as proficient as Hal, but I use them."

"You did fine," Hal assured. Casting his plate down, he added, "We should probably finish up and get you guys home."

"Home is a mess!" Chase blurted.

"Chase!" Cara started.

"What do you mean?" Hal asked.

"We have to move," Chase shared.

Hal looked puzzled, "You do? Where are you moving to?"

"We don't quite know yet," Chase shrugged. "We are looking at our options."

Hal nodded thoughtfully and gave Aaron and inquisitive look. Aaron waved him off.

"I tell you what, why don't you get the kids back. Hal and I can finish up, and I'll be home not long after you," Aaron suggested as they began cleaning up from dinner.

"Thank you for the pizza," Annie said.

Hal smiled, "Any time. Thank you for your help."

The stage sets completed, Hal drove back towards the farm. After a long, productive day, the two men rode in silence for most of the drive. As they started climbing into the hills, Hal asked, "So, what is this about your move? Not to pry, you don't have to talk about it…"

"No, it's fine. We were already on a short leash financially before the company shuttered. Not only were we surprised by the shutdown, we were expecting a healthy raise. We worked hard to get to break even. Unfortunately, we have not been able to build up any reserves. Chase had health issues when he was little, and it took us a while to dig out of the hole. Enough so that this latest snafu was, well... the last straw for our mortgage company."

"I see. I'm sorry to hear that," Hal said, "And Chase?"

"Oh, he's fine. A hundred percent," Aaron said.

"You don't know where you are moving to?"

"Not really. We had to sell quickly. I guess we were only able to manage one step of a two-step process so far. Not much available for rent, and we can't get a new house loan without me having a secure job," Aaron admitted.

The men rode in silence for a length of drive.

"One of those outbuildings, back behind the house. It is a guest cottage. Laura and I stayed in it when we were first married. Right now, it is just used for storage. You guys can move up here for a while...until you are back on your feet," Hal offered.

"Oh wow, that, this is so nice, but...," Aaron started.

"Come on, Aaron. It is no big deal for me. It would need to be tidied up a bit, and it only has a couple of rooms. It's not much, but the wood stove works great, and it has electricity. Besides, you would be ready there for work on the farm each morning," Hal pressed.

"Thank you, Hal. I will talk to Cara about it. It is very kind of you."

"I like your family. I would enjoy having you guys up there," Hal insisted.

"I appreciate that. We all like spending time with you as well," Aaron said. Sliding out of his seat, he closed the door and looked over the cab at Hal.

"See you in the morning, Aaron."

"See you in the morning, Hal," Aaron nodded.

Aaron returned home in time to kiss tired children and tuck them in their beds. Wading his way through moving boxes to the kitchen where Cara was packing less essential items and carefully marking the boxes.

Kissing his wife on the cheek, he thanked her for coming to help.

Slumping against the cabinet, Cara looked weary. "I was glad to help. Hal is a nice man."

"He is," Aaron nodded.

'What are we going to do? The car lender is up to three calls a day. We have already lost the house. My income is absorbed by our basic bills," Cara wondered out loud.

"I don't know. I send out resumes every night. I work all day at the tree farm. I don't know what else we can do right now," Aaron shrugged. "Hal has a bungalow on the farm. We can stay in until we figure something else out."

"That's sweet, but…"

"I told him we would think about it."

"How about your job leads, anything there?" Cara asked hopefully.

Aaron shook his head, "Nothing so far. Some bites for the new year."

Kneeling next Cara, he reached out to her shoulder and moved in for a hug. He was startled when she pushed him away. "I'm sorry, I'm just…I need to figure things out."

Aaron frowned, "Don't you mean we need to figure things out?

"Yeah, but I pay the bills. I see the stacks pile up. I need to figure out which to pay first…," Cara said.

"We are in this together. It was my decision to stay with the company and thought it was going the right way. I know we hung a lot on that," Aaron countered.

"Exactly!" Cara snapped.

Aaron looked away.

"I'm sorry, Aaron. I'm just overwhelmed," Cara said, realizing the heavy hand she dealt her husband.

"I know you are. So am I. But it's not your fight or my fight. It's our fight. When we are pushed to what we think are our limits, remember God never gives us more than we can handle. This is scary, it looks bleak, but I have faith that we can handle this, or anything else that we are given," Aaron declared.

"You're right. I'm sorry," Cara said, placing a hand on her husband's shoulder.

"We'll find a way," Aaron said.

"We always do," Cara added softly.

Twelve

Cara and Aaron followed Hal to the front porch of the cottage behind the house. "I haven't been in here for a couple of years, but I think we should be able to whip it into shape for you."

Pushing the door open, he led the family into the small bungalow. "There's a wood stove over there, works great for the whole cottage. Space isn't huge, but I think a realtor would call it 'cozy'," Hal ventured.

Pointing to the kitchen, the farmer continued, "Small galley, if you need anything more, you are welcome to use the house kitchen anytime. Bathroom is there, full running water and has its own septic. Main bedroom is there and the loft has a little room overlooking the living area, I figured the kids could make their home up there."

"This is all very sweet of you, Hal," Cara said.

"Aw, it's nothing. It will be good to see this place with a little life in it again."

"How much are you asking?" Cara asked.

Hal looked at Cara, confused, "Asking? I…uh…wasn't asking for anything."

"Come on, we can't just stay here for free," Cara pressed.

"I tell you what, would you be available to help out on Saturdays and Sundays after church at the store?" Hal asked hopefully. "The Ladies

Auxiliary usually comes and helps out. They haven't confirmed this year, and I would feel a lot better knowing I had such capable hands running the shop."

"Well, I suppose that would work. But the kids..."

"They are more than welcome. I'm sure they would have fun helping either you in the store or Aaron with the trees. I can even pay them, too," Hal offered. Seeing a concerned look on Cara's face, he adjusted his offer, "Or put something into a college account for them?"

Cara smiled and stuck out her hand, "Deal."

Hal shook her hand and then pulled her in for a hug, including Aaron in on the affection.

"Well then, this place isn't as bad as I thought, but if Aaron will help me carry some of these boxes into the barn, I'll get you some cleaning supplies and make sure everything is in working order," Hal said clapping his hands together.

Cara looked at Aaron and slid her arm around him.

"Will this work until we figure things out?" Aaron asked.

"I think cozy is the right word," Cara said, spinning around the room. "In all the right ways. It is a blessing."

"What do you think the kids will feel about living up here?"

"I think they will see it as an adventure," Cara replied.

"Let's bring them in, and we'll get to work," Aaron said.

Chase and Annie were waiting patiently on a little bench outside the window of the cottage's living room. "You two about done with your cocoa?" Aaron asked to a pair of nodding heads.

"What are we doing at this building?" Chase asked.

"Why don't you come inside and we will show you."

"It's like a little house," Annie said, her eyes moving about the small living space.

"Exactly. Farmer Hal is letting us stay here until we find our next home," Aaron told his children.

Annie looked confused, "Where are we going to sleep?"

"I'll show you," Cara said, looking over the banister of the loft. "Come up here."

Eagerly the kids marched up the steep set of stairs to the loft. A little round window with a seat inset flanked by the open wall to the living room below.

"This is neat!" Chase squealed.

Annie put her hands on her hips. "There is no wall."

"That makes is kind of cool, huh?" Cara said.

"There is only one room," Annie pressed.

"It's big enough. What if we made that window seat your bed?"

Annie's eyes brightened. "That would be kind of awesome!"

"It's just for a while," Cara reminded.

"Knock-knock," a voice called from the door. Hal poked his head in the cottage. "Ready to move these boxes?"

"I'm ready. You're sure this is no trouble?" Aaron asked.

"If you ask me again, I am going to raise your rent," Hal teased.

"Fair enough," Aaron said, hoisting two boxes off of the small dining table. "Where to?"

Once the boxes had been cleared, Aaron had left the cottage preparation duties to tend to his farm work. Following Hal's instructions, he continued prepping the trees for their big upcoming days and ensured the paths were clear of debris and obstructions.

As much as he was enjoying working the tree farm, Aaron was surprised by the new feeling of comfort and warmth that settled in his belly. Maneuvering the tractor around a bend, he smiled to himself. The work itself was calming and rewarding, but this new feeling, despite all of his worldly worries, was overwhelming. Having his family on the property, knowing that he could be there for them, and their warm smiles were back at the cottage waiting for him made him feel somehow complete, like his chaotic life had some semblance of order.

Hopping off the tractor, he tackled a section along the pathway, ensuring low lying scrub wouldn't infringe the Christmas trees. Aaron charted a path in his head for the guests, tugging on their sleds as they searched for their family's tree had a proper trail without snags, especially when the snow fell and obscured hidden objects underfoot.

Glancing over a ridge, he could see a little wisp of chimney smoke. Despite the chill around him, that bit of burning wood snaking its way into the air let him know his family was warm and cozy, a short trip down the hill.

Content, Aaron returned to his chores, tending to the field scheduled for the day. Tackling a plot higher in the elevation and further from the rest of the farm, the sense of peace was spectacular.

Lost in his thoughts and caring for the trees, Aaron was startled when branch up in the high ridge snapping called to his attention. Scanning the hillside above him, Aaron searched the maze of tall Douglas firs lining the ridge.

Neatly camouflaged among the speckled array of bark, he caught movement. Holding tight, he watched silently as the one artifact of motion multiplied. Moving carefully, though competently along the edge of the ridge, a bull elk led his herd through the brush. Occasionally snatching a bite while keenly observing the world around them.

Following the bull, Aaron counted nearly two dozen elk of varying sizes working their way as the bull had. Except for the occasional snapped twig, the entire herd moved in near silence. Massive, majestic beasts, yet calm, peaceful, and alarmingly stealthy for their size.

On their drives around the farm, Hal talked about how the farm, his family, and the animals all worked the land together and gave to one another. Aside from one or two culled each year, the herd had a safe haven for passage, shelter, and food on the farm and in the hills surrounding it.

Hal would often find elk and deer bedding down amongst the trees. Younger deer would use the valley at the base of the low lying fir branches as shelter from evening storms. Often Hal would change plans and work a different field so that he did not disturb them.

Aaron understood as he watched the herd mind their business high above him. The lead bull often tested the scents in the air and his keen eyesight and hearing. Eventually, even as still as he was, the bull caught Aaron down below. The bull did not overreact. Studying Aaron for a long moment, he sensed the man did not warrant immediate alarm, but instead, calmly and confidently led the herd into the tree line of the ridge and down into the valley below.

With a smile, Aaron watched the last elk slip through the trees. Surveying the work ahead of him, he enjoyed the brief respite, knowing he had a lot left to get done.

Settling in back to work, Aaron worked the field efficiently and with care. He began to comprehend what Hal had described as an eye for the trees. Almost as an artist tackling a canvas, he worked the trees and their shapes to be the best Christmas tree. In the field, the exercise would occur hundreds of times before the entire plot was ready for the families to visit and find their perfect tree for Christmas.

Finishing with another long day, Aaron drove back down to the driveway that served as the epicenter of the farm. Stowing the tractor in the barn, he closed the big doors for the night.

Out of habit, he started towards his car to drive home and stopped halfway across the driveway. Spinning nearly one hundred and eighty degrees, he headed up the little trail that curved behind the main house to the cottage where his family was waiting.

Aaron kicked his boots off prior to walking up onto the porch of the cottage. As he pushed the door open, he was welcomed by two giggling children in their pajamas standing in front of the stairs leading to the loft. A warm fire was more than adequately heating the small house.

In the small galley style kitchen, he could hear pans clanging. Cocking his head in that direction as he listened. Aaron turned back to his children, who were waiting patiently for him to take it all in. "Welcome home, Daddy!" they grinned in unison.

"Thank you, guys. Did you help Mommy get this place put together?"

Nodding, they added, "She's in the kitchen."

"I hear that. I hope she's cooking something good," Aaron said, ruffling their hair on the way back.

Poking his head into the kitchen, he found Cara wiping her brow with her sleeve as she stood in front of the sizzling skillet. "Smells good in here," he said as he walked behind her, putting his arms around her waist.

Turning to see him, she smiled, "Hi, honey."

"What ya got in there?" Aaron asked.

"Well, I clearly have not had time to go the store, so after Hal got the fire going for us, he brought over some steaks, huckleberries, and some root vegetables," Cara replied.

"That was nice of him. How's it going? The place looks great, by the way."

"Thank you. Annie and Chase were big helpers. As far as dinner goes…this is my first time cooking elk. We will see what becomes of it," Cara planted a kiss on her husband.

Aaron offered to help.

"No, I need to tend to said elk, why don't you go shower? Hal said the water heater should be up and running by now."

Aaron nodded, assuming he would be much more palatable to his family after he had washed up. The warm water, which he hoped would be so, would feel great on his tired and chilled muscles.

After enjoying their first home-cooked meal in the farm cottage, dishes cleaned, and dried with a little family teamwork, the Shepherds settled on the sofa opposite the woodstove. Arms stretched to encompass his entire family. Aaron asked, "What do you guys think?"

Both Annie and Chase took a moment to scan the cottage from their vantage. "It's small, but I like it. We are all close."

Aaron laughed, "That, we are."

"Yeah. It's like a cabin from a movie," Annie said, and then scrunched her nose, "But kind of far from friends."

"It is a little far, but I have to go into town all the time, so you'll get to see them," Cara said.

"And, imagine the sledding here when it snows. All of your friends will want to come here," Aaron shared.

"Yay!" the kids squealed.

"Besides," Cara added. "This is only for a little while. Think of it like a season-long adventure."

"I like adventure!" Chase said.

Annie nodded, "It reminds me of the books I read, especially the Christmas time ones."

"I guess we will make our own story, 'The Shepherd Tree Farm Adventure'," Aaron suggested.

"Part of the on-going Shepherd adventure series," Cara joined, the whole family enjoying their temporary home in front of the fire.

As the family huddled on the couch, Aaron felt content. For a brief moment, their concerns over jobs and bills and a place to call home were washed away.

He pulled his family even closer as he reached his arms around them. The kids were right. It was cozy in the little cottage living room. Yet, it was somehow more comfortable than the large home they had in town ever felt.

With a heavy sigh, Aaron allowed his mind to relax in the same way his weary body had sitting on the sofa.

Thirteen

Aaron woke up early, a little out of sorts until his brain connected that they had slept in a strange house. Heading into the living room, he put a fresh log on the smoldering coals and allowed the residual heat to ignite it.

Sitting at the dining table, he opened his laptop and connected it to his phone so that he could get on the internet. Starting with his email, he ran through the responses to his job inquiries. Setting times for calls and noting those who had declined his resume, he moved from his emails to the job search boards.

Sighing, he noticed that there were even fewer jobs available than the last time that he had looked. Sorting through the few new options, he found a couple that were reasonable and posted for them.

Heading into the kitchen, Aaron sifted through the cupboards looking for coffee and a kettle. Finding a French press and a sealed bag of coffee, he smiled appreciating that either Hal and Cara had thought of it.

Filling the kettle with water, he went to get dressed. Being quiet not to wake Cara or the kids, he filled a thermos with the pressed coffee and slipped out of the house. The crisp morning air hit him immediately. Instinctively, he pulled his arms close and held the thermos tight.

It was still dark out, and a light frost had settled on the farm. Heading out to the barn, Aaron set out to start his duties for the day. Thanksgiving was closing in fast, and Aaron had a few extra things he wanted to get done before opening day.

As Aaron moved from one field to the next, he saw Cara and the kids leave for school. Waving to them as he rode on the tractor, he realized that was a sight that he had never pictured. The thought made him chuckle, shaking his head over where life had landed him.

Hurrying through his day's chores, Aaron had checked off the mental list he had kept. Stopping outside of the barn, he went inside, finding the tools he was hoping to find. Piling the supplies in the tractor, he headed towards the end of the driveway. Carefully positioning the tractor, Aaron climbed into the front hydraulic scoop.

Reaching up, he went to work, touching up the tree farm sign that welcomed the guests that were soon to arrive. As he stood high on the tractor, he took in the vista he usually enjoyed from the farm in reverse. The farm looked amazing against the backdrop of the high ridge. The tallest trees stood like sentinels against the late fall sky.

It dawned on him, that these types of farms were disappearing and what a shame that was. The adventure of the family getting out of town, traipsing among the fields with saws in hand to find the perfect tree for their family was a memorable experience. He was glad that he, and now his family, were able to help Hal this season.

Aaron's thoughts were broken by the sudden ring of his phone. The caller ID let him know it was one of the companies he had applied to. Balancing himself on with one foot on the tractor's fender and the other on its hood, Aaron answered the phone. Despite the setting and his unusual perch, the phone interview was like all others. He went through the process of describing his work history and what he was looking for, asking a few on-point questions, his heart quickened a bit as the caller said that they wanted him to meet with them for a final interview. The decision would be down to him and two other candidates.

His heart sank as he learned that the interview would be in San Diego, and he would be responsible for his airfare and hotel. His brain scrambled as he tried to calculate the expense, and he rationalized it didn't matter, because whatever the expense was, they didn't have it.

Urged to decide on the spot, Aaron had no choice but to reluctantly decline the final interview. Dejected, he sighed as he slid his phone back into his pocket. The job would have been perfect – a thirty-minute commute with occasional trips to the home office in San Diego and even a modest increase in salary compared to his last job.

It was frustrating to have a solution to his family's needs so close, and yet he was powerless to take advantage of it. They had leveraged every bit of help and resource they had to try and keep their house. There was no other help to go to wrangle the expense of the trip. Even they had just enough, Aaron couldn't justify the cost of thirty-three percent shot.

Aaron's shoulders slumped as he stared down towards town below. He knew somewhere down there was his family. His family was counting on him to improve their situation and provide for them. Yet, he couldn't.

Standing on a tractor, with a paintbrush in hand, he had to decline an opportunity that would have gotten them back on their feet. With a shrug, he stared at the paintbrush and back up to the sign. The contrast between the worn and the fresh section that he was working on was stark. It gave Aaron a strange sense of accomplishment.

Resigned to the circumstances, Aaron returned his focus to completing the touch-up work on the farm sign. When he was done and admiring his work, he chuckled to himself. He found work around the farm strangely satisfying, in fact, more so than the job he had worked so hard at for so many years.

Part of him wondered if accepting that job out of San Diego would provide him with the same satisfaction.

Hopping off the tractor, he placed the lid back on the paint. Admiring his handiwork with the sign ready to welcome visitors to the farm.

Fourteen

"The sign looks great! Did you do that?" Cara asked as she and the kids returned home from school.

"That was me," Aaron admitted, nodding his head.

"I don't usually allow paint brushes in your hand, but you did good," Cara said. "Any news from the job front?"

Aaron eyed the stack of bills, most marked "past-due" on the table. "Yes…and no." He went on to tell her about the phone interview.

Cara's eyes also lit upon the bills. "Are you sure? We need to be able to find a way."

"I thought about it. But it would be two other candidates and me, so we could be hit with the expense, which is money we don't have anyway, and still end up not getting the job," Aaron said.

Cara looked away as if searching for insight.

"I think we had to try," she said, sounding disappointed in her husband's decision.

"It would be a gamble, and that was if we could even come up with the money at all in the first place. Unfortunately, they needed a decision right then," Aaron shrugged.

"I guess. It is just so frustrating. It seems each day we slip in a deeper hole. Our bank account is empty. As soon as my check from the school comes, it is spoken for, as is the money that you get from working here at the farm," Cara said.

"I know. Digging a further hole out of desperation wouldn't help us either, though," Aaron defended.

"Aaron, you don't understand. I barely have gas to get to work. We won't have anything for the kids this year…I just…I just," Cara spun away, covering her face.

Aaron walked up and put his arm around her shoulder and said softly, "I know."

When the kids were in bed, Aaron and Cara sat at the table. Aaron double-checked the latest job postings. Cara tried to put the bills in order of importance and number of payments behind. The exercise did little to encourage her.

"I have to find a part-time job. There are seasonal jobs, weekend work and over Christmas break, I would have extra time," Cara reasoned.

"What about the kids?" Aaron asked.

"I don't know. We'll have to figure something out. Stay here with you at the farm?"

Aaron shook his head, "It depends on what I am doing, whether they can be there – for safety sake. Sometimes it would work. Besides, working the store here on the farm is our rent."

"Right," Cara sighed.

"There is this one job, they already said they would hire me, but there is a catch," Aaron said.

"Oh," Cara asked, already dubious.

"We would have to move."

"Move where?"

"Biloxi, Mississippi," Aaron shared. "Similar job to what I had, lower pay."

"How much lower pay?"

"Two-thirds. We would need to move over the holiday to start January second."

Cara frowned, "I can see why you didn't run that one by me."

"I'll keep digging. I'm trying."

"I know," Cara ran her hand over his shoulder. "I'm just scared and frustrated."

"I am too," Aaron acknowledged. "We'll find a way."

Cara laughed in spite of herself, "We always do."

Fifteen

The Shepherd family woke up wearily on Sunday. This was the Sunday of the month that they volunteered to help at the early service before they attended their usually later service that followed. Aaron put on a pot of coffee while Cara assembled peanut butter toast for breakfast and helped the family rush out the door.

Dropping Annie and Chase off at the children's worship program, Cara headed for the nursery. Aaron caught up with his friend Bob on the way to join the rest of the usher team.

"So, how's it going? I heard you guys moved?" Bob asked.

"Yeah, it was a short notice kind of thing," Aaron admitted.

"Oh? Where'd you move to?"

Aaron paused momentarily and replied, "We are staying up at the Maple Hill Tree Farm. I have been helping there for the past few weeks."

"Maple Hill Tree Farm...I almost forgot about that place. We used to go up there to get our tree when I was a kid. I loved doing that," Bob reminisced as they walked.

"Yeah, it's a great place. We have only gone up once with the kids, it is a lot of fun."

"I guess people just get busy and find it easier to grab a tree from the shopping center," Bob surmised.

"Hey guys," Aaron's friend John joined them on the way to the pre-service prayer. "How're you guys doing?"

"We're fine, just telling Bob we moved up to the Maple Hill Tree Farm for the holidays," Aaron said.

"Maple Hill Tree Farm, I haven't been there in ages," John said, rubbing his chin. "You guys doing alright? I know these things can be tough on a family. Money, help moving, a job reference...whatever it is, you just ask, okay, pal?"

Aaron nodded, "Yeah, absolutely. Just prayers, that's all we really need."

When service let out the families gathered in the lobby. Tables decorated for the annual Angel Tree stood for families to select gift requests from those less fortunate in the community.

In years past, the Shepherds each would take on an angel request, and they would also provide a Christmas meal for an entire family.

Annie walked up to the table, and one by one, began reading the tags. Aaron became absent in his conversation as he watched his daughter. He watched as her eyes brightened, clearly finding a card for a little girl that she had hoped to find a gift for.

Chase followed his sister, frowning. Once Annie found the one that she selected, she nudged Chase to where the requests for boys were and helped him as they began reading those tags.

By the time Aaron had broken away, Cara joined them from the nursery. Excitedly, Annie held her tag up, "Mommy, this girl wants a Purrfect Kitty too!"

Cara glanced at Aaron. Taking the card from her daughter's hand, she closed her eyes briefly, and then turned to return it to the tree. "We'll see if there are any left next weekend."

"Why, Mommy? We always get angels," Annie pleaded, confused at her Mom's gesture.

Aaron joined them, giving his wife a glance, "Sometimes, we help those we want to help, which is not such a bad thing. But what can be even more amazing is helping those we don't have a connection to or might not even want to help."

"Like at the Mission Kitchen," Chase said. "The people there weren't our friends. And then we made them our friends."

"Yes, something like that," Aaron nodded.

"Are we still going to do a meal for a family?" Annie asked, her eyes big and still bewildered.

"If we can," Aaron nodded.

"Come on, guys. This is a workday for us," Cara said, taking Annie's hand.

"It is?" she looked up at her mom.

"We are going to open the store on the farm and see what kind of work needs to be done," Cara said.

"I've wanted to go in there," Annie said, exuberance returning to her gate.

"You are going to get your chance. In fact, you can be a helper in the store when it opens the day after Thanksgiving," Cara said.

Annie's face brightened.

Before they could leave the church, they were stopped at the door. "Hey Shepherds," the youth pastor called out.

"Hey, Danielle, the kids love serving the kids' service," Cara said.

"They're great. They do a great job with their respective groups," Danielle said, "I wanted to ask if you guys would be willing to serve at the youth Thanksgiving dinner next week."

"Uhm, uh, sure. Yes, we can help," Cara nodded.

"Great," Dannielle clapped her hands. "We are short on food. Would you guys be able to pitch in for turkeys?

"Turkeys…" Cara repeated.

"I think if we got two more, we would have exactly what we need," Danielle said, "You guys are so wonderful, thank you."

Cara and Aaron stood somewhat stunned as Danielle joyfully fluttered to say hello to a family that was in her youth group.

"Turkeys, huh?" Aaron cocked his head at his wife.

Cara looked at him and shrugged.

Sixteen

Putting together a quick lunch, the entire Shepherd family walked over to the store at the far end of the parking lot. Hal met them there and let them in.

Opening up the store was like a peek into a page from Christmas past. Buried beneath the dust from being neglected since the year prior, were objects of joy and the excitement of Christmas from a simpler time.

A sizeable wooden sleigh took up much of one side of the store. Converted as a display for wool blankets. In the back of the sled were handcrafted ornaments while the front of the sleigh displayed syrups and treats from fellow area farms.

A red wagon suspended from the ceiling with two playful elves peeking out from either side. An empty tree stand stood atop a red rug, a tree skirt folded neatly next to the stand.

A bank of coolers were unplugged and propped open to allow them to air out while not in use. Next to the counter was a warming shelf.

"It's cozy, like the cottage," Annie chirped.

Chase wrinkled his nose, "It's dusty and smells funny...but somehow, it feels sort of like Christmas in here.

Cara and Aaron laughed. "It will air, and our job today is to get rid of all that dust," Aaron said.

"Well, how you put this all together is completely at your discretion and whim," Hal said. "Do you need anything? What can I do to help?"

Cara shook her head and watching Hal wince a little and instinctively put his hand on his back. "I think we have everything we need to get the shop in ship shape. You go relax. It looks like you back is acting up."

"Yeah, relaxing is not really my cup of tea. I do think I will get off my feet for a while. I'll grab a handful of saw blades and see if I can't them sharpened and ready for opening day. It will be here before we know it," Hal said, leaving the Shepherd family to the store.

Annie and Chase went from item to item in the store, inspecting everything. Cara and Aaron took stock of the space. Aaron began making a to-do list while Cara gathered the supplies that they needed.

Putting the list down, Aaron grinned as he walked behind the counter. Blowing a layer of dust away, he flipped a switch. In moments, the store filled with the crooning of Andy Williams.

Cara instantly began swaying humming "It's the Most Wonderful Time of the Year".

Annie and Chase joined their mom while Aaron began wiping down the stereo and then moved onto the counter.

Cara was drawn to the old sleigh, running her hand down the side, imagining it gliding through fresh snow along the ridge with a white horse adorned with a red leather halter and reins strung with bells.

Finding a rag and polish, she began carefully cleaning and bringing what luster she could of the sleigh back to life. Smoothing the cloth across the crackled lacquer and then the brass hardware.

Aaron watched her, nurture the sled to the beautiful centerpiece of the store that it deserved to be. While he straightened up the check stand, the kids pulled everything out of cupboards so that they could take stock in the leftover wares from the previous season.

Annie tabulated while Chase sorted items. "Twelve nutcrackers, nine angel ornaments, ten star candle holders…" Annie said out loud as she scribed. As Chase pulled out a box, Annie frowned, "What's this?"

Aaron looked out across the check stand, "Let's have a look."

Annie brought the box over to her dad. "Ah…," Aaron muttered thoughtfully as he pulled the contents from the crate and quickly put it together. Searching around the check stand, he found a box of matches. "Here, let me show you."

Lighting four candles, he said, "Watch for a moment." As the candles flickered, the piece began to move. Slowly at first, a little brass windmill rotated as the heat from the candles created a slight convection. As the fans turned, little brass cherubs took flight in a circle around the assembly, trailing them were small strikers which softly lit upon small bells perched below. Picking up speed, the angels played their song, driven by the wind produced by the candle heat.

"Swedish Angel Chimes," Aaron replied. "My grandmother used to display these every Christmas. I would watch them dance around as I sat on the floor next to the side table she placed them on."

Aaron watched as the kids were mesmerized by the simple feat of Christmas engineering. Smiling, he winked at Cara, who had stopped her work on the sleigh to watch the kids herself.

Leaving the angels to their dance, the family dove back into their work. Aaron, done with the check stand, headed into a little storeroom tucked behind the refrigerated units. Clicking on a light, he found shelves crammed with boxes. Pulling one opened, he found them full of decorations.

Poking through each box, he began to determine an order to it. The first three boxes were all tree decorations, presumably for one from the farm that would ultimately be placed in the tree stand in the store.

Rummaging through the contents of the remaining boxes, Aaron found several strings of lights, an entire box of red bows, and an assortment of classic decorations. Pulling them all out, he placed the tree ornaments on the rug with the stand. The rest, he lined up in front of the check stand.

As the dust cleared, the shelves cleaned, and the floor swept, as Aaron found another Christmas record to play, they began to decorate the store. Seeing the box of ribbons, Cara asked Aaron and Chase to gather some boughs.

"And holly?" Annie asked.

Aaron snapped his fingers, "You know what? Yes! I saw some near the edge of the western field. Come on, Chase!"

Together, Aaron and Chase ran across the driveway to the barn. Tossing the barn doors open, they hopped in the Gator and tore off of the western field. Stopping along the edge, they found several holly bushes scattered amongst the wild brush and the outer tree line.

Lopping off a few sprigs, they carried them back to the Gator. Finding a couple of trees that had low boughs that would need to be trimmed anyway, they cut a few branches and added them to the Gator as well.

With a high five, they returned to the store and the girls.

Clapping in excitement, Cara and Annie began assembling garland from the tree boughs, adorning them with red bows, pinecones and holly sprigs with bright red berries. "Wow, that looks great!" Aaron cheered.

Aaron and Chase followed the girls, stringing lights around the evergreen garland. When they completed their circuit, they stood together at the front of the store.

"This looks...amazing," Cara gleamed.

"Nice work, Shepherd family!" Aaron grabbed everyone in his arms and pulled them in for a warm hug.

Their admiration was snapped by the sound of boots on the porch of the store. The door swung open, and Hal stepped in, his face in awe at what he saw.

"Wow. I haven't seen the store this beautiful since...since Laura," Hal said softly, taking it all in.

"I don't know about the rest of the farm, but I would say the store is ready for business...well, once the goods are stocked," Aaron said.

"I'll let the rest of the farms know. Laura and I, we stocked the purchased items- the local farmers, they bring homemade pies and eggnog, quilts, crafted decorations, cider...like a real old-fashioned shop," Hal explained, his voice trailing as he found himself lost in a memory.

Snapping himself out of it, he addressed the Shepherds, "You all have been working so hard, and it shows. I was guessing perhaps, that you might have lost track of time. I took the liberty of making you all dinner, if you would like to come to the house."

Cara glanced at her watch, "Oh my, you're right. Hal, you are the best."

"Don't get too excited, you haven't tasted the food yet," the farmer grinned. Taking a last look around the story, he shook his head, "Wow."

Seventeen

Bellies full, the Shepherd's thanked Hal for dinner and made their way to the cottage. Aaron stoked the fire while Cara got the kids ready for bed.

Checking his emails, Aaron saw that he had a few replies on his job inquiries, but nothing imminent. Closing the laptop, he joined Cara in tucking the kids in bed.

"That was so much fun," Chase said, giving his father a big hug.

"It really was. Like Christmas has come early," Aaron replied, "Well, Christmas season, at least. Christmas comes when it does."

"You two were such big helpers today," Cara said, taking her turn.

"And we get to help when the store opens?" Annie asked.

"If you want to, yes," Cara nodded. "Now, my little ones, time for bed."

Aaron and Cara took turns with hugs from Annie.

"Sweet dreams, guys," Aaron said, switching off the loft light.

Cara and Aaron made their way to the sofa in front of the fire. Looking at her husband, Cara said, "One blessing in this, no television. When I'm not grading papers, and you aren't job searching, we get to dial down and enjoy a little no distraction time, just the two of us."

"It is nice. I don't miss the television. Don't get me wrong, I like the occasional football game, and I shamelessly admit, I will miss our Hallmark movie time during the holidays," Aaron said.

"We can catch a movie or two online, just for tradition sake," Cara suggested.

Aaron smiled, "How about some tea? I can put the water on."

"That sounds great," Cara nodded. "Then come back, and we'll cuddle by the fire."

Aaron went into the kitchenette to start the water. He retrieved two mugs and placed a tea bag in each one. Pausing, he flipped through the mail at the end of the counter. Nearly every one was a bill. Nearly each one was stamped "overdue".

One of the envelopes, in particular, caught his attention. Recognizing the logo, he opened it. It was a note from the jeweler where he had placed a deposit on the diamond ring for Cara. He had lapsed his time for payment, and the ring was no longer on reserve for him. The deposit he had placed was forfeited as well since the ring had been held out of circulation.

With a big sigh, he folded the envelope up in buried it deep in his pocket.

Returning the other bills to their stack, he slid them aside. They would remain a problem for another day. Tonight, he just wanted to revel in the fun day the family had and to enjoy time with Cara.

The water heated, he filled the mugs and grabbed one in each hand. Walking briskly into the living area, he stopped short as he looked at the couch. Cara was fast asleep, slumped against the armrest of the sofa.

Grabbing a blanket, Aaron slipped between her and the armrest, carefully covering her. Leaning his head on hers, he traded conversation with listening to the rhythm of her breath.

Eighteen

The next day, Aaron got another early start. This was the first day for harvesting the trees that would be picked up for the in-town lots opening the day before Thanksgiving.

With thermos in hand, Aaron opened up the barn. Grabbing a hand saw and a chainsaw, he stowed them in the large trailer and hitched the tractor. Firing up the engine, he pulled the tractor out of the barn. Deciding to start on the lower field, so that his family could find him when they got up, he went to work.

Not wanting to wake anyone, he used the hand saw for the trees on this parcel. Noting the tags that Hal had placed for the lot-bound trees, Aaron began felling them one by one. As each was cut down, he hoisted it over his shoulder and tossed it into the trailer.

Aaron had completed half of the first parcel before he saw his family pause on their way down the driveway, the exact reason he had decided to start on the lower lots. Setting down his saw, he trotted over to the car.

"Good morning, guys," he smiled.

"Good morning, Daddy," Annie and Chase chorused.

Leaning into the window, he kissed each one of them. Hurrying around the car, stood outside of Cara's window. "Hi, honey," he said.

"Hi, baby. Be careful out there," she warned.

"I will. Have a good day," Aaron replied, and the brightened calling to the kids in the backseat, "Almost Thanksgiving break!"

"Yay!" the sang as they headed down the driveway.

Looking up at the house, he noticed the smoke had stopped spilling out of the chimney. Jogging up the driveway, he decided to check on Hal.

Rapping on the door, Aaron waited. Several minutes passed by with Aaron knocking and no response. Pulling out his cellphone, he dialed Hal's phone number. Before the call was picked up, the door opened.

Hal stood in the doorway, stooped over, and looking extremely out of sorts.

Aaron frowned, "You okay, Hal?"

"Well, I just, I…no," Hal shook his head. "This darn back. It has just gotten worse. I want to

be out there with you today. There is so much work
to be done."

"Don't worry about the work, Hal. I've got it
covered. I got an early start, and I am in a groove.
You did a great job marking them. I've got the big
trailer so that I can stay out in the fields longer,"
Aaron said. Seeing the concerned expression on the
farmer's face, Aaron stressed, "Seriously, I've got it.
You get yourself situated where you are
comfortable. You look like you're in a lot of pain.
Do you need anything? Are you sure you don't
want to go get checked out?"

Hal snapped, "I don't need some doctor to
tell me to rest it. I've got some ointment. It helps a
bit."

"I see," Aaron nodded. Noting the slight chill
in the house, he remembered what brought him up
to the house in the first place.

Heading to the stove, he noticed that the rack
Hal kept in the house was empty. Aaron reasoned
that gathering more wood had been too much for
Hal's back. "I'll be right back!" he called.

Heading out to the woodpile, he gathered up
a hefty armload and staggered to the house.
Leaning against the door so that he could lighten
his grip on the wood enough to nudge the knob
with his hand, he pushed into the house. Setting the
stack down, he stoked the failing coals to a crystal
glow and added a few pieces of wood.

Soon, the bed of coals ignited the new logs brought the stove ablaze again. "There, that should help," he muttered to himself.

"You didn't have to do that!" Hal called from his sitting room by the front door, opposite of where the wood stove was.

"Yes, I did. Besides, being cold only makes sore things feel even more sore," Aaron called back.

Poking his head into the sitting room, Aaron said, "I'll be back at lunchtime…to make lunch."

"Now, I don't need…," Hal started to growl.

Aaron looked cross, "Hal, I'm making lunch. Period."

"Now, you're starting to remind me of Laura," Hal muttered.

"Good. I'll take that as a compliment. Now behave so that I can concentrate on getting my work done," Aaron said and headed back to tackle the tree harvest.

Returning to the fields, Aaron parked the tractor alongside the next parcel he had to tackle. Wielding a chainsaw, he cut down the trees as marked by Hal the previous week.

He moved swiftly through the field, finding a rhythm of felling trees, stowing them in the trailer, and stacking them next to the barn for the big trucks to pick up.

Feeling a bit odd about spending his day away from a phone, email, and direct contact with others, Aaron had to admit, he was enjoying the manual labor for a nice change of pace.

Tossing the last tree from the parcel into the trailer, Aaron started the tractor and headed back towards the barn. Making a long loop around the next plot so that he did not have to perform a humiliating sixteen-point turn with the tractor and trailer, he did a mental assessment of what was left to be done. By his estimation, he should be able to complete the harvest in another day or maybe a day and a half.

Stopping in the driveway alongside the barn, he climbed inside the trailer and began hauling the trees out and lining them up in their assigned stacks. By the time he had the cart unloaded, he glanced at his watch. It was nearly lunchtime, and he wanted to ensure that he head Hal off from trying to fix lunch himself and was probably overdue for tossing another thick log on the fire.

Nineteen

Aaron grabbed an armload of logs on his way towards the house. Stomping up the steps to kick some of the dirt off of his shoes, he rapped on the door to alert his entrance as he walked in the house.

"Hal...!" Aaron called. "Lunchtime!"

Dropping the load of logs by the stove and tossing one in, he headed to the parlor where he left the farmer. Hal was there, with White Christmas playing in the background. Head slumped and loud snores rocking the room, Aaron chuckled.

Heading into the kitchen, Aaron plundered the pantry and began to work out a plan for lunch. Frying some bacon and then eggs in the bacon grease, Aaron assembled some sandwiches, his BLET rendition of a BLT.

Finding a tray, Aaron placed the sandwiches, a glass of milk, and a glass of water down and carried it to the parlor.

Setting the tray on the coffee table, he nudged Hal. "Hal, hey bud, time for lunch."

"Huh...what?" Hal snorted awake.

"I made lunch. Nothing extravagant, just poking around the kitchen, I hope you don't mind," Aaron said.

"I never balk at a meal prepared by the hands of others," Hal admitted. "Whew, took some pills for my back, and I guess I kind of zonked out."

"It's alright, you probably needed it," Aaron said, handing Hal a plate. "I recall you having milk at lunch."

"Thank you, Aaron. I wish I were out there to help."

"We're fine. I'll be done at worst case, a half a day before the trucks come," Aaron shared.

"I don't know where I would be without you," Hal said, "And your family."

"With all respect, I think we could say the same. Regardless, I am happy to be here, happy to help," Aaron professed.

"Well," Hal hoisted his milk glass, "To shared...benefit?"

"To friendship," Aaron suggested.

"To friendship," Hal agreed.

A few bites into the sandwich, Hal blurted, "Without your help...without your help, I can't help think that the farm would be done."

Aaron frowned, "What do you mean?"

"Well, the farm's revenue has been decreasing each year. I do okay on the commercial harvest, but there just isn't a lot of traffic out here anymore. Not like it used to," Hal explained. "The mortgage has been paid off awhile. I'm not hurting. But as you can tell, I need to hire help or call it quits. If this year's sales aren't enough to hire a hand or two for next year, I think this will be my last."

"Hal...," Aaron started, his voice showing his concern.

The farmer waved him off, "It's not like that. I love the tree farm. I love the trees. I love seeing the families come out. I just think maybe it's time is passed. Selling wholesale has been the most profitable these past five years, but that is my least favorite part. That is work. Running the U-cut with the families visiting, that is the joy. People just don't do it that way anymore."

"I see. I suppose you might be right. We haven't been here in a few years. People we have spoken to about me working here have said the same. It is a piece of family tradition that has started to erode away. Local tree lots, grocery stores, and department stores are where most folks get their trees," Aaron admitted.

"Just a factor of times changing," Hal surmised.

"Perhaps," Aaron said thoughtfully as he took a bite of his sandwich. "What if there was some way to bring that nostalgia and tradition. Remind folks in town about the experience of hand-selecting a tree."

"Sure, just turn back the calendar a few dozen times," Hal scoffed. "Christmas comes in a box. People don't go to the store anymore to shop for gifts, never mind slog through the snow to find a tree. Click a button, and two days later it's on your doorstep."

"Tough to argue that convenience and hectic lives converge to make a perfect storm mail order holidays, but some things are worth holding onto," Aaron defended.

Hal smiled, "A few thousand more like you, and I've got a profitable farm again."

"It's worth fighting for," Aaron pressed.

"I'll fight to the end, don't get me wrong. Even that end is closer than I might like," Hal said, a sparkle in his eye.

"Let's see what we can make of this season," Aaron declared in defiance.

Twenty

Starting up the tractor, Aaron made his swing around the driveway and up the trail leading to the high ridge. Passing the tracts along the way, he cataloged the remaining parcels yet to harvest.

The more extended lunch set him back a bit, but he intended to make it up by working a bit later into the evening. Pulling his jacket collar tighter, he noticed the day had gotten darker and colder.

Reaching the top of the ridge, he swung the tractor around the turn-around and aligned the trailer near the field for harvest. Just as Hal and his wife had, each time on the ridge, Aaron could not help but pause to take in the scene. Either direction held its own spectacular vista, whether the expansive valley, the current of the ridge as it flowed and met with other crests, or the towering Douglas firs resting atop the ridge itself.

As Aaron enjoyed the firs, looking up at the peak, he noticed small objects spinning and floating down from the sky. Smiling, he held his hands out wide, gathering flakes as they landed.

Knowing that he was nearly a thousand feet higher than the farmhouse and well above the floor of the valley, he was confident that he was witnessing the areas first snow of the season. Aaron couldn't help but feel warm inside despite the increasing chill in the air. He loved snow, the beauty as it fell, the beauty as it collected, the stillness and silence that it brought with it.

Pulling himself out of his thoughts, he knew he would need to get back into action as he had time to make up to complete the parcels he had planned for the day. He further knew the task was going to be more challenging as he studied the sizes of the trees tagged on this lot.

Grabbing his gear, he set to gathering the trees Hal had marked for harvest. Starting the chainsaw, he kneeled at the base of a tree and began cutting through it. It fell to the ground with a much more ferocious crash than the trees on the previous lots.

As Aaron hoisted the first tree, he quickly determined the trees on the top lot were a lot heavier. Carrying the tree over his shoulder and tossing it into the trailer, he began to reluctantly recalculate how long it would take him to complete the harvest.

The snow stopped falling, leaving behind it a light dusting on the ridge. The boughs of the trees were powdered with snow. Aaron loved how the beautiful trees were made only more beautiful accented in white. And though while somewhat more cumbersome, he didn't mind the extra effort in working through the snow.

Making a stop by the barn to unload the trees, Aaron welcomed Cara and the kids as they arrived home from school.

Cara eyed the ever-growing line up of trees ready for transport, "Wow, you are really getting a lot done."

Giving his wife a quick kiss, he nodded, "Lot's left to do." Adding another tree to the stack, his eyes brightened. "You should come up with me on the ridge."

Cara glanced up and saw the dusting up high. "Yes, that sounds like a great idea. How about this, I would like to check in on Hal and maybe get dinner started? You guy's head on up, I will see you in a bit."

Eagerly, Annie and Chase climbed aboard the tractor with their dad. Powering it up, he brought the tractor to life and began its climb. Aaron used the trip to ask his kids about their school day, partially because he always asked and was genuinely curious, but a bit to distract them as well.

As they hit the higher elevation and the light dusting blended into a solid coating, the kids' eyes widened, grins spreading across the faces, "Snow!"

"Pretty exciting, right? The first snow of winter!" Aaron said.

"Can we play in it?" Chase asked.

"Of course. Let's get to the top and get this thing pointed in the right direction," Aaron nodded.

"It's so beautiful," Annie crooned.

Aaron hugged his daughter tight, "I love it."

Climbing to the top of the ridge and using the turn-around to spin the tractor, he again faced the valley.

"It's like it snowed just for us!" Annie exclaimed, noting the only the ridge was graced with snow.

"Hmm...," Chase frowned. "It's not enough to make a snowman."

"Maybe not," Aaron grinned. Holding out his arms and falling backward on an unscathed blanket of snow. "But, it is enough for really thin snow angels!"

Flapping his arms and legs, Aaron laughed as his kids joined them. Making three distinct snow angels. Aaron sat up as Annie stood and inspected their efforts. "Not the best angels I have ever seen."

"What?" Aaron looked flabbergasted. "First snow of the year snow angels are supposed to be a little...special." Grabbing his daughter, he pulled to the ground and squeezed her in a big bear hug.

Reaching out for Chase, they played in the snow and giggled with each other.

Three more angels, a six-inch snowman and a snowball fight which more resembled a snow dust fight later, they returned to the barn with another load of trees. Hearing the tractor approach, Cara walked out on Hal's porch to greet them.

"I have cocoa waiting inside," Cara said, as the family came to meet her. Gathering the kids and ushering them inside, she added, "And Hal has been waiting for someone to play board games with!"

"Hey," Aaron called. Cara turned to face her husband, "What about you?"

"Me?" Cara said. "I...uh, I am working on dinner."

"Oh? Roast in the oven?"

"Yes."

"How long is it in for?"

Cara shrugged, "About two more hours."

"More than enough time, come on," Aaron smiled, holding his hand out for his wife.

"You two are good?" Cara asked.

"We're good," Annie nodded.

"Alright. Your cocoas are on the kitchen counter. Be sure not to spill," Cara said.

"Great, let's go!" grasping her hand, Aaron led the way to the tractor. Getting her to snuggle close to him, he hit the starter and slid the tractor into gear. Heading up into the hills, daylight was quickly fading. It wasn't far from the house that snow began to fall again.

Heading up further into the hills, Cara leaned into her husband, his arm around her shoulder, pulling her close. As they reached the upper elevation, the snow was falling enough that it was difficult to see the angels that Aaron had made with the kids not too long ago.

Pointing them out to his wife, they laughed together, enjoying the moment Aaron had with the kids. Cara giggled at the tiny snowman that Annie and Chase were so proud. She quickly snapped a picture with her phone.

Inspired, she held her phone out as far as she could and took a photo of her and Aaron on the tractor. "I don't think I ever pictured this moment in my head. You and me on a tractor in the middle of snowfall," Cara said.

"I can't say that I had ever had that vision either...until this afternoon," Aaron admitted.

Hitting the peak of the ridge, Aaron wheeled the tractor around and shut it down. The hill was silent amidst the cascade of snowflakes that were making their way all around them.

"What do you think?" Aaron asked, watching his wife take in the wintry scene.

"It's beautiful. It's so peaceful," Cara replied.

"Nice to have a bit of peace, even if it is only momentary," Aaron admitted. He kissed his wife on the temple.

Cara looked at him in the eyes, content for the first time in weeks. Leaning in, she kissed her husband deeply.

Twenty One

Aaron had a full day's work ahead of him. Taken off course with helping Hal around the house and taking liberties to play in the snow with his family, he would need the entire day to have the trees ready so that they could be on the lots the day before Thanksgiving.

With a full thermos, Aaron headed out into the field. Tackling the plots between the ridge and the house, he worked quickly and efficiently until it was time for lunch. Pulling a full load down the barn, he quickly unloaded and headed towards the house.

With an armload of wood, he pushed through the door. He was instantly hit with aromas of kitchen activity. "Hal!" Aaron called.

"In here, Aaron!" Hal called.

Setting the wood down, Aaron followed the smell of lunch. "Feeling better?"

"A bit," Hal nodded. "If I don't bend over, move too fast, try to lift anything…"

"I've been there before. A tweaked back is just affected by everything," Aaron said.

"In all my years, I have had one season where I had to have so much help. I'm grateful for what you have done. I hope it isn't taking you too much away from your job search."

Aaron shrugged, "I check my email at night, and fortunately, my cell phone has service nearly anywhere on the farm. The reality is, it is pretty slim pickings this time of year."

"It will pick up in the New Year, I'm sure," Hal encouraged.

"Yeah, I'm sure it will," Aaron agreed. "So, what's for lunch?"

"French Dip sandwiches. You like mushrooms?" the farmer asked.

Aaron nodded.

"I find most of them up on the ridge, some I grow myself on logs in the little stand of trees and ferns behind the garden," Hal explained.

"Smells great," Aaron admitted.

"So…how's it going out there? Trucks come tomorrow."

"I know. We'll be ready," Aaron assured.

"Yeah," Hal nodded, seeming a bit more distant than usual.

Aaron looked at the farmer, his brow furrowed, "What's going on, Hal?"

Hal bristled at the question. "I just can't help thinking this is the farm's last year. I've had offers from commercial outfits in the past. They would put this place on an eight to twelve-year rotation – raze everything for harvest to send to stores around the region, replant in the spring, and do it all over again eight or so years later."

"I see. They make you a fair offer?"

"I suppose so. They threw in some money for the buildings though they said they would knock them all down and plant over the entire property," Hal said. "I just, I just am not sure I can do it anymore. Without you, this entire year would be lost."

"It sounds like a solution. But…you don't seem so keen on it," Aaron said.

"Not exactly the legacy I wanted to leave, but…" Hal started.

"We'll just have to make this a great year, then!" Aaron said.

Hal patted him on the shoulder, "That we will. That we will."

The rest of the day, Aaron kept a mental countdown of how many parcels were left. By the time Cara and the kids returned from school, he was down to his last half-section to harvest. Stopping the tractor, he hopped out to greet his family.

"Hi, guys!"

The kid gathered on either side to hug him.

"Hi, honey," Cara said. "Don't forget, we are leading youth group tonight."

"Right...yeah, of course," Aaron nodded, clearly haven forgotten. Glancing at his watch, he knew he would struggle to get the last field done. He also wouldn't have time to follow up on any job calls that he missed during the day. "I'll be ready, probably, coming in hot, though."

Cara smiled, "Coming in hot, huh?" She gave him a quick peck on the cheek and then frowned, "Time for a shower, right?"

"I certainly hope so. No promises," Aaron admitted. Giving the kids another quick hug, "I better get going!"

Waving, he blew kisses as he climbed aboard the tractor and steamed towards the final parcel.

Twenty Two

"That was a great meeting," Cara said, tossing her keys on the counter.

"Yeah, it was," Aaron agreed, flopping onto a dining chair exhausted.

He looked past the stack of bills and flipped on his laptop. Skimming through the emails, he recognized one from a man he had interviewed with on the phone. Clicking on it, he quickly read through it. It was a short paragraph thanking him, but stating there were going in "a different direction".

Sighing, Aaron continued his scan. Seeing the job title that was perfect for him sent through a recruiter, he opened it. The job description read perfectly. Glancing at the interview times, he realized they were for that day or the next morning. Aaron's mind raced with how he could help with loading the harvest trees and partake in the interview. Reluctantly, he slid the laptop away, knowing there was no way he could do both.

He leaned both elbows on the table and rested his head between his hands. Cara walked over and began rubbing his shoulders, "What's wrong?"

Aaron explained what he had read.

"Are you sure there is no way? I mean, it is important for us," Cara pleaded.

"And what? Leave Hal without help on probably his most labor-intensive day?"

"I guess not."

"Maybe it's just too much. Helping out around the farm, at church. I'm missing too many opportunities. This family, we need me to be making money. Not seasonal labor money, real money," Aaron said, his frustration leaping out of him.

"I know, I know," Cara said softly.

"I don't know what to do. The farm at least gives actual money and a place to live, for now, at least. Abandoning it and focusing on job searching leaves us with more immediate cash downfall and no roof over our heads. Plus, I would feel bad leaving Hal in a lurch," Aaron shrugged.

"At least make Hal aware. I think he would understand if you had to take intermittent job search time outs during the day," Cara suggested.

Aaron nodded, "I am sure he would."

"What are we going to do about the car?" Cara said, mentioning their older second vehicle.

"Transmission acting up again?" Aaron asked.

"It took me about fifteen minutes to get it into gear after school, and it dropped out of gear at the stoplight on the way home," Cara said.

"It's getting to the point it's dangerous," Aaron said.

"The guy who owns the storage unit place we put our furniture said he would take it for a year's worth of storage fees," Cara offered.

"As long as he is aware of everything that is wrong with it. We wouldn't get anything more by trying to sell it outright," Aaron agreed. "It would take another bill off our plate."

"Can we get by with one car?" Cara asked.

Aaron looked contemplative, "As long as I am working at the farm, I suppose. We can always worry about a second car when we have the appropriate money to purchase it. We will just have to get by."

"We'll find a way," Cara grinned.

"We always do."

Twenty Three

As is usually the case with Aaron, a good night's sleep and the arrival of a new day brought with him a refreshed spirit. He kissed his still-sleeping wife and hopped out of bed.

Getting the hot water boiling for coffee, he quickly got dressed. Sitting on the cottage porch, he drank his coffee and waited for the trucks to arrive. Huddled in his thick work coat, he slipped off his gloves so that he could manipulate the keys on his laptop.

Using every spare moment he had, he tried to manage his job search while helping at the farm. Running through the latest possibilities, he sent off his inquiries and closed the computer. Placing it inside on the kitchen table, he jogged over to Hal's house. Blowing warm air on his hands before slipping his gloves on, he grabbed a stack of firewood as he heard the diesel engines roar up the driveway.

Quickly stowing the logs, he saw Hal fully dressed, work boots donned for the first time in days. "Hal? You sure you're up for this?"

"I'd be lying if I was up for lifting trees, but I figured maybe I could lend a hand running logistics," the farmer admitted.

"Alright, glad to have you in action, even if it's behind a clipboard," Aaron said. "Trucks just got here."

Walking out together, the men greeted the first two truck drivers.

Hal introduced Aaron and set a course of action. The drivers would climb in the back of their trucks, and Aaron would bring the trees two at a time, one for each truck from the requisite stacks.

The first two trucks left just as Cara was leaving with the kids for the last day of school before Thanksgiving break. Stopping the car, Aaron leaned in and gave them each kisses. Watching them head down the driveway, he waved.

"Next trucks should be here any minute," Hal said.

"Mind if I run back to the cottage real quick? I'd like to check emails," Aaron asked.

"Of course. I'll grab us a snack and some fresh coffee," Hal said.

Aaron jogged to the bungalow. Not stopping to take his boots off, he slid into the dining chair and clicked on his laptop. Most of the emails were junk and filler. One caught his attention. Opening it, he read through the job description. It was an advanced role of his last job. Scanning the details, he spied one significant caveat. Hovering over the submit button, he pressed send just as he heard diesel engines return to the driveway.

Turning off the computer, Aaron ran back out to the stack of trees by the barn. Seeing Hal on his porch, ambling towards him with a plate piled with biscuits and a large thermos of coffee, he waved.

Lining the trucks up, Aaron took Hal's lead and had the drivers mind their own truck beds as he brought them trees marked for their respective destinations.

Before long, the pair of trucks were pulling out, and Aaron leaned back on the rail of the fence alongside the barn.

"Finally ready for a biscuit and some more coffee?" Hal asked.

"Absolutely," Aaron nodded, resting his hands against his knees.

Thanking Hal for the snack, he looked up at the farmer. "You have done this every year for the last...."

"Forty-seven years."

"Right. This is a heck of a job," Aaron panted.

Hal grinned and raised his eyebrows, "It is, isn't it? I admit, I usually didn't load the trucks quite so fast as you."

"Come on, you're being kind to the desk guy," Aaron said.

"No. You're a heck of a worker, Aaron."

"Thanks," Aaron said. Looking up as he heard tires on the gravel drive. "That's no diesel."

A white car pulled up, and a young man hopped out in front of Hal and Aaron. "Shepherd?" the man called.

"I'm Aaron Shepherd."

"This is for you," the man said, handing Aaron and envelope. Without another word, the man got back in his car and drove back down the driveway.

Tearing the packet open, Aaron scanned the contents. His heart sank as comprehended the gist of the document. The lender of their car was taking legal action against them for failure to pay.

With a deep sigh, Aaron looked away and crammed the envelope and document in his back pocket.

Hal observed him quietly, noting something wasn't right. He wanted to ask, but instinct told him to let Aaron be.

Aaron was relieved to hear the next diesel engine heading up the drive. Putting his gloves back on, he focused on work.

With frustration and stress at its peak, Aaron worked with even more fervor the rest of the day. The more he worked, the less he fretted over finances. For him, that was a blessing. Like an addict, he pined for the next truck.

Hal watched with concern. He could tell something was amiss and wanted to see if he could help somehow, but let Aaron work through his frustration in his own time, in his own way.

When the last truck pulled away and the massive stand of trees Aaron had amassed through the course of the week was bare, the two leaned against the fence.

"Nice work today," Hal offered.

"Yeah," Aaron said distantly. "Anything else you need done this afternoon?"

"No, I think you did more than enough work today."

"Are you sure? I noticed the barn door was sticking a bit. It opens now, but when it snows..." Aaron suggested.

Hal waved him off, "That happens every so often. I'll clean it out with a planting shovel. It works perfect."

"I can work on the woodpile. Weather is getting colder, good to get it done before it snows down at this level," Aaron said.

"I tell you what. There is something you can help me with. Wait here. I need to grab something from the barn," Hal said and walked off.

Aaron stared out at the light mist gathering in the valley towards town. The absence of focus capturing work allowed his mood to sink once more.

Hal returned with a box in his hand. Leaning next to Aaron, he blew a layer of dust off of the box.

Patting more off of the edges, he opened it up.
Tilting up two small glasses nestled in their
compartments, he pulled a bottle out of the center.

"My dad and grandad weren't big drinkers,
but a couple times a year, they would visit over a
glass. The end of harvest day was one of them," Hal
said, eying Aaron. When Aaron didn't object, he
popped the cork top and poured two modest
glasses of whiskey.

Handing one to Aaron, he held his in the air.
Aaron followed. "Salud!"

"Skol!" Aaron replied. Each took a sip.
Aaron winced and let out a fiery breath.

Hal smiled. His mind full of questions and
concerns for his new friend and his family, but
remained content to share the peace of the farm in
silence after so much activity and hard work. Hal
knew how he was at that age, and knew that if
Aaron wanted to share, then he would do so. Hal
was not going to push him.

Twenty Four

"What are we going to do?" Cara asked when Aaron shared the notice with her.

"All we can do, keeping moving forward," Aaron shrugged.

Cara frowned, "How can that be? 'Just move forward'? We are supposed to be responsible adults, parents…"

"I know that. We are doing what we can. We are both working. We are cutting expenses. I am looking for another job," Aaron said. Then reluctantly added bitter fuel to the fire, "Oh, got an email today that the kids are out of lunch money."

"They have been for a week. The school was just letting them slide," Cara acknowledge. "Wanda from the lunchroom whispered in my ear as I walked down the hall. By the time we are back from Thanksgiving break, the PTA will have us on a list to consult with to see if we need school lunch assistance. And you know what? We do need it!"

Aaron rubbed her arm tenderly, but she pulled away. "I can only imagine how challenging that would be for you."

Cara sighed, a hand on her forehead, "It's not your fault. I mean, you are working your tail off for us."

Aaron hugged her, and she relented, leaning in close.

That night, Aaron walked out on the porch after the family had fallen asleep. He had put a final log in the woodstove and closed his laptop for the night.

He looked up, hoping to see something – stars, snow, the moon – but the night was black. Under a thick layer of clouds and without spoil from the lights of town, the farm was especially dark.

Sighing, he dropped his head. "God. Thank you for granting me the strength to work on the farm and be your blessing to Hal. I pray that you continue to provide me strength. I pray that you help me find my way, light my path where I am supposed to go, how I can provide for my family. Help be the provider for them that I am supposed to be.

"I'm nervous, God, that I am not on the right path. That I am not focused like I am supposed to be. That I am spending time on church projects and the farm when I should be spending that time on the job hunt. That maybe I am not being responsible. Please show me…what I am supposed to be doing."

Sitting in the deep silence of the night, Aaron did something he had not done in a while – he sat still.

Twenty Five

Aaron navigated around the house even more quiet than usual. Cara and the kids were enjoying their day off from school. As he made his coffee and perused his emails for the morning, he was pleased to see an email from a recruiter.

The job that fit his previous role well was requesting a phone interview. He scanned the times and found a slot in just a few hours. Aaron always performed stressful scenarios better when he could react as opposed to ponder for a length of time.

Finding a quick breakfast of nuts and fruit, he grabbed his coffee and his laptop. Slipping on his boots and jacket, he carried breakfast, his phone and laptop to the barn.

Stepping out onto the porch, Aaron found a light dusting of snow on the ground and very soft flakes meandering down from the clouds above that were suspended above him the night before.

Leaving the barn door open so that he could watch the light snowfall, he set the laptop on the engine of the tractor and leaned back in the seat.

Opening up his resume, the company website, and the job ad, Aaron leaned back and finished his breakfast. He laughed at his set up. As offices went, he didn't mind this one.

At the top of the hour, the phone rang. Muddling through the usual pleasantries and regurgitating what was in the resume, they arrived at the crux of the conversation.

"Aaron, I have to tell you, I am enjoying speaking with you. You certainly have the base skillset for the role, but the company you primarily have experience in is, well…let's just say Jans and Barnett is in another league," Joe Fitch, the hiring manager, said.

"Oh, I know. We competed directly against you quite often. It wasn't easy winning cases against your brand. The clients felt as though Jans and Barnett would have a better back office and support because of your size and breadth, but by the same token, I was able to win a number of cases against you," Aaron boasted.

Joe laughed, "Yeah, I see that. I had my admin pull the cases that we pitched against you. It is humbling data, to be sure. Maybe it would be better to have you with us than against us."

"I'd like to think so," Aaron said.

"So, this position will be based out of our Chicago headquarters…," Joe started.

"Chicago? I thought this was a regional role," Aaron asked.

"Like a lot of companies, we have pulled back from regional offices and run everything out of beautiful Chicago. That's not a problem, is it?"

Aaron's heart sank. He was quiet for several long seconds, lost momentarily in the snowfall. "No, that's not a problem."

"Good. Well, I still have several strong candidates to interview. Have a good Thanksgiving, and we will be in touch after the holiday," Joe said.

"Happy Thanksgiving to you, too. I look forward to our next discussion," Aaron hung up the phone. Closing his laptop, his mind reeled. The posting was unclear where the role would be stationed. It was an issue he wouldn't fret unless the conversation went further.

Heading back to the house, to stow his laptop, he peeked into to see if anyone was awake. The house was quiet, so he tiptoed to the kitchen table and set his things down. About to sneak back out, he heard a low whisper, looking around, and then up, he saw two little hands wrapped around the spindles of the loft rail. Moments later, a little grinning face appeared between them. "Daaaady!" Chase whispered.

Aaron waved him downstairs. By the time Chase reached the third step, he launched himself into his father's arms.

Holding him tight and giving him a big squeeze, Aaron asked, "What are you going to do with your day off?"

"I don't know. Be with you?" Chase said, his voice hopeful.

Aaron thought for a moment and nodded, "Sure. Go get dressed. I'll make you some breakfast and write your mom a note."

Heading out of the house, Chase looked up at his dad and asked, "What are we doing today?"

"Today, we are going to set up the area where families will come to load the trees that they picked," Aaron replied.

Stepping off of the porch, Chase's eyes went wide as he finally noticed that snow had reached the level of the house. "It's even less than the other day on the ridge, but it is still snow!"

A little shed behind the store held most of the tree prep supplies. Aaron took inventory of what was in there and what was needed. He plundered in the storage space and item by item, handed Chase things to bring out to the lean-to covered tree prep station.

First came a large spool of twine, followed by red flags to tie onto oversized trees. Aaron grabbed the heavy tree shaker himself and brought it out to the station. In the back of the shed, an entire rack of sleds were stacked from floor to the ceiling. He got them down, and Chase leaned them against the wall of the tree station.

"Hi, boys!" Cara and Annie called.

"Hi, Mom!" Chase waved, carrying a sled out to the station.

Cara gave her husband a kiss.

"Annie and I are going to get the shop ready," Cara declared.

"Perfect timing," Hal said, walking up to the family. "I was just about to make my annual run to the local farms and load up the old truck with their goods to sell at the store. Would you two like to join me?"

Annie looked at her mom, who shrugged, "That would be fun. Will you two boys be alright?"

"We'll be fine!" Aaron said.

Hal escorted the girls to the 1951 red Ford truck. The wooden rails of the bed still had a light dusting of snow and frost, but the old truck fired right up. "No air conditioning in the summer, but the heater works," the farmer assured.

As they climbed in, Hal added, "I did retro-fit lap belts in the eighties."

Strapped in, they headed off to gather items for the store. The old truck roared along, turning onto the winding foothills road.

The first stop was the local goat farm. Annie giggled as she watched the goats play. Parking alongside the fence line, Hal smiled as he watched Annie admire the goats, and the goats run excitedly up to the fence to admire her. "You can pet them. They love it."

Annie looked up at her mom, who nodded. As she neared the fence, the goats stuck their noses up to her as they put their front hooves on the rail to crane closer. Cautiously, Annie rubbed them on the head. As they jockeyed for petting position, she pet them all with abandoned, being sure to spread the attention as fairly and thoroughly as possible.

She was disappointed when her mom and Hal returned with a Styrofoam cooler bound tight with packing tape. "Make some new friends?" Cara asked her daughter. Cara nodded.

"Those guys love the attention, far sweeter than you might think. Make great pets," Hal said.

"What did you get?" Cara asked.

"Goat cheese," Hal said triumphantly. "These are dairy goats."

"Ah," Annie nodded, having no idea what goat cheese was.

"We should move on to the next stop, but I bet if we asked, Marnie would let us come back and play someday," Hal suggested.

"That would be fun!" Annie declared, hopping back into the truck.

"Our next stop has critters too, but you won't see them this time of year," Hal grinned.

Annie looked at the farmer curiously. "Bears?"

"Not bears, but they do like to eat what these little guys make," Hal raised his brows. "Bees…"

"Ooh," Annie wrinkled her nose. "I don't want to pet them."

"I suppose not. These bees, all honey bees, are amazing. They help the crops grow, the flowers, the trees…they are a farmer's, really all of our, best friends," Hal said.

Climbing into the truck, he assured the young girl that bees, these ones, in particular, were most certainly her friends.

Making a big circuit around the rural loop on the outskirts of town, they amassed their haul of cider, quilts, fudge, and wooden toys. Stock complete, they returned to the tree farm. Aaron and Chase had completed the set up for the tree loading area and waved as the truck chugged up the driveway.

Annie ran out excitedly and filled her family in on her farm adventure. "There were goats and chickens and bees!"

"Wow, you got quite the farm tour," Cara said.

"Yep. I pet the goats," Annie declared. Screwing her face a bit, "I didn't pet the chickens or bees, though. The bees are friendly bees, nevertheless."

"They are, are they?" Aaron laughed.

"Yep, they help the farmers grow things, and they make honey!" Annie exclaimed.

"That they do," Aaron nodded.

Hal looked thoughtful, "My grandfather used to keep bees on the farm. Great for pollinating the trees. Not everyone...enjoyed maintaining them, however."

"You know, I know a guy. Maybe I could connect him with you and other farmers. Kind of a traveling beekeeper," Aaron suggested as he inspected the contents of the truck.

"Sounds like a good idea. I know plenty of folks who might benefit," Hal nodded.

Circling to the bed of the truck, Aaron began lifting items out and hauling them into the store. Cara and Annie started placing items in their requisite spots.

Handing Chase lighter items, they quickly got the truck unloaded and stocked in the store.

"This place looks even better with things in it," Hal beamed.

"I think we are ready for business," Cara chimed.

"You guys...are wonderful. I don't know how to ever thank you," Hal said.

"You did put a roof over our heads," Aaron reminded.

"I rented you a cottage that hadn't been used in years. You guys have gone way above and beyond," Hal argued. "Let me take you all out to dinner, my treat."

"We would love to," Cara said, "But we are running late for our church's youth Thanksgiving. I delivered our turkeys on the way to school yesterday, and gratefully, my friends Stephanie and Sharon agreed to cook them for me."

"Two turkeys?" Hal asked, frowning, knowing the Shepherds were short on money.

"Oh, in all of the excitement of visiting the farms, I forgot to ask you to Thanksgiving. We don't have an extravagant spread, we have ground turkey, I was thinking of making a turkey meatloaf with a cranberry ketchup," Cara wrinkled her nose.

"How about, if you don't mind, I turn the tables and invite you all to Thanksgiving dinner," Hal suggested. "I'll get a turkey and…"

"We can't, that's not what I meant…" Cara defended.

"I know. And I can," Hal said. Clapping his hands, he declared, "So it's settled."

Aaron stepped into the conversation, "On one condition, we come and help you cook."

"Great, it will be like a big family Thanksgiving. I haven't had one of those in a long time," Hal smiled.

Twenty Six

The Shepherds arrived at the church just in time to help Cara's friends unload the turkeys. Cara went to the kitchen to help with the rest of the cooking prep.

Aaron walked the kids to the nursery, where they would help entertain the little ones for the volunteers while he began setting up the long community table that would run the length of the hallway for the teens and young adults of the church.

After placing the 24th table, he began to work on chairs when other volunteers started to arrive.

"Shepherd!" John called out as he arrived. "What can I do to help?"

"Well, I've got the eating area almost done, if you could start on the buffet line and then the dessert area in the multipurpose room, then I think we will be ready from our end," Aaron instructed.

"Sounds good. Hey, how are you guys doing, you know, at home? Can we doing anything to help you?" John asked as he started to peel away.

"No, we're great. Thank you," Aaron replied.

"Alrighty, to work then," John smiled and sped off to haul out tables for the buffet line.

When the last seating was in place, a pair of helpers coordinated the kids to decorate the tables with orange tablecloths and ears of dried corn. Aaron and John were called on to help carry out the serving dishes and set them up on the buffet.

Just as the set up was completed, the doors opened, and excited teenagers came streaming into the church. Skirting by the dessert table, they called their shots while the youth pastor ushered them into the sanctuary.

Aaron rejoined with Cara, and they walked hand in hand to the sanctuary themselves. The youth band was playing an upbeat worship song, and kids sang along.

A few songs into the set, the sanctuary was nearly filled with young people. A line of parents gathered in the back of the room. After an opening prayer, kids were called up to describe their perspective of thankfulness before the youth pastor began a prayer to bless the food.

Thanking the volunteers, the youth pastor dismissed the teenagers to get their meals.

"You guys are so great," Danielle, the youth pastor, approached Aaron and Cara. "We couldn't have done this without you."

"We're glad to help," Cara smiled.

"You wouldn't be able to help with the Christmas production, would you? We could always use the help, or at least donations for props and the cast dinner," the pastor asked.

"I'm sure we'll be able to help in some way," Cara said.

"Right, what am I thinking? Let's get through tonight, right? Thank you two again."

After helping serve the dinner and ration desserts to treat-loving teens and young adults, they reversed the process of setting up and put away the tables, chairs, and serving ware. Chase had fallen asleep in the car, and Annie was out the moment her head hit her pillow.

Aaron and Cara looked at each other, exhausted. They fell in a heap on the sofa. Aaron wrapped his arms around Cara, and she settled in next to him.

"Nice work, I think it went well," Aaron told his wife.

"Yeah," Cara nodded. "I am exhausted."

"Nice to be able to do that for the kids."

"Yep," Cara yawned.

"Don't sign us up for donations for the Christmas production. I'm happy to volunteer my time, though," Aaron suggested.

"Yep. Time. We've got lots of that," Cara snuggled in close to her husband, her eyes shut. Yawning, she added, "And energy."

Twenty Seven

Not surprisingly, Aaron found his email inbox empty in regards to his job search being Thanksgiving morning. With a fresh cup of coffee, Aaron stoked the fire in the woodstove and sat on the couch, enjoying a few moments of quiet.

Even in times of strife and challenge, a holiday was a great time to put the stressful world on pause and just be. A switch of focus entirely on enjoying family and friends and being together.

Aaron didn't have to wait long before his family began to stir. Chase was the first. He slumped down the steps dragging his blanket behind him. Finding his dad on the couch, he snuggled in next to him.

Wrapping an arm around Chase, Aaron pulled his son in close next to him. No work, no concerns over money, just a morning with his son.

By the time Cara and Annie awoke, and the Shepherd family got ready for the day, it was time to help Hal fix the turkey. Gathering up a few items from their stock in the kitchen, they headed out of the cottage to the main house.

Hal greeted them at the door, the fire well-stoked in the woodstove. Smiling, he declared, "Happy Thanksgiving, Shepherd family."

"Happy Thanksgiving, Hal!" One by one, they gave the farmer a quick hug.

"So, what's the game plan?" Hal asked.

"I'll tackle the turkey. Cara will work on the sides," Aaron suggested.

"If it is alright with you, I'd like Annie and Chase to help me with the pies," Hal suggested.

"Pies?" Cara asked.

Hal shrugged, "I learned a little something from Laura in all those years."

"Sounds good, you two game?" Aaron asked Annie and Chase.

The kids nodded their heads eagerly.

Before long, Aaron was elbows deep in turkey, Cara was simultaneously preparing mashed potatoes, bacon-Brussel sprouts, and homemade cranberry relish. Hal had Chase peeling apples and Annie measuring ingredients for the pie crust.

There was a warmth in the gathering that belied worldly troubles, the family and Hal focusing on the moment, together.

Hal raised his glass, "Happy Thanksgiving." Across the table adorned with a bronze turkey, colorful bowls of green vegetables, and deep burgundy cranberries, the Shepherd family raised their glasses. "May I?" the farmer asked, holding out his hands and bowing his head.

Aaron nodded, and Hal began, "Dear heavenly Father, we are so grateful for your presence and the wonderful people you put in our lives. Bless the people of this country, this town and this table as we celebrate Thanksgiving. May families find peace in their days and their travels safe. God, I am personally so grateful that you have brought the Shepherds to this table. Bless the food that nourishes our bodies so that we may serve strong in your name. Amen."

"Amen," the Shepherds chorused.

"Well, this is undoubtedly the most amazing Thanksgiving dinner that I have sat down to enjoy since…well, my last with Laura. I am so glad you are all here to share the day with me and clearly surpassing what meager meal I would have churned out," Hal gushed.

Cara smiled, "We are happy to be with you too, Hal."

"What do you say to family board games, if you are all up to it after dinner," Hal suggested.

Annie and Chase cheered.

"That sounds like a perfect end to a great day," Aaron nodded.

Twenty Eight

Aaron gently kissed Cara awake. "Hon, it's opening day. Time to get up."

"What? Coffee. Sleep. Open later," Cara mumbled.

Aaron chuckled, "Come on, babe. Your coffee is on the stand next to you. I'll get the kids."

Leaving Cara to wake up fully, Aaron jogged up the steps to the loft. "Good morning, guys!"

"Why so early?" Annie yawned.

"It's opening day for the tree farm. All hands on deck," Aaron reminded.

Chase rubbed his eyes, kicked his blankets off and jumped out of bed.

"Now that's the spirit!" Aaron mussed Chase's hair.

Aaron left while the family finished getting ready and had breakfast. A half an inch of fresh snow had blanketed the farm. Looking down the hill towards town, he could see that the snow level reached about a third of the way to town. A snowplow's chains clanked loudly down the road, ensuring the drive was clear and safe.

Heading to the tree prepping station, he began setting out sleds with a tape measure and saw. By the time he had ten neatly lined up, the rest of the Shepherd family arrived for duty.

Cara had Annie help her get cocoa, coffee, and cider ready.

"What do I do?" Chase asked.

"You have a very important job. You hand out candy canes, encourage people to warm up in the store, and grab a hot drink, and when I am helping tie trees onto their cars, you can restock the sleds like I have them there," Aaron explained, pointing to the row of sleds.

"Can I have a candy cane?" Chase asked.

Aaron looked at him with a serious glance, "I believe you are allotted one morning candy cane and one afternoon candy cane."

"Ok," Chase nodded.

Hal joined the Shepherds as the first car arrived. Hal greeted his guests, and Chase passed out candy canes. Aaron provided them a sled and gave the family the layout of the farm so they could determine where they wanted to go for what type of tree and what size they were looking for.

While the first family headed up the trails, Aaron pulled over a firepit and set it up just outside the tree prep area. Grabbing large logs, roughly the same size, he set them around the fire as seats for guests to gather, warm up and drink their cocoas or ciders.

"Nice touch," Hal said, patting Aaron on the shoulder.

As the first family descended the hill with their special tree, a second family and a third were just heading up.

Aaron greeted the family, grabbing their tree for them and putting it on the shaker to free any of the loose needles or random things and critters that found their way into the boughs. Chase did as he was instructed and urged the family to head into the store, while he restocked the sled.

The family gathered around the fire, sipping hot drinks as Aaron lifted their tree onto the top of their car and began tying it down. When the tree was secure, he wished them "Merry Christmas" and found himself greeting the next family.

The routine continued for hours. Hal brought down turkey sandwiches midday, and the family saw a steady stream of guests at both the tree farm as well as the store.

Later in the afternoon, during a lull, the Shepherds gathered around the firepit. Aaron had just tossed a fresh log on the fire, and Cara brought out cocoas for everyone. Even by the fire, the latter half of the day was chilly. Hal recognized Cara's shiver and ducked into the store.

Returning with a wool blanket that he had noticed Cara admiring when they were prepping the store, he tossed the sale tag into the fire and stretched it around her shoulders.

"Hal, you didn't have to do that," Cara said.

"I know," the farmer admitted.

"Well, how'd we do?" Aaron asked.

"It was a good day. Per family, we sold more at the store, and I think everyone enjoyed themselves," Hal admitted. "As busy as we were, each year, we get fewer visitors. We make most of our revenue from the harvest."

"Everyone seemed happy," Cara said.

"They did," Hal acknowledged. "Thank you all for a great day."

"Cheers!" Aaron raised his cocoa in the air.

"Cheers!" the rest echoed as they raised their cups.

Cara enjoyed the moment with the family. Inspired, she began to sing, softly at first, "Hark, the herald angels sing…." as her voice grew, her family, and Hal joined in.

Twenty Nine

The second day of the tree farm being open to the public started in similar fashion. A weary Shepherd family made their way to the store. Coffee, cocoa, and cider were brewed, sleds were laid out, and the firepit stoked to a roaring blaze.

Aaron found an extra pair of speakers and wired the store stereo to play in the tree prep area as well. Chase gathered a fresh arsenal of candy canes.

Families began streaming in, Hal greeted them on the way out to their search. Aaron met them as they returned with their prize trees. As the modest but steady flow of families arrived, the Shepherds and Hal cared for them in a well-oiled fashion.

Losing track of time, enjoying being amidst families that found their trees, browsed the store and gathered by the fire pit, Aaron didn't realize he was hungry until Hal brought lunch out to the family.

Thanking him, Aaron sat with his family on the firepit logs and ate his lunch. As two more cars pulled up and a family returned down the hill, Aaron set his plate down and picked up his phone to slide back into his pocket. As he did, he realized that he had missed a call.

Quickly checking the number as he met the family returning, he recognized the number as Joe's, the Vice President for the company that he had interviewed with. Reluctantly, he slipped the phone into his pocket and focused on helping the family.

For an hour, he tried to tear himself away so that he could listen to the message, each time he was interrupted to answer questions, shake a tree or string one to a rooftop. When he finally did steal a moment, he had trouble hearing as another carol played on the speakers he set up, or a family sang a song at the fire.

Seeing a family head down the hill and another family arrive, Aaron was becoming stressed and frustrated.

"There's another one, Daddy!" Chase tugged at his jacket.

"Aaron, would you mind grabbing a load of wood for the fire?" Hal asked.

Aaron's phone buzzed in his pocket at that very moment. "I...I have to go."

Chase, Hal, and the family stood with their tree, watching Aaron run off towards the bungalow. Cara, who was just returning to the shop with Annie, watched the scene unfold.

"Hello," Aaron said, trying not to breathe heavy into the phone after running to find a quiet spot. The line was already dead. He had missed the call.

The voicemail indicator flashed, and he listened to the message. His heart raced. Joe shared that they had tried him earlier in the day and are down to the final slot for the final interview to take place on Monday. He had wished Aaron were among the candidates, but is sorry that they couldn't wait.

Aaron stopped in his tracks. Sighing, he tried to determine what he should do. Without another moment's hesitation, he streaked to the cottage and barged inside. Hitting the call button, he tried to slow his heart rate as he listened to the dial tone.

Reaching Joe's voicemail, Aaron shared his desire to attend the interview and apologized for being in an area of poor reception. Slumping against the kitchen counter, he stared at his phone. His frustration was peaking. He liked helping Hal and the families visiting the farm, but they were not going to bail his family out of their financial strife. He needed this job.

Resigned, he slowly started back toward the tree prep area. As he reached the door, his phone rang. "Hello?"

"Aaron, I caught you. Good," Joe's voice rang through the phone.

"Yes, sorry. I was…at a tree farm with my family. I didn't have great reception," Aaron replied.

"Well, I hated to have time pressure put on you, but the executive team wants this next hire in place immediately. I was just leaving for the day, sorry to say you would have missed the cut."

"I understand, I'm glad we connected," Aaron said.

"So, you can make it on Monday?" Joe asked.

"I can."

"Excellent, I'll have our travel department send you a plane ticket and set you up with a hotel. Do you prefer the window or aisle?"

"Aisle."

"Excellent. See you on Monday."

With that, the phone went dead. Aaron pumped his fist in the air.

His mind was on the to-do list he needed to put together for Monday. As he looked out of the window, he saw Cara walk from the barn with a load of wood in her arms. He watched Hal make three attempts to get a tree on top of a car, but the stiffness in his back did not afford him the range needed to do so. Two more families waited behind that one to get their trees shaken.

Aaron burst through the door and sprinted back to the tree prep station. Cara had just reached the fire pit and dumped the wood in a pile, tossing one log onto the fire. Glancing at her husband with a knowing look, she returned to the shop.

"Hey Hal, sorry about that. Let me give you a hand," Aaron called, rushing over to lift the tree on top of the car. In quick work, he got the tree tied down and headed to the next family.

Hal stood back, straightening his back.

Aaron attacked the afternoon with renewed vigor, getting the farm caught up and back into full swing.

Thirty

"So, what was taking off all about this afternoon? You kind of left Hal...all of us in a lurch," Cara asked.

"Yeah, I felt bad about that. The big interview I had earlier in the week called back. I had missed two calls already while working the farm, and they were about to move on. I just caught them before they passed on me," Aaron said.

"So, you made their list?"

"Final three."

"Good job, honey," Cara said. "Which one is this?"

"This is just like my last job, but the next level up. It will mean a bump in our last pay. It solves our problems."

"That's great. It has been hard these past couple of months," Cara conceded. "What's the next step?"

"Final interviews are on Monday, in Chicago," Aaron replied.

"Chicago?"

"Yes, they are emailing me a ticket and arranging a hotel for Monday night. I'll be back mid-day Tuesday," Aaron said.

"Oh, is that the company's headquarters?"

"Yeah," Aaron scuffed his foot on the floor. "So is the job."

"In Chicago?" Cara shrieked.

"Yeah, I didn't realize that at first since the position is for this region, but I guess they have their regional guys work out of the home office and travel as needed to their territory," Aaron defended. "This job, it fixes everything for us."

"Yeah, but Chicago? This is our home. What about the kids and their school? What about my job? Our church?" Cara demanded.

"I know all that. I do. But…we have bills to pay. The salary for this role, you will only have to work if you want to," Aaron said.

"I do want to. At my school," Cara said.

Aaron frowned, "You have to be reasonable. We are in a tough spot. I have to find our way out of it."

"You do, or we do? Last I checked, we were in this together, Aaron."

"We are, but what else are we going to do?" Aaron asked. And then softened. "Look, nothing is settled. I might as well hear them out. We can pray on it."

"Ok," Cara tried to soften herself. But couldn't resist muttering under her breath and exasperated, "Chicago…."

Thirty One

The air among the Shepherds was heavy the next day. Aaron and Cara were particularly short with each other. Both prayed and asked for prayer on the job situation.

Joy, the head of the church's Angel Tree program, bounded up, "So, can I count on you two for sponsoring a family this year?"

"I...uh..." Cara started, fighting for the words to say.

"We can't. Not this year. I'm sorry," Aaron said. Being spread too thin both financially and from a time perspective, he was at wits end. A glance at Cara as if to make his point on Chicago.

When the youth pastor came and reminded them about their ability to donate or volunteer for the Christmas production, Aaron's response was the same. He could tell Cara was conflicted, he was himself, but he didn't think they had much of a choice. They were backed up to the edge and had to push forward.

In service, they prayed. In worship, they sang. Aaron and Cara were hollow and weak in their efforts. Their minds and hearts remained terribly distracted.

Even as he sat in the service and prayed, Aaron questioned the decision to attend the interview in Chicago. As the offering was passed their way at the end of service and Aaron had to pass it along without adding to it himself. At that moment, he was convinced he was doing the right thing by agreeing to the Chicago interview.

Though they typically lingered in the lobby with friends, the Shepherd's left quickly. In part, because they needed to get back to the farm, but in part because they didn't want to have to decline any more requests for donations or participation in events that they typically enjoyed during the holiday season.

At the farm, the family found their spirits strangely lifted. Though Aaron had the final interview and travel on his mind, he found helping Hal and working on the farm, a welcome distraction.

The family working together warmed their bond as they served the guests and helped them with their trees. The Christmas songs from the stereo mixed with the harmonization from families around the fire brought their Christmas spirit back.

Snow began to fall as the afternoon faded to evening. Aaron loved seeing the flakes drift down over the scene as he and his family cleaned up for the night.

"Another good day," Hal said.

"Yeah, business seems pretty good," Aaron agreed.

"Not quite like it used to be, but consistent with the past few years," Hal shrugged.

"Listen, I need to fly to Chicago tomorrow. I'll be back late Tuesday," Aaron told the farmer. "Are you going to be okay around here?"

"Well," Hal scratched his chin. "We'll make due. You take care of your business, and I'll pray for your success and safe travels."

"Thanks, Hal," Aaron said. "This and all you have done for us means a lot."

Hal nodded, "I'm happy to help."

The old farmer gave a wave and began walking quietly towards his house. Aaron watched him slowly make his way towards his porch, clearly hobbled by his sore back. Aaron wished he could pull the job interview and all of the stress over finances away until after the holidays, but he had to take care of his family.

Thirty Two

Aaron snuck out of the house early to catch his flight. Clearing off a snow-packed car and carefully navigating the wintry roads until they gave way to clear pavement in the lower elevations, he had gotten to the airport in plenty of time for his flight.

He searched his pockets for enough change to get a coffee, but found himself short. He was nervous about how he was going to get to the headquarters for the interview but determined he would tackle each hurdle at a time, as they presented themselves.

Reviewing his resume and researching the company on his phone, he felt ready for everything except for the details of food, transportation, tipping, or anything else that required money on his trip.

Aaron felt foolish in his lack of funds. That was, however, the incentive that propelled him for this trip. Cara was not happy with his decision to go forward with the interview knowing the job was in Chicago. Leaving on December first, the second busiest day of the year for Hal on the farm, was another factor that weighed on him.

He watched Hal try and load a tree while he was on the phone talking with Joe. Hal was not going to be able to manage that for his guests. Aaron was unsure whether his family could carry the extra burden. Chase was too little to be left unattended, and it did not appear that Hal's historical help from the Ladies' Auxiliary was able to pitch in at all this season.

Aaron didn't have long to focus on concerns over the farm as he had landed in Chicago. Deplaning, his most significant worry formed a giant pit in his stomach. He still had no idea how he was going to get to downtown Chicago with three dollars and forty-seven cents to his name.

Wandering his way to the transportation section of the terminal, he aimed for public transportation, hoping he could somehow get on with what he had. Coming home would be an issue for another day.

"Mr. Shepherd...Mr. Shepherd..." a man called to passersby.

Aaron froze. He turned his head to face the man. "Aaron Shepherd?"

"Yessir," the man nodded. "Here, I will take your bag."

The man grabbed Aaron's carry on and led the way to a big, black luxury SUV. Opening the door, he held it for Aaron to enter in the back and load his bag in the rear hatch.

As they settled in the car, the driver adjusted the climate controls to Aaron's liking. He turned and handed Aaron an envelope, "For you, sir."

Aaron thanked him and opened the envelope. Inside, he found two one-hundred-dollar bills, a hotel key card, and a welcome letter. Reading the note, Aaron shook his head. The cash was for incidentals, but he could charge his meals along with his stay to the hotel room, and the company was picking up the tab. The driver service was at his disposal, and tipping was already included.

Aaron clutched the envelope and said a quick prayer of gratitude. His heart climbed out of his belly as he felt an enormous sense of relief. His immediate concerns resolved, he walked into the home office with a lightness in his step, a confidence that he had not felt in months.

Finding the appropriate floor on the directory, he held the elevator door open as people milled in. "Aaron?" a voice called.

"Katlyn?" he asked in surprise.

"You're here for the regional manager spot, aren't you?" Katlyn. "You will love it here. I'm sorry to hear the company closed, but I guess I'm not too surprised. I am glad I got out when I did.

Good luck, I'll put a good word for you." She smiled as she exited the elevator on her floor.

As the doors opened for his floor, Aaron was quickly met by an elegant woman. "Mr. Shepherd? Welcome to Jans and Barnett. My name is Christina, I will be your assistant while you are here and perhaps, if you are successful in your interview today," she smiled.

Aaron stepped out of the elevator into a luxurious lobby. A reception desk in the center was flanked by sweeping views of the city seen through conference room windows.

"May I get you an espresso or sparkling water?" Christina asked, still moving as Aaron had paused to take it all in.

"Mr. Shepherd?"

"Oh, still water would be fine. Thank you. Call me, Aaron."

"OK. Aaron," Christina said, leading him to an office with a large bank of windows. "You may wait in this office. It is the western-most office for our western regional manager, cute, huh? If you need to freshen up, there are washrooms down either hallway. I'll be right back with your water."

Aaron undid his scarf and removed his overcoat, carefully placing it over the back of a high back chair opposite the desk chair. Walking to the window, he overlooked western Chicago, watching a light snow flurry brush by.

A large flat screen on the wall showed a series of reports with a business news station in one corner and a corporate memo in the opposite corner.

Aaron rubbed the grand mahogany desk with his hand as he sat in the luxury car seat worthy desk chair.

"Is everything alright?" Christina stood in the doorway. A glass of ice in one hand and a bottle of imported water in the other.

"Yes, just getting acquainted," Aaron replied.

Christina sat the glass and bottle on the desk. "Your interview will begin shortly. Janice will come and get you here when they are ready for you."

"Thank you," Aaron said.

Christina wheeled around and stepped out into the hallway. Pausing, she poked her head back in and smiled, "You look good behind that desk."

Aaron reviewed his notes one last time before a woman stood in the doorway of the office. "Mr. Shepherd, the executive team is ready for you."

"You must be Janice," Aaron smiled, grabbing his portfolio and rising to follow her.

"I am," the woman nodded. "I am Mr. Baronosky's Executive Assistant. He, as I am sure you know from your readings, is the head of HR. Joseph Fiske, the gentlemen you have been speaking to, is the Vice President of sales, he will be your primary interviewer, though the entire executive team will have a hand in the final decision."

"Thank you," Aaron said, appreciating the bit of insight.

Janice stood outside one of the large glass conference rooms. Her arm held out towards the room. "Gentlemen, Mr. Shepherd is here."

Aaron walked in and announced, "Good morning."

"Good morning, Aaron. Nice to finally meet you in person," Joe rose. Nodding towards the door, he said, "Go ahead and get the door, and we will begin."

Sharing the usual pleasantries and rehashing both the role, the foundation of the company, and Aaron's resume, one by one, the executive team took turns asking their questions of Aaron. Each impressed with his experience and depth of knowledge, questioning his ability to move from a smaller company to a much larger global brand.

Aaron assured him the principles that allowed the smaller company to perform well, even beating out the larger company in many cases, would translate only to further success with the backing of Jans and Barnett.

Seemingly liking his responses, most of the interview was met with nods of the head, though genuine smiles rarely cracked the stern expressions. Fielding the barrage of inquiries until the CEO glanced at his watch and signaled the end of the meeting.

Shaking everyone's hands, Aaron thanked them for their time and interest and impressed upon them that he was beyond confident that he was the right choice to run their western region.

"I'll walk you out," Joe said, point the way. As they entered the hallway, "So, what do you think?"

"I am impressed with the entire company. First-class personnel and every facet of the organization from my experience, so far," Aaron admitted.

"Life in the big leagues, if you will," Joe smiled. "I believe that you are first-class people too. While our process is not done yet, I feel that you are an excellent choice for the position. You already have the contacts and the relationships in the west region. Leveraging your connections will only accelerate the growth of our sales in that market with you leading our salesforce."

"I have no doubt that I can bring my connections to Jans and Barnett," Aaron nodded.

"So, here's the thing. If you are selected, we will need you to begin right away. We would need you in Chicago officially by January second. We will, of course, pay for an executive suite for your first six months here, for your whole family and cover any moving costs. Will that be an issue?" Joe asked.

Aaron tried to hide his momentary pause, "No, not a problem at all."

"Excellent," Joe beamed. "So, enjoy your evening. Treat yourself to a great meal. You deserve it. I will reconvene with the executive team, and we will connect with you later this week with our final decision."

"Thank you. I look forward to it," Aaron shook Joe's hand and disappeared into the elevator. Standing tall and confident, as soon as the doors closed, he collapsed against the wall of the elevator and let out a deep breath.

Thirty Three

The driver from the airport was waiting for Aaron as he left the Jans and Barnett building. As Aaron approached, the driver opened the door for him.

"Thank you," Aaron said. Stopping short of entering, he paused and looked at the driver, "I'm sorry. In all of the chaos and stress of the morning, I forgot to ask your name."

"Finley. Charles Finley," the driver said.

Aaron held out his hand, "Charles, it is a pleasure. Aaron Shepherd."

Finley shook Aaron's hand and smiled, "It went well then, I take it."

"I think so," Aaron nodded. "I think so."

Aaron waved goodbye to Finley, who assured Aaron that he was only a phone call away if he needed a ride anywhere, and he would pick him up three hours prior to his flight home.

Without the stress of the interview, Aaron could see Chicago fully. The luxury hotel the company had put Aaron in was spectacular. Walking up the steps into the lobby, a giant Christmas tree stood front and center.

Evergreen garland interlaced with Christmas lights adorned much of the entrance and hallways. Already having his keys and room number, Aaron did not need to check-in, but went straight to the bank of elevators. Soft holiday carols played throughout the hotel halls and elevator.

Even the hallways had boughs with red ribbons tied to the sconces that lit the hallways. Sliding his keycard into the door at his assigned room, Aaron nudged the door open.

Pushing into the room, his jaw dropped. The suite was giant. Aaron set his portfolio down on the counter and wandered the room. A kitchenette with stainless steel appliances, a full-size refrigerator, and the most luxurious granite countertops that he had ever seen. A large living room with floor to ceiling windows allowed the city of Chicago to peek through the lace curtains. The fireplace, complete with roaring gas-fed fire, had a mantle with a wide evergreen bough and holiday lights.

In the corner of the room was a tall Christmas tree that filled not just the floor Aaron was on but stretched up to a second story.

Ascending the stairs, Aaron found the bedroom suite. On a bench in front of the bed was Aaron's luggage. He laughed, in the commotion of the day, he had completely forgotten about his bag.

Aaron lavished in the moment, wising his family was there with him. Excited to tell Cara about the meeting and missing his family, he dialed her number. He was dejected when the call went to voicemail. Looking at the time, though nearly evening, he realized that his family would be in the busy December first mid-day swing with Hal at the farm.

Walking back down the stairs, he studied the Christmas tree. The decorations were gorgeous. Mostly traditional items like stars and snowflakes, intermixed with nature-inspired pieces like birds and glass pinecones.

Under the tree, he noticed a small package. Wrapped in attractive paper and with a bow adorned with pinecones and cinnamon sticks. A tag with his name was attached to the bow.

Curious, he opened the package. It was a glass ornament, like one on the tree. A little note said it was from the hotel, a memento of his stay.

On a dining table, he found a basket wrapped in plastic, tied together with a big red bow. Pulling off a card, he read it was a thank you from Jans and Barnett. Inside was a candied nuts, a bottle of wine, and other goodies to make his evening stay more comfortable, as the note suggested.

Taking the entire experience in- the car and driver, posh office and appointed assistant, the fabulous hotel suite and what was sure to be an exquisite steak dinner he was going to seek in the hotel's restaurant – it was all a far cry from the past few months of sweating whether or not they had enough gas to get to town and back.

Aaron's search for succulent steak was indeed rewarded. He was sure the one he had just finished was the best he had ever tasted.

Returning to his room, he tried his family again. As he looked out of the grand windows at the sparkling city lights, Cara picked up this time. "Hi hon!" he sang cheerily into the phone.

"Hi. How did your day go? Did you find a way into town?" Cara asked.

Aaron went on to tell Cara about his experiences throughout the day.

"It all sounds very exciting," Cara said, her voice a bit dry.

"You don't sound as excited as I am," Aaron suggested.

"Well, unless you learned something different, this job is still in Chicago," Cara said.

"Yeah, it is. If I am selected, they want me to start right away," Aaron said.

"How is that going to work? What about the farm? What about the Christmas projects at church?"

"I get all that. If they need me to start right away, we get paid right away. We need that. We need this," Aaron defended. He decided to avoid the discussion of having to officially move by January second out of the conversation for now. "How was your day?"

Cara scoffed, "I'm not going to candy-coat it. It was a tough day here. I think my arms are going to fall off. The kids were great. Hal ran the shop with Annie while Chase and I did what we could with the trees. I learned anything under six-feet I could handle. Anything above, the guests had to do themselves."

"I'm sorry I wasn't there to help."

"Yeah. We worked well together as a family when we were all here," Cara admitted. "I worry about Hal. He was pretty sore and tuckered by the end of the day."

"Maybe this is all sign. Maybe the farm, as it is, has run its course. Maybe change is needed," Aaron offered.

"Change. Like moving to Chicago? Really?"

"If we do move, they will absorb all of the expenses. They'll put us up for the first six months while we figure out our next step," Aaron said.

"I don't want to uproot the family," Cara said.

"I know. I don't want the family to have to live under a bridge," Aaron quipped. "Look, my idea is I get up and running, I wow them with success and I encourage them that I can work remotely and instead of traveling to my assigned geography, I travel to the home office as needed. It just might take a little time to get there."

"I get it hon, I'm just scared about this whole thing," Cara said. "Look, I'm tired, the kids are tired. We look forward to seeing you tomorrow. We'll all pray for safe travel for you, Aaron."

"Okay. Good night, Cara."

Aaron flopped on the bed, his head spinning with his call with Cara, understanding her distress, but still arguing that they needed to take the path forward.

He patted the thick down comforter, momentarily distracted by the bed, "Wow. Wow. This bed is…ridiculously plush." Enjoying yet another luxurious experience with the trip, he was confident that things would work out, even if they had to move.

He had to admit, he harbored his own reservations with taking the job and moving. His family was ingrained in their community in Maple Valley. The people at church weren't just part of a congregation. They were like family. Cara is known throughout the town as she had touched so many of its young lives. Now there was Hal and his tree farm. It had been a wonderful experience this past fall. He knew without performing well enough this year for Hal to hire help next year, the farm was done. Hal's hand would be forced.

Still, his mind reeled with the bills and the pressure and the stress. To find a way to wipe all of that away, that was an opportunity extremely difficult to deny.

Thirty Four

Aaron waited in the exquisite hotel lobby after a breakfast of eggs benedict and asparagus. Checking his watch, he saw Finley arrive precisely five minutes before he was due.

Aaron waved off the bellman and grabbed his bag. Before Finley could open the door for him, Aaron slid into the backseat and tossed his carry-on next to him.

"Good morning, Finley," Aaron said.

"Good day, Mr. Shepherd. Traffic is...well, Chicago traffic. We will use all of our available time to get you to the airport on time, but you'll be fine," the driver said.

As they slogged through traffic, Aaron's phone rang.

"Aaron, it's Joe."

"Good morning, Joe."

"I trust you had a good evening at the hotel, and your accommodations were up to par," Joe prompted.

"Yes, everything was fantastic. Thank you."

"Well, I wanted to call this morning with some news," Joe started. "Jans and Barnett would like to extend you an offer. All the details we had already described, with one small change. We understand the disruption to your family this holiday season, so we would like to offer you a bonus if you are able to start this week."

"This week? I suppose I should be able to. Do I need to stay in Chicago?"

"No, no. You can work from your home office, though we may need to ask you to travel a bit once you review the initial training. Again, we would want you officially in Chicago by the second of January," Joe explained.

"What bonus are you suggesting?" Aaron inquired.

"The equivalent of two month's salary. We could wire it to you as soon as we receive your banking information in the employment paperwork."

Aaron stifled his excitement, "That sounds reasonable."

"Excellent, I will have the paperwork emailed to you. Congratulations and welcome aboard," Joe said.

"I look forward to joining you as well," Aaron said, beaming as he hung up the phone.

As Aaron rode to the airport, his mind wandered. The new job would not only provide them a stable income, but it would be a sizable increase as well. The bonus alone would bail them out of their immediate financial strife.

They would also receive fantastic benefits, as explained to him, including exceptional healthcare for the entire family, longer vacations and an expense account along with a company car.

The opportunity seemed to be just what the family needed.

Thirty Five

Aaron pulled into the drive, excited to see the family. Parking by the barn, he saw a couple of families milling about, either on their way to find a tree or having just returned with their selection.

The family had assembled as Cara had described on the phone she and Chase outside, Hal and Annie inside. Each manned their post and tried to help as best they could.

Aaron got out of the car. Seeing Cara struggle to get a tree on the family's car, he jogged over and, despite being in business attire, helped loft the tree onto the car's roof rack.

Chase seeing Aaron, ran up and hugged his dad.

Draping an arm over Chase, Aaron smiled, "I missed you too, pal."

The family thanked them as they finished tying the tree down with twine and drove away. Aaron took the moment to steal a kiss with his wife.

"I am glad to be home," Aaron admitted.

"We're glad to have you home," Cara said. "Now, go change your clothes, because we need you on the farm."

Aaron nodded. "I'm going to say hi to Annie real quick, and then I'll change."

Poking his head in the store, he saw Annie's head perk up, and a smile stretch across her sweet, freckled little face. "Daddy!"

Running around the corner of the check stand, Annie ran and leaped into her father's arms. "Hi, baby."

"I missed you, Daddy."

"I missed you too. Have you been a huge help for Mom and Hal?"

"Oh, yes. It hasn't been too busy, but we have taken care of everyone," Annie grinned.

"Yes, we did. And I could not have done any of this without your help," Hal concluded. "Welcome back, Aaron. Have a good trip?"

Aaron looked thoughtful, "Yeah, I did. It was a very good trip."

"Good, I was praying for you."

"Me too," Aaron grinned. "Speaking of which, I have an email I need to respond to, and then I will change and get back to my farm duties."

Managing his email took longer than he expected as he carefully reviewed the offer from Jans and Barnett. They wanted several forms returned right away so that they could begin processing his employment.

He completed everything right then, with the exception of the official acceptance, which he respectfully wanted to wait until he had a chance to discuss the job with Cara before signing and submitting it.

Closing the laptop, he quickly changed his clothes and rushed out of the house. As he descended the porch, he found Cara once more trying to get a large tree on to the roof of an SUV. Running over, helped to heave it in place and tie it down. Cara shot him look as if to ask what had taken him so long.

"Alright, I am officially on duty," Aaron said, clapping his hands together.

Cara took her gloves off and retreated into the store.

The rest of the afternoon was relatively quiet. Few families made their way up the hill to the tree farm. Aaron used the downtime to start snowball fights with Chase or split wood for the firepit, as well as a few extras for Hal's stockpile.

By closing time, the sky was dark, Hal and the Shepherds retreated to their respective homes. The kids played in the living room in front of the fire.

Cara began fixing dinner, and Aaron slid in to see if he could help. "You know, this is barely a kitchen for one, never mind two," Cara said. "Why don't you sit in the stool on the other side of the counter and relax after your big trip."

Reluctantly, Aaron conceded and rolled around the counter to take a position on one of the stools. "Sorry I wasn't around to help yesterday and most of today."

"We managed," Cara shrugged. "I do worry about Hal. I know the type. My dad was like him. They could be hurt, tired, sick, or broken, and they just don't stop. He told me this will likely be the last year of the farm. I can see it makes him sad."

"Yeah. He's a good man. This is a great place. Getting to experience this, while certainly not planned, has been a real blessing," Aaron admitted.

"So, are you going to tell me about it?" Cara asked.

"Tell you what?" Aaron grinned.

"I can tell you have had further discussion," Cara said.

"I did."

"And?"

"They offered me the position," Aaron said, leaning across the counter, his hands clasped in front of him.

Cara kept working on dinner without much of a response.

"I know we would have to move, at least for a while. But, they are offering us a two-month's salary bonus. That would fix our finances, immediately," Aaron pleaded. "Not to mention the increase in salary."

"We've talked about this, I don't want to move," Cara spat, her voice hoarse.

"I don't either. But we don't have much of a choice. We have financial responsibilities that we are not able to meet. We need a solution, and this is it," Aaron argued.

"We have responsibilities here. At church, my work…"

"You won't have to work. We'll find a new church. I am pretty sure we will find that there are plenty of people in need in Chicago," Aaron quipped.

Cara sighed, slamming her wooden spoon down. "When is all of this supposed to happen?"

"They sent me the paperwork today. I need to respond tomorrow. They want me to start right away," Aaron replied.

"In Chicago?" Cara gasped.

"No, not right away. I have home study that will largely take me through the holidays," Aaron said. Cara seemed somewhat relieved that they could get through the holidays unscathed.

"What about Hal? How are you supposed to work for this new company and work at the farm?" Cara asked.

Shaking his head, "I don't know. Maybe I can work around the peak farm hours. We'll have to see. What about the kids? We don't have anything for them for Christmas, and every dime we have is spoken for and then some. We sweat each trip to town, not knowing whether we will have enough gas to get us home. This way, we can relax and enjoy Christmas."

"What happens after the holidays?" Cara asked.

Aaron slumped his head down, "They want us there by January second."

"They what?" Cara exclaimed, raising her voice to the point the kids whirled the heads around.

"It's...it will get us back on our feet," Aaron urged.

"I know it will, I know. I know you deserve a job like this. You've worked hard your entire career, but...I always thought we would raise our children here, in Maple Valley. Or at least somewhere not too far from here. Be a part of the community," Cara said.

"I did too. No one says we can't return. But right now, we are financially broken, you know that. We need this relief," Aaron said. "We need to take this job."

Cara breathed deep and wiped her brow with her sleeve, "I don't know."

Aaron circled the counter and gently squeezed her shoulders, "It will be okay."

Thirty Six

After a couple of days in suits in the big city of Chicago, Aaron couldn't help but admit to himself that a day in jeans and boots at the farm was rather comforting.

He prepped the tree station so that the farm was ready to receive guests. He stacked a pile of wood on Hal's porch and left coffee and breakfast prepared for his family.

As he got the fire going in the firepit, he sat on a stump and relished the mountain air.

"Snowed a bit last night." Aaron looked up to see Hal walking next to him and sat on a nearby stump. "Supposed to have reached to the valley floor."

"I always liked it when it snowed," Aaron said and laughed, "Town drivers don't always handle it so well, though."

"No. No, they don't. Probably mean a lighter than normal day for here at the farm," Hal said.

"How's it going this year?"

"We're doing okay. If I was a few years younger, I think we'd be just fine. But without a bigger turnout, this will likely be the last year," Hal said solemnly.

"Well, we've still got time," Aaron encouraged.

"Yeah."

The rest of the family joined them. Cara made cocoa for the kids, and they all gathered around the fire. A light dusting of snow drifted down over the family and settled around them.

It was an hour before the first guest arrived and an hour after that before another. Hal and the Shepherds afforded exceptional care with the reduced crowd. At lunchtime, those had been the only visitors they had.

Heading into the house, the sound of chains against the pavement chugging up the highway and turning into the driveway.

A brown delivery truck stopped just outside the house. The driver called out, "Delivery for Shepherd?"

"That's us!" Aaron raised his hand.

"Here you go," the driver said, handing over the package.

"Merry Christmas!" Aaron nodded, reading the package. He read from the label that it was from Jans and Barnett.

"I'm going to run this up to the house. I'll be right back," Aaron said.

Setting the box on the kitchen table, Aaron split the top of the package open to reveal the contents. Removing a blanket of bubble wrap, he found a welcome letter and manuals for the new job, complete with a study and testing schedule for him to complete over the next few weeks. A glance told him he would have his hands full to meet their expectations.

The next sheet, an ACH receipt, reminded him that he was on the clock, as the sizable bonus Jans and Barnett promised was now in his bank account.

Underneath the receipt was a moving guide for the city of Chicago. Aaron slipped the guide under his study manuals. He was torn. He wanted to tear into the materials and get to work, but he knew Hal and his family were waiting for him back outside.

Reluctantly, he left his documents on the table, slipped his gloves back on to head outside.

Most of his day was tending to the fire and entertaining Chase. Occasionally they would all huddle inside the store or around the fire. Aaron would regale them with the wonders of the

Christmas décor at the hotel and the grandeur of his holiday-decorated suite.

"So, you had a chauffeur?" Chase asked.

"Well, something like that," Aaron nodded.

"Laura and I spent some time in Chicago," Hal said. "Nice town. You guys will like it there."

Annie looked down, "I'm gonna miss my friends."

"Moving is always tough, but you are so much fun, you will have absolutely no problem making all sorts of new friends," Hal comforted. "You like art, right? Chicago has amazing art museums and galleries. In fact, they have an entire art district."

"We have some time before we worry about moving," Cara cautioned. "Your father and I haven't worked out all of the details, just yet."

"Right. For now, we can all focus on the holidays," Aaron smiled.

The workday at the farm had been quiet. Less than half a dozen guests had made their way up the hill. Putting Annie and Chase to bed, Aaron pulled out his first training manual and began reading through it.

Cara sat down on the couch, blowing the steam off of a cup of tea. "I think I have a plan. It won't be easy, but I don't know how else to make all this work."

Aaron set his study materials down. "What do you mean?"

"Chicago," Cara said. "I am in the middle of a school year. The kids are too. We have a lot of projects we are working on at church…"

"Cara, we talked about this. I had to take the job," Aaron said.

"I know. And you did," Cara nodded.

"So…?"

"So, if you have to go to Chicago, I think the kids and I should stay here…just for the school year, and then we can see where we are at," Cara said.

Aaron was stunned by the idea. Shaking his head, he frowned, "I don't understand?"

"You have to travel out here anyway, as part of your geography. We can come up on Spring Break, and by then, we'll have a better picture of what is going on. Besides, your plan is to get them to let you work out of a home office out here," Cara said.

"Yeah, but we are family. Family's stay together. We weather the storms, together," Aaron protested.

"I know. And we are and will. It is going to take us time to find a place," Cara said. "This is just a stepwise way to get there."

"I don't know," Aaron said, dubious.

Cara sipped her tea, "Let's sleep on it. Like you told the kids, we'll get through the holidays and go from there."

"Yeah, sure," Aaron said. "I've got to get my studying in. I have several tests each week."

"I think I am going to turn in," Cara said.

Aaron nodded, "Goodnight."

Dropping his head, he focused back on his work.

Cara got up, setting her cup on the counter.

It was the first time in their marriage that Aaron could remember either going to bed without the other not giving a kiss goodnight.

Thirty Seven

Aaron started his day with a cup of coffee and his study manuals. With an eye on the clock and another on his work, the morning slipped by.

As his family woke up and gathered, he realized it was the latest that he had started for the farm. "Good morning, guys!" He sang, putting his studies down.

Annie groggily yawned her way over to him and laid her down on his shoulder.

"Are you going to help us today, Daddy?" Chase asked.

"Yep, I am on duty. I got up early so I could get some of my other work done," Aaron replied.

"I like it better when you are with us," Chase said.

"Me too, bud. Me too."

Bundling up and manning their respective roles for the tree farm, the family readied for any guests that would venture out that day.

"These in-between days can be a bit slow," Hal said. "But with December first coming up, that is our busiest day. Busier than Thanksgiving."

"That's good. I'd love for you to get a solid boost this year," Aaron said.

"I'm sure we'll do fine," Hal said. "Say, why don't you take some time with the family today. With your travels and all..."

Aaron smiled, "Yeah, that's sounds good. Maybe we'll take a break and head up on the ridge for some sledding."

Chase's eyes went wide, "That would be awesome!"

"Let's make sure this place is ship shape for any families that do come up," Aaron suggested. "Tell your sister the same thing. We will go right after lunch."

Chase ran off to talk to Annie.

"You sure have a fine family, Aaron," Hal remarked.

"I do," Aaron nodded. "I do."

A fresh dusting of snow had settled onto the hills and continued to sprinkle through the air. Aside from several phone calls from families planning to come to the farm over the weekend, the morning was exceptionally light.

In anticipation of sledding after lunch, the Shepherd's retreated to the cottage while Hal manned the shop. Cara had promised to bring a sandwich back for the farmer.

As the kids ran off to don their snow gear, Aaron flipped on his laptop. A reminder popped up that a test was due. Moving to a corner of the dining table, he entered the exam.

"You aren't going to have your laptop open during lunch, are you?" Cara asked.

"I have a test I need to take. Shouldn't be too long, probably done about the same time as the kids finish their sandwiches," Aaron explained.

Buckling in, he focused on the test questions. The kids joined him at the table, their snow pants rustling, tossing their hats, mittens, and coats on the couch. "Dad, no electronics at the table," Annie scolded.

"I know. I got special permission from Mom," Aaron said.

"Well, not permission, I just didn't argue," Cara quipped.

"I have to get this done so we can play," Aaron said, taking a bite of his sandwich.

Chase gobbled his sandwich and peeked over the top of his father's computer, "Are you done yet?"

"Not yet, buddy. They are very detailed in their testing," Aaron said.

"When are you gonna be done?" Chase asked.

"I will be done sooner if you let me focus," Aaron said.

"Come on, guys, why don't you walk back to the shop with me. Your father can come get you when he is done and you guys can go sledding," Cara said.

"Thanks, hon," Aaron said, not looking up from his work.

As Cara and the kids left, the quiet in the house did help Aaron focus, he twisted a little, feeling bad about having his nose in his laptop during lunch and not being ready for the kids when lunch was over.

Cycling through the final battery of questions he hit submit, held his breath and smiled scoring a ninety-eight percent. Feeling good about his effort, he closed the laptop and crammed the remaining bits of his sandwich in his mouth. Grabbed his winter outerwear, he started tugging it on when his phone rang.

Aaron hesitated to answer, but knew he was officially on the clock. "Hello?"

"Aaron, its Joe. I see you aced your first exam, nice job. Listen, I hate to spring this on you, but your predecessor left the western region budget and business plan in a bit of shambles. The executive team is meeting first thing tomorrow to review all the regions. Since you will ultimately be held accountable, I figured it would be a good idea if you took what you could glean from Harry's report and make it yours."

"Yeah, that should be no problem," Aaron said, slipping his arms into his weatherproof coat. "I'll have it on your desk first thing in the morning Chicago time."

"I appreciate that, but I need to review it this evening. You got some daylight left, with today's test out of the way, you should be done in time for dinner with your family," Joe said.

"Sure," Aaron nodded to no one who could see him. "No problem."

"Great, I knew I could count on you," Joe said.

Aaron hung up the call and stared at his phone. Sighing, he trudged out of the house towards the store.

As soon as he stepped off of the porch, he heard Annie and Chase squeal, "Daddy's ready!" Their arms in the air, they celebrated in anticipation of their trip up the ridge to go sledding.

Aaron's heart sank as he walked. The last thing in the world he ever wanted to do, was disappoint his children. Seeing them so excited and knowing he had no choice, made him feel miserable.

"Let's go!" Chase shouted, his hand raised in the air, running towards his dad.

"Hang on there, bud," Aaron stretched his arm out to corral Chase. "So..." Aaron began. Cara's head snapped up, anticipating what was coming.

"I just got a call from my new boss. There is a project he really needs me to do," Aaron admitted.

"Can't you do it tonight?" Annie pleaded.

Aaron pointed at his daughter, "That is exactly what I suggested, but he needs to review it tonight, so I...so I have to go do that...now."

Chase's arms fell from his dad and his shoulders slumped.

"So, why don't you two sled down the hill on the inside fence line along the driveway? Your Mom can watch you. It would be like practice for the big hill," Aaron suggested.

"Yeah, I guess," Chase moped. "I wanted to sled with you."

"I know. I wanted to sled with you too. Trust me, I would much rather be sledding than reviewing budgets and sales forecasts."

"What are those?" Annie asked.

"Like reading a really boring book, but that boring book is going to pay the bills and ensure we have money to help at church and buy sweet little kids Christmas presents," Aaron said.

"Well, I guess it is for a good reason. But you have to do it now?" Annie asked.

"I do," Aaron nodded.

"Alright. Come on, Chase," Annie waved for her brother to follow.

Aaron reluctantly turned and headed back towards the cottage. The look on Chase's face was something he would struggle to cleave from his mind.

Thirty Eight

After working all day on the reports for the western region, taking a break to spend dinner and the evening with the family, Aaron stayed up late to get a jump on the next day's studies. Taking the test at two in the morning so that he could free up his time on the farm and with family.

The next morning, Aaron woke, and instead of waking up with the laptop in his lap, he drank his coffee in the kitchen, making pancakes for the kids.

Chase and Annie joined him downstairs, and Aaron set out plates with a giant pancake topped with two smaller pancakes to look like ears. Strips of bacon laid placed to look like whiskers. The kids giggled.

"What is going on in here?" Cara asked.

"Dad made mousecakes!" Annie said.

"Mousecakes!" Chase grinned, pointing at his plate, which was missing a whisker and half of an ear.

"I see. You are lucky to have such a fun dad," Cara said. "Hardworking, too. What time did you get to bed last night?"

"Late. I wanted to get today's work done, so you all have my undivided attention," Aaron said.

"Now that, I like," Cara kissed her husband.

"I'll meet you guys at the shop?" Aaron asked, slipping his boots on.

Aaron met up with Hal as he walked across the driveway to the tree station.

"New job has you really tied up, huh?" Hal asked.

"Not too bad, the whole last-minute report thing was certainly a setback yesterday. That is a part of corporate life I did not miss," Aaron admitted. "I did today's work last night, so I should be good to go."

"You didn't have to do that. I understand you have to work. You all have done so much to help already," Hal said.

"I'm good. I want you to have a good year at the farm," Aaron said.

The men were distracted with the sound of a powerful engine churning up the hill. A flatbed truck swung into the driveway and parked in front of the shop. A driver hopped out, "One of you, Shepherd?"

"I am," Aaron raised his hand.

"Alright, sign here," the man handed Aaron a tablet. Checking that the signature was accepted, the man tossed the tablet into the cab of the truck. Walking to the rear, he pulled a lever, and the rear of the bed sunk to ground level.

Climbing into a European sedan, the man backed the sedan off of the truck and parked it alongside the shop. Tossing Aaron the keys, he called, "She's all yours!"

Climbing back into the truck, the man backed out of the truck and headed down the drive and back down the hill.

"Nice car," Hal said, eyeing the sedan. It was gleaming black with its high polish.

"I guess this is the company car my boss told me about," Aaron said,

Chase and Annie ran over to investigate.

"Who's car is that?" Chase asked.

"It's ours," Aaron said. "Go on, check it out."

Chase and Annie dove into the car.

"It seems like your new job is treating you well," Hal noted.

Aaron nodded, "They are. I was always a little dubious with them as a competitor. They have a reputation as being a bit cut-throat, but they have been nothing but first class with me so far."

"Wow," Cara called as she joined the family.

"Should we take it for a spin?" Aaron asked.

"Sure," Cara grinned.

The Shepherd family piled into the car. They all took time to smell the new car and leather

aromas that were so pleasing. Aaron fiddled with
the buttons for the front and back heated seats and
opened the roof panel revealing giant sunroof that
spanned both the front and back seats.

Aaron fired up the potent engine. Putting it
into gear, he backed out of the parking spot and
drove down the driving. Carving the curvy
backroads, they admired the giant sunroof and
richly appointed leather upholstery of the car.

After a quick circuit, they returned, and
Aaron parked the car by the main house. "See, the
new job is not so bad," Aaron gloated with his
family.

"Not bad at all." Annie chimed.

The family let the new car collect a soft
dusting of snow while they helped Hal prep for the
busiest weekend. Restocking the store shelves,
prepping the sleds, and saws. Aaron worked on
chopping a large pile of wood for both houses and
the tree station fire pit.

Aaron had just made a dent in the to-do list
when his phone rang.

"Aaron, it's Joe. It sounds like your car
arrived. Do you like it?"

"Yes, it's great. The entire family has already
checked it out," Aaron admitted.

"Good, good. Listen. We need to put your
studies on hold, or shuffle them around a bit at
least. As long you get them done by the end of the
year, we are good. Anyway, we need you to visit

the key clients in your region before the holidays. It would be a tight turn as I know you have a lot of real estate to cover," Joe said. "I have sent you the target list."

"It sounds like I will put the new car to good use," Aaron said.

"Great. I knew we could count on you," Joe said. "Make a daily report and a summary of the completion of the target list by the 24th."

"Will do," Aaron assured and snapped off the phone.

When the farm waved goodbye to their last customer of the day, Aaron retreated to his laptop at the kitchen table and opened the file that Joe had sent. Aaron started mapping out the geography. As he filled in the routing, he sighed. In order for him to hit their prescribed objective, he would have to be on the road for most of December.

For many of the appointments, Aaron calculated that he would have to leave on Sunday to hit Monday appointments and stay on schedule. Pushing back from his work, he reasoned Cara and the kids would not like the scenario. He also knew that he would be putting Hal and the farm in a difficult spot as well.

Double-checking the calendar and being as creative as he could be with the trips, he could barely make a dent in the road time that he would need to schedule in December.

Still, the job was fulfilling a gaping need for the Shepherd family, Aaron knew that he had to comply.

Thirty Nine

Aaron set his alarm early and snuck through the cottage as he got ready for the day. He had placed what he needed for work by the door before going to bed so that he would have less of a chance to wake anyone.

Pausing to toss a log on the fire for his family, Aaron grabbed his new car keys. Taking a last look at the cottage where his family were sleeping warm in their beds, he grabbed his bags and left the house.

Starting up the car, he fired up the defrost and the heat to help melt the layer of ice and light snow that had fallen that evening. When the windows were cleared enough for him to see, he put the car in gear and pulled out of the drive.

The road along the farm had a sheen that reflected off of his headlights. Aaron knew leaving so early, he ran a higher risk of icy roads. In order to hit the key clients, especially those further away from home, he had to travel while people slept so that he could make his appointments throughout the day.

Pressing the accelerator gingerly, eyeing the navigation and the roads carefully, he began his first road trip.

Cara snuggled the kids awake, hating to make them get up out of their cozy beds, but her heart warmed when her effort met with sleepy hugs and smiles. "Good morning, babies," she cooed.

"Good morning, Mommy," they whispered back in little, hoarse morning voices.

"Farmer Hal says today is going to be a big day, so we need to make sure we are up to help him," Cara informed Annie and Chase.

"Is Daddy already up?" Chase asked.

"He is, but he left for his trip, remember?" Cara reminded.

Chase's head slumped, "Oh, yeah."

"It's alright. He is doing his job and got up early to work for us. I have a feeling he would rather be here loading Christmas trees than driving through cities and meeting with people in boardrooms," Cara said.

Helping the children don their snow gear, they made their way to open the shop for Hal.

The scene at the farm met Hal's prediction, being the first of December, it was as busy as Cara had seen it. With Hal's back not allowing him to do the heavy lifting, he manned the store with Chase while Cara worked the tree prep station with Annie.

Getting families on their way for their tree search was a smooth process with Cara giving the lay of the land and Annie handing out the sleds and saws. Together, they kept the fire pit roaring and directed families towards the shop for cocoa and coffee.

When families returned with their trees, the process was not nearly so fluid. Cara struggled to get the trees onto the shaker and keep it supported while it did its loose needle banishment. On more than one occasion, the tree flung itself out of Cara's grip and out of the shaker across the tree station, sending her and Annie into a frantic dash to rescue it.

Getting the trees onto vehicles, in particular, taller SUVs, was its own area for frustration and frequent hilarity. Helping one family in particular, Cara was proud of herself for getting the tree lofted up and over the edge of the SUV's roofline, only to have gravity to send it rolling off of the roof's edge, crashing back down on top of her.

Annie couldn't help but to giggle, Cara was less humored, as the day was painting her from head to toe in tree sap.

Finding a small stepstool, Annie brought it to her mom to assist with tying trees to the cars, a much more successful venture.

The girls found a rhythm with helping, still their efficiency and organization couldn't match the times when brawn would have been a useful trait in taming the crowds when multiple families stacked together. Where Aaron could have carried two trees at a time to the shaker and could hoist the trees overhead with the ease, the extra effort required by Cara, left them running and feeling behind all day.

With their attention on keeping up with the demands of shaking, loading, and restocking for the next family, they never quite felt like the experience for the visitors was what it should have been. Not like it had been the day after Thanksgiving when they were able to work as a family.

Exhausted, Cara and the kids gathered around Hal's dining table. Cara offered to cook, but Hal wouldn't hear of it. "You, Chase, and Annie had the tough jobs today. I just had to stand behind the cash box and smile," he reasoned.

"Can I at least help?" Cara asked.

"Nope," Hal replied flatly. "You guys relax, I'll have something hearty and delicious, I hope, before too long. "

Cara ran her fingers through her hair as she leaned to prop her head in her hands as elbows rested on the table. "Ouch!" she gasped as her fingers got stuck and tugged at her hair.

"What's wrong, Mommy?" Chase asked.

"I have sap in my…well, everything," Cara laughed.

Hal appeared with a small dish with a citrus smelling liquid, "A little dish soap. Works great. If it is really bad, use a little hand sanitizer."

"Thanks," Cara called, dabbing her fingers in the bowl and finding the worst snags to work through.

As she combed through her hair, smoothing dish soap through it until the sap was freed, her phone rang. Nodding her head towards her phone, she looked at Annie, "Would you?"

Annie clicked the glowing green button on the phone.

"Hello?" Cara called.

"Hi hon!" a tired sounding Aaron called back through the speaker.

"Hi, Daddy!" the kids called across the table.

"Hi, guys! How was your day?" Aaron asked.

"Busy," Annie replied. "Mom had a tree fall on her and flung two of them out of the shaker."

"She did? Is everyone alright?" Aaron pressed.

Cara laughed, "We're all fine. I don't know if my hair will ever be the same, I think I bathed in sap."

"I wish I had been there to help you," Aaron said.

"I know. Overall, I think we did an...okay job today all in all," Cara admitted.

"Where are you?" Chase asked.

"I am in Boise, Idaho," Aaron replied. "Tomorrow, I will be in Spokane, Washington."

"When will you be home?" Annie asked.

"Uhm...the way it looks now, not until sometime on Saturday."

"Saturday? I thought you'd at least be home tomorrow night," Cara asked.

"That was my plan, but with winter roads, I have had to add margin to my appointment schedule. I have a client that I meet with Saturday morning for coffee and then come straight home after that," Aaron explained.

"Well, drive carefully. I worry about you on icy roads," Cara said.

"I will. I love you guys!" Aaron called.

"Love you too!" the kids sang.

"I love you, Aaron. Good night," Cara wiped her dish soap hands on her pants and swiped to end the call.

"I want Daddy home," Chase said.

"I know. I know," breathed Cara.

She put the phone down, staring at it as if it had some answers to provide her. She didn't like seeing the kids disappointed, and she didn't like how the new company was running her husband around, and it was only the beginning.

Her thoughts were broken by Hal calling that dinner was ready. Carrying a large roasting pan towards the table, a towel tossed over his shoulder, the farmer said, "Had some beans and meat and tortillas. Pretty easy to figure out what to do with all that."

"Hal, it smells delicious," Cara said. "Thank you."

"Not a problem at all. How is Aaron and his travels?"

"He's traveling. He won't get back until sometime on Saturday now," Cara informed.

Hal looked concerned, "Sure are running him ragged, aren't they?"

"They are," Cara nodded.

"And how are you doing with all of this?"

Cara looked away for a moment and with a breath, addressed Hal's question, "I am not exactly in love with the idea. It's like we traded one stress for another."

"Out of the frying pan and into the fire," Hal scoffed.

"Something like that," Cara nodded. "I felt like in a time of stress, we got conned into selling our soul."

"When you're struggling, sure is an apt time to be taken advantage of, but this sounds like a pretty good job," Hal suggested.

"It is. I mean, it pays well, provides Aaron with perks he's never seen before and likely deserves. I'm just not sure it's…it's worth it," Cara admitted.

"I'm sure things will work out. Aaron is a solid man, and he puts his family first, even if he has to take a short step away to do so," Hal said.

"Yes, you're right. I'm sorry to burden this all on you," Cara said, feeling sheepish for pouring all of that out and in front of the children.

"Not at all. I asked the question, you were just being open with your concerns," Hal said. Glancing at both children, he added, "What I am most impressed by is how much you all truly care for one another. That is what family is all about."

Cara let out a little laugh, "It is. We'll figure things out, we always do."

Forty

Aaron swirled his coffee cup, disappointed to find that he had already reached the bottom of it. Smoothing his hand over his face, he yawned and flexed his eyes open as he navigated the luxury car off of the highway and up the twisting roads of the hills.

It was afternoon by the time he pulled the car into the drive of the tree farm. Though it had only been a temporary home to them for a while, he felt good as he drove along the evergreens flanking the gravel road.

The snowy hills presenting a majestic backdrop behind the main house and the barn were postcard perfect. The handful of families milling about the farm with prized trees or cups of cocoa along the firepit was a picture that warmed his heart and mind.

Aaron was in particular awe as he watched his beautiful wife smile and help a family with this part of their family tradition. Cara admired a tree that a family had selected and motioned towards the shop as she reached her hand between the boughs to grasp the trunk of the tree.

Standing outside of the car, pulling the lapel of his overcoat up to ward off the chill, he looked on as Annie rested her hands on her knees so that she could stoop over and be eye level with a little girl who was telling her some sort of story. With a big smile, Annie reached her hand in her pocket and produced a candy cane.

The little girl grasped it and bounced a little as she offered Annie her thanks.

Sacrificing the fact that he had dress shoes on, Aaron walked across the snowy driveway. "This doesn't look like the chaotic scene described to me on the phone," he smiled. "You guys look like a confident, well run tree farm to me."

"Things are admittedly a bit calmer today. That said, we would welcome your manly tree lifting skills," Cara admitted.

"Sure thing. Let me get out of my suit, and I'll be right back," Aaron said, leaning in to kiss his wife. "Nice tree!" he called to the family.

Despite being exhausted from the work trip, early hours, and long drive, Aaron felt refreshed in the crisp mountain air, never mind energized by being with his family.

Changing out of his professional attire, he transitioned into what had become his work clothes – a pair of jeans, a flannel shirt covering a thermal henley, and work boots.

In minutes, he had taken over the tree hoisting duties. As the families drove away with their trees atop their vehicles, Aaron poked his head into the shop to receive a sprinting Chase leaping into his awaiting arms.

"I missed you," Chase said, burying his face into his father's shoulder.

"I missed you too, pal," Aaron said, giving his son a big squeeze.

Turning to Hal, Aaron asked, "How goes the farm?"

"Oh, pretty good. Yesterday was busy, as predicted. Down from previous years, but busy enough to give us a run for our money," Hal declared.

"I heard," Aaron nodded.

Hal looked taken aback, "I didn't mean to imply..."

"I know. I didn't take it that way. I do wish I was here to help," Aaron conceded.

"That family of yours, they sure gave it all they had," Hal said.

"They're a good crew," Aaron admitted. Eying the register, he asked, "So how is the farm doing?"

Hal paused prior to replying. "Our two biggest days are behind us. We've had a nice stream of families, but…"

"Yeah," Aaron sighed in acknowledgment. "Well, this place sure makes those families that do make it out here happy."

"It does, it really does," Hal smiled. "Hey, why don't you and your family take the rest of the day and find your own tree?"

"Are you sure? There are still a few folks out there…"

"I insist. They'll be fine. Now go," Hall shooed Aaron and Chase out of the shop.

Annie ran up and hugged her father.

"So, Hal has kicked us all off of the clock. He says, no he demanded, that we go and find our own tree. What do you think?" Aaron said.

The kids clapped their hands together, and Chase darted to grab a sled. Annie selected a saw and held it up. "Let's go."

Pulling Cara in close by her shoulders, "Well?"

She smiled at her husband, "I think that is a great idea."

Having spent a month on the farm, the kids knew precisely the plot they wanted to search. Running off ahead, they left their mom and dad to walk arm and arm trailing behind them.

"This is a moment we have needed," Aaron declared.

"Getting our tree?" Cara asked, looking up.

"Just being together."

"Guys, over here!" Annie waved her arms. Chase was the first by her side, freezing next to his sister, eyeing her find.

Aaron and Cara filtered in behind them.

"I saw this one when we were helping you," Annie said. "I can't believe it is still here. It's beautiful."

"I like it," Chase agreed.

"It's perfect," Aaron admitted. "Who wants to do the honors?"

"I'll do it!" Annie exclaimed.

Dropping to her knees, she ducked under the lowest bough and started working the saw back and forth. Aaron held the top of the tree to prevent it from falling.

"Ugh, the saw is stuck!" Annie called.

"Here," Aaron tilted the tree so that the trunk didn't pinch the blade of the saw.

"That's better!"

Soon, the tree was down and loaded on the sled. "For old times sake," Aaron paused, looking at Annie and Chase.

Knowing what their father meant, they piled on top of the tree like it was a sturdy and compliant horse. Aaron grinned, grabbing the lead and march the sled through the snow.

Cara laughed as she took a picture with her phone. She loved seeing her family so thoroughly enjoying their time together. This moment was one of those that would etch its way into the granite of heartfelt memories.

Putting the tree in a stand that Hal left for them on the cottage porch, Cara went to fill a pitcher of water for it while the kids admired their selection.

Aaron left to help Hal close up the shop for the night. Hanging up the saws, stacking the sleds, and straightening the shelves, the two men made quick work of the nightly duties.

"You got decorations?" Hal asked.

"I didn't even think about it," Aaron answered. "Ours are all in storage."

"I have tons of lights up in the loft in the barn. You are welcome to whatever you find up there," Hal offered.

"Thanks, the kids would love it if we could light up the tree tonight. I'll take a look," Aaron nodded.

"That about does it around here, and you have a family tree to decorate," the farmer said, patting Aaron on the back.

"You know, Hal, you keep telling us how helpful we have been to you and the farm, but I need you to know that you have been a blessing for our family as well," Aaron said. "I wish I could be more help."

"Laura used to tell me, 'Be happy for what you get, don't waste time pining for things that you don't get'," Hal shared.

"Wise woman."

"You have no idea," Hal grinned.

Aaron went to the barn and used his cellphone to light his path up to the loft. There, amongst a wide array of items and boxes, he found a whole section dedicated to Christmas decorations. Aaron stopped counting after half a dozen that were completely filled with string lights. Selecting one appropriate for indoors, he headed back to the house to string the tree before dinner so the family could enjoy it while they ate together.

Poking his head in the cottage, Aaron was surprised by what he saw. On the dining table was a centerpiece made from discarded boughs. Hand-cut paper snowflakes strung throughout the living room.

"Wow, this place looks great," he remarked.

"Chase and I made the snowflakes, Mom made the centerpiece," Annie said proudly.

"I like it. And the smell, this place smells like Christmas," Aaron said, breathing deep.

"It smells like a Christmas tree!" Chase rejoiced.

"Speaking of Christmas trees, I found Christmas lights. You two want to help me string the tree?" Aaron placed the box down. Pulling a strand out, he plugged them in to make sure they worked. Satisfied, he began unbundling the string and, with the children's help, began weaving it around the tree.

"It's so pretty!" Annie exclaimed.

"I like it," Cara approved from the kitchen.

"How else are we going to decorate? Do we have our ornaments?" Annie asked.

"Well, I thought about getting them out of storage after church tomorrow, but then I had another idea," Cara suggested. "Why don't we decorate the tree with what we have, like the way they used to in the old days."

"Like what?" Annie asked.

"We can string popcorn. You guys can make paper ornaments like the snowflakes," Cara suggested.

"We can make pinecone ornaments and find more holly berries," Aaron added.

"Like we did in the store!" Chase said.

"That's right," Cara replied. "First thing first, I need to feed you guys."

After dinner, they fashioned decorations for the tree. Cara and Annie made bows out of red ribbons and two yellow ribbons for family friends with military ties overseas.

Aaron and Chase found pristine pinecones and sprigs of holly with bright red berries. Popcorn was popped and strung.

"I think this is one of the prettiest trees we have done," Cara stepped back and admired.

The family stood by her and agreed. They were surprised by a knock at the door. Aaron opened it to reveal Hal standing on the porch.

"I found this among our things in the attic, I thought it might work for your tree," Hal said, holding up a star.

"Yeah, let's hook it up," Aaron said.

"You want to help, pal?" Aaron asked Chase. Lifting him, he had Chase place the start on the very top of the tree. "Let's plug it in."

Aaron made the connection, and soft colored lights reflected off of the ornate glass star. The lights themselves were beautiful, but the shards of beams that they scattered along the ceiling were spectacular.

"Wow, I thought it was beautiful before," Cara said.

"That one was Laura's mother's. We had it on our tree for our first year before we bought one together. I'm glad it still works," Hal replied.

"I made some gingerbread cookies. They should be ready to eat if you don't mind undecorated. Or, better yet, why don't you join us for decorating?" Cara suggested.

"I could try my hand at decorating, just no judging," Hal grinned.

"Oh, there might be judging," Cara warned.

Rolling up their sleeves, the Shepherds and Hal made gingerbread men, stars, snowmen, and reindeer.

Cara preferred simple white frosting for decorations while the children, Chase, in particular, made rather colorful representations.

Chase looked at his father's plate and frowned, "Really, Dad?"

Aaron had simple designs. Two small dots for eyes, a thin smile for the gingerbread men. For the snowmen, he added little buttons, and the reindeer merely adorned with eyes and a jingle bell collar.

He smiled and shrugged at his son, "What? I like my cookies bare, if I'm completely honest."

Looking over at Annie's creations, Aaron exclaimed, "Wow. Those should be on Food Network or a magazine. Those are beautiful."

Annie blushed as her father gushed.

The family and Hal enjoyed their slow-paced, festive evening, together.

Forty One

Church during the month of December always carried a different feel to it. The activity, the pageants, the songs, and even the message had extra special energy and warmth to them.

Aaron didn't know what to make of the pastor's message on living within the margins, especially during the busy holiday season. Not overcommitting and building enormous piles of stress, but allowing for downtime and moments of just being still. He could hear the message over and over. He wasn't sure how he could comply. Not this season.

As he entered the lobby following the services, he quickly learned how prophetic the message was as some margins were taken out of his control.

"Hey, guys!" Cara's friend Stephanie called them over. "We wanted to invite you guys over for a wrapping party for the Angel Tree. No need to bring anything, snacks will be served, just able wrapping bodies. John was hoping you could help with assembling the bikes and dollhouses. We are short-handed in that department."

"I think we can make it. We can come over as soon as the tree farm is closed for the night," Cara suggested.

"Great, John will be especially relieved," Stephanie said.

"Uhm," Aaron interjected. "We didn't get to talk about it because we got so busy with the tree yesterday. I have to take off this afternoon so that I can make my appointment in Southern Oregon."

"What?" Cara exclaimed and then collected herself. "Well, the kids and I will make it. I can pitch in with the bikes and dollhouses. I've been building up my handyman skillset working on the farm."

"We'll miss you, Aaron, but I'm glad the rest of the Shepherds can make it."

As the family walked towards their car, Aaron confessed, "I tried to tell you I have to be gone all week. We were just having such a good day yesterday."

"It is what it is," Cara shrugged. "Are you helping at the farm today?"

Aaron shook his head. "I need to take off not long after we get home. I have a long drive ahead of me, and I need to get over the pass before the next storm comes in."

"If you have to go, we need you safe," Cara conceded.

"I'm sure once this initial phase in under my belt, things will settle down," Aaron assured.

"You mean when you are in Chicago?" Cara snapped.

The drive home was quiet. A pit settled in Aaron's stomach as he battled the feelings of being away from his family even for a week, never mind any extended time apart as Cara had suggested if they did not immediately come with him to Chicago. He hated leaving them, but this job and the bonus came at the very moment the final financial straw had dropped. It was a blessing in so many regards. He had to see it through and make it work. They had to, as a family.

Forty Two

Aaron had worked from sun-up to well past sundown before he finally stopped for the night. Three states away from where he started, he was checking off the clients on the list that Joe had provided for him.

Checking into his hotel, he called his family.

"Do you have a Christmas tree in your room?" Chase asked.

"Not this time, pal," Aaron laughed. "How was your day?"

"Pretty good. Not many people came for trees, so Annie and I played in the snow," Chase shared.

"We miss you!" Annie said into the phone.

"I miss you too."

"When are you going to be home?"

"Not until Friday. I told you, I had to be gone all week," Aaron said. "How did the Angel Tree night go?"

"Great. I got to help wrap. Chase helped entertain the younger kids," Annie said.

"There were Christmas cookies!" Chase exclaimed.

"It sounds like I missed quite the event," Aaron said.

"They were still building bikes when we left," Annie told her father.

"Yeah, I guess I was the main bike builder last year. Maybe next time," Aaron said.

"Where did you end up today?" Cara asked.

"I'm in…Utah," Aaron laughed. "I had to stop and think where I was."

"How's the weather?"

"Snowed off and on, especially the more east I drove. I try and stick with lower elevations once it gets dark. As nice as the car is, I don't know how it will handle on wintry roads," Aaron said. "Speaking of cars…"

"I set the payment to autopay, it will catch up all the payments on the next cycle, the next week or so," Cara said.

"It will be nice to get that behind us," Aaron said. "I have to be doing all this crazy traveling for a good reason."

"You are," Cara sighed. "Be safe and call tomorrow night."

"I will. Love you guys," Aaron said and hung up the phone.

Aaron hated being away from his family. He was missing out on their adventures. Missing out on serving with the church, which was an essential part of the Shepherd household.

When Annie was born, he vowed not to travel regularly and not miss things that were important to his family. A day into the week-long trip, and it was already miserable. He couldn't even fathom if they were apart for an extended period living in two separate states, as Cara had suggested.

He laid down on the bed, thinking of a more efficient way to manage the new job and the looming living situation. His thoughts were broken, his email reminding him another test was due. Sighing, he opened his laptop and, instead of resting from a long day on the road, tackled yet another corporate quiz.

Aaron's week clicked off the miles and days with much more of the same. Two to three different cities each day. An exam to take nearly every evening. A non-descript hotel room and phone call back home.

The calls were his respite and his anchor. Hearing that the kids were having fun and hearing in Cara's voice that she missed him was a haunting mix of warmth in his family doing well and sadness for not being there himself.

"How's the farm doing?" Aaron asked.

"It's been really quiet," Cara said. "Hal said there is usually an occasional second bump after the first, but it hadn't come this year. He seems to be content that this is likely the last year. I'm glad we are here. I think we have helped him enjoy one last hurrah."

"I was hoping he would have a big enough of a year to continue from a managerial perspective, but seasons change, I guess," Aaron offered.

"That, they do," Cara agreed.

Picking up on Cara's implication in her words, he countered, "Rainbows and flowers benefit from storms."

"I get it," Cara laughed. "No one said this would be easy. You didn't ask for your company to shut down, and you have put yourself in a position to provide for us and well, at that."

"I am doing what I can," Aaron said.

"I know. Listen, I am going to get the kids ready for bed. I love you and drive safe tomorrow."

"I love you too. Goodnight. Give the kids hugs for me," Aaron said.

He tossed his phone on the bed stand. He had never wanted to be "that" dad. The one who wasn't present. His thoughts were interrupted by his email chime, reminding him to take another test.

"I know," he cursed at the laptop.

Forty Three

Pulling into the farm driveway was like coming home for Aaron. He felt his heart swell up with excitement in anticipation of being with his family and in familiar surroundings.

It was already dark, and the farm had been closed for hours. Aaron dragged his weary body and week's worth of luggage towards the cottage. The Christmas tree lights casting a soft glow through the small cottage windows and the familiar smell of birch and pine burning in the woodstove were welcoming him home.

Slipping into the tiny house, an even better greeting met him as Annie and Chase ran up and gave him hugs. Aaron dropped his bags at the door. Cara walked up, stirring something in a bowl and gave him a kiss on the cheek.

"Glad to be home?" Cara asked.

"Oh yeah. I thought I would make it hours ago, but Friday traffic and winter weather had other plans for me," Aaron replied.

"Well, you're home now. Relax with the kids. I was just about to bake a batch of cookies," Cara said.

"Sounds great. I have been on the run all week long," Aaron said. Sitting down on the couch, flanked by the kids, Aaron kicked his dress shoes off.

Chase and Annie looked at their father intently.

"Yes?" he asked suspiciously.

"Mom said now that you have a paycheck, we can think about a Christmas list," Chase said.

"She said nothing too..." Annie tailed off, fighting to recall the word her mom used.

"Extravagant!" Cara called from the kitchen.

"Right, extravagant'," Annie continued.

"What's that mean?" Chase asked.

"Think of one, reasonable item that you would like for Christmas this year. That means no televisions, game systems, computers, things like that," Aaron replied.

Chase looked thoughtful at his dad. "I know what I want for Christmas," he said definitively.

"What's that?" Aaron queried.

"You, home."

Aaron's heart twisted. "You know, I'm asking for the same thing." He kissed his son on the forehead and squeezed Annie in close. Shattering the moment, his laptop chimed, reminding him that he had another exam to complete that evening.

Forty Four

The morning was quiet. Chase ran into the store to ask his mom for a cocoa. Aaron and Hal sat by the firepit.

"Long week for you," Hal noted.

"Yeah, hoping it levels out once I am up and running," Aaron admitted.

"I'm sure it will," Hal said, poking the fire with a stick.

"Sounds like it was a quiet week," Aaron said.

"Yeah, I think this year's rush is over. We could consider shutting the store down and just running the farm as a true do it yourself U-pick lot," Hal said.

"That would lighten the load," Aaron nodded.

"Just not the same. Kind of what I'm afraid of if I sell."

"What's that?" Aaron asked.

Hal leaned back, supporting himself with his hands on his knees, "Oh, the commercial operation will just sweep in, making the entire farm part of a major rotational harvest. No more families, just cut the whole thing down, replant and do again eight years or so later."

"Yeah, I think that is sort of like the new company. They run a first-class business, but they buy up smaller companies. Sometimes just to dissolve them to get rid of competition or they just want some small component of the business and throw the rest away," Aaron said.

"Is that what happened to your last company?" Hal asked.

Aaron scoffed, "Maybe. Maybe that's why I got hired too. In our region, we are their biggest thorn to contend with. A lot of their deals are shrouded in secrecy, so unless you are at board level, you might never know."

"How's the family with the move to Chicago?"

"I don't know, none of us want to move there. Scratch that, I do know. I just don't think there is anything we can do about it," Aaron said.

"Yeah, sometimes the course is set, and all we can do is navigate to avoid the rocks and icebergs on that path," Hal nodded. "More travel on tap?"

"I have to complete the circuit of clients by Christmas Eve. By my calculation, if I head out each

Sunday and return late Friday, I will just complete what they have asked me to do," Aaron replied.

Hal was thoughtful as he played with the fire. "Tough time of year to be traveling so much. I can tell holidays and family mean a lot to you."

"They do. I think it is just an initial jolt. I carved out this Sunday so that I could watch the kids in their Christmas production. It just means I'll need to head out about three or so Monday. I'll get through it, and things will settle down.," Aaron surmised.

"I'm sure they will."

Reluctantly checking his email on his phone at lunch, Aaron pulled open a message from Joe. Reading it and rereading it, he put the phone down.

"What?" Cara asked, recognizing the reaction.

"Another trip to Chicago. I have some big state of the region report Joe wants me to present to the board," Aaron said.

"You just started."

"Yes, but I have experience regionally from my last role. Likely, they want to tap into that experience. It is the reason they hired me," Aaron replied.

"What about this ridiculous tour they have you on?"

"That is their way of using me to mark their territory. Most of the clients are familiar with me.

They wanted the connection drawn back to them," Aaron said.

"When do you have to go?"

"Tomorrow," Aaron said, his voice sullen.

"But that's the kids' play!" Cara exclaimed.

"I know."

"Can't you tell them that?" Cara asked.

"Tell the entire board in Chicago that I cannot attend a meeting at their request, two weeks into my job..."

"Yes."

"No, I can't do that," Aaron said.

"I don't know why you took that job. Running you around, owning your schedule, demanding we move to Chicago..."

Aaron was exasperated, "You know exactly why I took that job. We were going under. We lost our house, we are already down to one vehicle and are three months behind on those payments. Once we pay our base bills, we are empty. Nothing left. I had to get a job, that is the only one who answered the call this time of year. The pay is great, the benefits are unbelievable, they sent me a car, and not only that, a really nice one."

"I hope it is worth it," Cara said.

"What else am I to do? Hal is great, but the farm doesn't come close to paying our bills. Not close," Aaron argued. "Look. I need to pack and get ready. I have to put together a presentation that Joe wants to review while I am flying tomorrow. This will work out. It will be okay. I promise."

"I'll hold you to that promise," Cara said. "I've been praying about Chicago."

"I have to," Aaron admitted.

Cara looked at her husband, "I keep getting that I am not supposed to go. I am supposed to be here."

"I keep getting that I need to take care of my family," Aaron said. "That is why I took this job. I need to take care of my family. Our family. So, what do we do?"

"I don't know," Cara shook her head. "We'll figure something out. We always do."

"Yeah," Aaron nodded solemnly, lacking conviction, "We always do."

Forty Five

"How's it going today?" Cara asked as she pushed her way into the shop.

"Hi there, Cara," Hal looked up. "Oh, we've had a couple of families up, you haven't missed much. How was church?"

"Good. You should come with us," Cara invited. "That's kind of why I stopped in. I wanted to remind you that I'll be at the kids' Christmas production this afternoon."

"Of course, I don't think I'll have any trouble minding the shop today," Hal said.

Cara cocked her head, "Why don't you come along? Could you with families possibly driving all the way up here?"

Hal looked thoughtful for a moment, "You know what? Yes, I can. And I will. I'll set a sign out and an honor bucket. I would love to see Annie and Chase in their play."

"Great! I am going to gather up cookies, and we can head into town," Cara smiled.

Aaron boarded the plane and settled into his seat. Once in the air, he planned on pulling out his laptop and reviewing his presentation once more. Joe had emailed first thing that he wanted Aaron to be more aggressive when he spoke in front of the board.

They wanted to see every former client, partner and competitor in his region, identifying those he thought were struggling. Since his last company worked with smaller players in the industry as partners instead of competition, he had solid insight into their requests.

While he waited for take-off, he thumbed through the inflight magazine. One caption caught his eye. It had one word in bold, "Priorities". The image that dominated the spread was the silhouettes of a family looking out at the ocean, their arms around each other. The picture struck Aaron. The family used in the photo could have been his. One boy, one girl, each roughly Annie and Chases' ages and a couple, their widespread arms connecting one another.

He found himself mesmerized by the photo and the word. Even as he flipped through the rest of the magazine, he would return to that page. He thought of the kids. Their play was in a few hours. He knew he should be there. He wanted to be there.

Aaron thought of the impact of decisions. Taking the farm job was interfering with the job search. The job he did get was interfering with the family. Bills without a job were crushingly stressful. Each its own priority. He questioned how you balance them all or when you can't, how you would possibly choose between them. He knew family was first, just behind God. He prayed. Each time he got the message that he needed to take care of his family. That is what he was doing, he reasoned.

He shook his thoughts, he was doing what he had to do, and that was consistent with taking care of the family. Confident in his rationale, he opened his laptop and diligently worked on his presentation.

Hal offered to drive Cara in the farm truck. "Shouldn't we take the SUV? It has four-wheel drive."

Hal laughed, "How do you suppose we got up the hill for nearly a century without four-wheel drive?"

Cara folded her lip, "I guess that is a good point. I would love another ride in the farm truck."

After a few moments of silence, minus the Christmas carol played over the old radio, Cara blurted out, "I don't know what we're going to do, Hal."

"What do you mean?"

"Chicago. Aaron's job. Our lives are here. He's not here," Cara confided. "I don't know how he could have felt alright about this."

Hal drove for half a mile or so before he responded, "Hmm. Maybe you need to look at it from his perspective. Right or wrong, a husband, especially a father, is going to do what he can to provide for his family. Safety, love, provision, not much will stand in a husband's way to provide that. Worse yet, when they do hit a hiccup and struggle or fail to provide, well, it becomes the conflict above conflicts for them to resolve."

"I guess, but I never cared how much money he made. We had a nice, modest life with his last job," Care protested.

"And yet, was there a push to find a job, to turn things around?" Hal asked.

"Well, sure, we had bills to pay," Cara defended.

"Did Aaron find a way to pay those bills?"

"He did. And then some," Cara sighed. "But to uproot and move the family?"

"If that is what it took, you bet," Hal said. "Like I said, right or wrong, that is how men think."

"I see," Cara said softly.

Hal chuckled, "Look, he isn't deciding to not be there for the kids tonight. Or when he couldn't help on the farm December first. He decided to provide for his family. That removed these other options for the table."

"Thank you, Hal. I think I've needed your advice for a couple of weeks now," Cara said.

"Never said I was right, but you're welcome to chat with me anytime," Hal grinned.

Cara and Hal got to the church. Annie was looking through the crowd and danced a little when she saw her mom and Hal. Waving, she continued looking around them. She knew her dad was traveling, but she was hopeful just the same.

Taking their seats, they watched the performance. A story about Saint Nicholas and finding the spirit of Jesus in giving, especially to those most in need. Both Annie and Chase played supportive roles. Chase, a natural ham, took to the stage well. Annie, a bit shy, slid partially behind a prop. Concealed, she felt the most comfortable.

Cara sat in a spot where she could record the whole play on her phone. Each child circled their heart and pointed to the phone, something they both did with their father since they were small.

When Aaron got to his hotel, he found that he was in a smaller room, but it still had an elegantly decorated tree and was as plush as the previous stay. He knew he should have cracked open the laptop and reviewed the presentation once more, but he received the recording of the play from Cara on his phone.

Kicking off his shoes, he hopped on the bed. Leaning on an elbow, he watched the play. The church always put on an impressive production. Aaron was amazed by the quality of acting and stage design pulled together by the time and hands of family volunteers.

Cara had been able to capture Chase's giggle when it was his time to speak. His colossal grin illuminating the stage as he delivered his line. Behind the shield of a large palm tree and a sheep, Cara captured Annie moving in and out of view. The audio barely picking up her softly spoken verse before disappearing back behind the stage props.

Aaron smiled when he saw the kids do the motion from their hearts to his. Subconsciously, he did the same back to the phone.

Forty Six

The executive car dropped Aaron off at the corporate headquarters early. He pushed into the building and found the right bank of elevators.

As the elevator doors opened, he swiveled his head a few times before he recalled which direction his office was. Despite his early start, there were already a handful of employees milling out about, working east coast hours and likely a few, like him, preparing for a presentation with the board as they were assembled that day.

Finding his way to the western regional manager's office, he flipped on the lights and opened his laptop. Settling into the strangely comfortable desk chair, he sat at the extravagant mahogany desk.

He had barely scanned the presentation before a voice called into his office. "Aaron, welcome back. May I get you an espresso or tea?"

Aaron looked up to see Christina standing in the doorway. She wore a glamorous dress and was as put together as the first time that Aaron had met her.

"You're here early," Aaron noted.

"Joe said to expect you," Christina replied. "I cannot assist you if I am not here when you are."

"Careful what you wish you for," Aaron laughed. "You know, coffee would be great. Thank you."

Aaron flipped through the presentation. He had been through it so many times that he was struggling to concentrate on any of it. Catching a small tweak or word to rephrase, but overall, he felt the presentation was as good as it was going to be.

"Here you are," Christina sang as she placed the mug of coffee on Aaron' s desk.

"Did you grab one for yourself?" Aaron asked.

"What? No...," Christina shook her head.

"Why don't you? If you are to help me, the best help you can provide is with some background on the company, the board...," Aaron offered.

Christina looked slightly confused, "Well, okay. Sure. I'll be right back."

Aaron jotted some notes of things that he had pondered regarding the board, the company, moving to Chicago.

Christina returned and sat down across from him, holding her coffee mug in her in lap as she crossed her legs. "What can I help you with?"

"I always like to know as much about who I am presenting to as possible. The better I understand them, the better I can drive the conversation and the presentation to fulfill their needs, not the ones I think they have. Presenting, selling isn't about getting someone to think they need or want what you have, but it is about solving a problem that they have with what you have to offer. Client or board, it is the same," Aaron said.

"Alright, fire away," Christina said, sipping her coffee.

"Tell me about the company...not the stuff I can read about, but what it is really like," Aaron asked.

"It takes itself pretty seriously. If you work hard and perform well, you do well," Christina shrugged.

"How long have you worked here?" Aaron asked.

"A year and a half," Christina answered.

"How many people have you...assisted?" Aaron asked.

"Three...four, including you," she replied.

Aaron frowned, "Chase them all away?"

"Seems that way," Christina laughed. "Working in the home office is an acquired taste. When they pulled the regional employees from the field in-house, more than a few struggled. You have a leg up since you started this way."

"Right," Aaron nodded. "Tell me about the board?"

"You can probably tell from the activity this morning, when the board assembles, it is a big deal. What they say goes, and it filters quickly downward throughout the organization. Don't get me wrong, they listen, but once they make a decision, it is a done deal," Christina answered.

"It seems really busy this holiday season, is it always this way?"

Christina wrinkled her nose, "This is my second year, but yes. The board and executive management seem to get all keyed up for year-end. The marketplace is "vulnerable" as they like to put it."

"I see, you need to be ready to take advantage of opportunities, I suppose," Aaron shrugged. "Are you able to take time off to spend the holidays with family?"

"It's tough. It tends to be all hands on deck. We get Christmas day off, of course," Christina replied.

"What is the board like?" Aaron asked.

Christina let out a little laugh, "As you can tell, they levy a lot of sway around here. Mostly old-time execs from other companies. A lot of experience. They like growth."

"Any good board would, right?" Aaron said, digging for the positive.

Christina touched her ear, nodding, she said, "Right away."

Looking at Aaron with a raised eyebrow, she motioned, "Earpiece. Always on. Joe would like to see you,"

"Sure," Aaron nodded and stood up, "Uh, where is Joe's office?"

Christina grinned, "I'll show you. Come on."

The assistant led Aaron down the hall and to a grand office, about three times the size of Aaron's already sizable space.

"Aaron, good to see you. Have a seat," Joe welcomed. "Thank you, Christina."

"Of course, Joe," Christina said and walked away.

"Your report looks good. I appreciate you making the changes I requested," Joe said, leaning forward across the desk. "We have about ninety-three minutes before you present to the board. I will already be in there, Christina will take you in at the appropriate time. I would encourage you to be even a little more aggressive. I sold you strong to the board. They are going to expect, with your experience and relationships, some serious growth in the western region."

"I gave it a reasonable, attainable, though worthy stretch goal," Aaron said, reading his boss, he added, "I will dig in and find any areas that I can push even harder."

"Excellent," Joes stood up. "I am due in there. We'll see you in a little bit."

Aaron retreated to his office and pulled open his presentation slide deck one last time. He was used to making challenging but realistic goals. Perhaps they had a strategy that he wasn't aware of. He figured he would soon learn.

Forty Seven

Aaron was reviewing his routing as the Chicago trip took him off schedule for two days, he needed to determine how to make up for the change. He was removed from his thoughts with a light knock on the office door.

Aaron looked up to Christina leaning in. "It's time," she said.

"Ready as ever," Aaron said.

"Did you submit your updates to the server? I can send them to the conference room for you," the assistant asked.

"Yes, I named it with today's date," Aaron replied.

"Great. You're all set. Here you go," Christina pointed to the room where the board was waiting for him.

"Thank you, Christina," Aaron said.

Aaron took a quick breath, cognizant that he was in complete view of the glass windows and entered the room.

"Gentlemen, Marcy, I would like to introduce you to Aaron Shepherd, our new Western Region Director. As we had previously discussed, he is well-engrained in that marketplace and will be a driver of strong growth," Joe said and then turned the meeting over to Aaron.

"Thank you all, Joe, for that warm introduction. The Western region is historically, a challenging marketplace. Like Hawaii and similar marketplaces, they can be very wary of outside influence and new relationships. That is where relationship is the keyword. I know most of the key players and have been making the rounds turning them into Jans and Barnett clients based on my relationship with them," Aaron started.

"Yes, your projections for the base are strong and better than historical performance for us in that region," one distinguished gentleman noted. "And I see later in the slide deck that you have uncovered some additional partnerships and untapped clients that we might be able to break into, that's good. But what our research suggests that there are players in the space that are struggling. They are either new and therefore have a weak foundation, or they have never cleared the hurdle of the last economic downturn. How many of them do you have on the list?"

"A number of them will make great partners. Because of their...challenged positions, they would be more than welcome to revenue share as we co-market in that space. I had experience with several of them in my last role..." Aaron shared.

"Why partner and share revenue when we have the stronger position?" the woman named Marcy asked.

Aaron cocked his head, "We can leverage their positive relationships and gain access to their clients with minimal disruption."

"True, and there may be some advantages to that, at least in the short run," Marcy admitted and then added, "But then we have to share revenue and run the risk of propping that vendor up without us with that client."

'What would your suggestion be?"

A portly man who had been silent, cleared his throat, "You capitalize on their weaknesses. If they are financially strapped, you pressure them to the point where they sell out to us, or they fold. This time of year, a lot of companies find themselves vulnerable, but they push through the end of the year with the hope of improvement in the next. Some even give Christmas bonuses and time off which weakens them more and tanks their productivity. A perfect storm for us."

"If they are teetering, we help them over the edge," Marcy added. "We lower our prices, give our services away, if we have to, until they break and then we can adjust back to market levels and even above market levels. Think of it as an investment in that marketplace."

"What the board is suggesting is for you to identify those opportunities and strike while we can, this season, right now," Joe said.

"I see," Aaron said. Inexplicably, his mind went to Hal and the farm. He imagined a commercial tree supplier taking advantage of him the same way. "So, we look at a business. Maybe it started as a family business or some idealistic entrepreneur working out of his garage. Through time, determination and hard work, whether a recent company in relatively a short run or a long-standing family business they find themselves in a rough patch, distracted with the holidays, employees taking vacation to be with their families and we swoop in, put them out of their misery."

"That's a harsh way to put it, but yes. That's it exactly. It's business. If some don't take it as seriously as us, they put themselves at risk," Joe explained.

"These companies, these owners may be on the brink of losing their legacies. While the right thing might be for him to sell or to know when to call it quits, it should be on their shoulders. It should be their call. They should have the ability to fight to the very end, without some industry bully taking advantage and forcing their hand," Aaron argued, the words coming out almost without him fully processing them, especially in context of the group. "Jans and Barnett should be a beacon on a hill, welcome clients. Reminding them that we are here and present, when they need us. We should draw them to us, not force them into some terrible situation that breaks them to the point that they give in to us."

"Aaron, this is the business world. You can't focus on whatever sad situation they put themselves in, all you need to focus on is what is best for Jans and Barnett," Joe demanded.

Aaron separated himself from his presentation and squared up to the board table, "I am going to do what is best for Cara, Annie and Chase. And maybe a nice old farmer named Hal. We all have legacies to manage. I need to own mine. I appreciate the opportunity to have joined Jans and Barnet, but I am sorry to say, my legacy…is not here."

Joe looked cross, his cheeks enflamed in red, "Aaron, be careful. You are about to make a huge mistake."

"Not being careful enough, is what landed me here," Aaron said.

"If you walk out of those doors, you are done. Everything we have provided for you is gone," Joe bellowed.

"I figured as much," Aaron nodded. "Merry Christmas, everyone."

Aaron excused himself from the meeting. He was surprised by how comfortable he was with his exit. He had zero reservation that he did the right thing.

By the time he reached his office, Christina was waiting for him with his things. "I'm sorry, and I'm not sorry to see you go," Christina said, a kind smile washing over her face. "Maybe I need to consider that myself."

"I wish you well…and good luck," Aaron said.

Christina escorted him to the elevator. "Good luck yourself, Aaron."

"Merry Christmas," Aaron said as he climbed in the elevator, turning as the doors closed.

Forty Eight

Aaron stepped out of the office building and out onto the busy Chicago sidewalk. Seeing the executive SUV out front, he rapped on the window.

Charles Finley rolled down the window, "Mr. Shepherd."

"Hi Charles, if you could take me to the hotel so that I can collect my things, and then to the airport, that would be great," Aaron inquired.

"I am sorry, Mr. Shepherd. I would love to. Unfortunately, I received notice of your termination and can no longer provide you service," Finley said. "Between you and me, I like you. If they didn't have me GPS-tracked, I would just do it."

"I understand. I appreciate it. Merry Christmas, Finley!" Aaron waved and walked down the sidewalk to wave down a taxi.

Pulling up to the hotel, Aaron pulled out his corporate card to pay the fee. The driver rolled his eyes and went through a dramatic process to run the card. Even after the fuss, the driver held the card back over his shoulder, looking cross, "This does not work. Cash."

Nodding, Aaron dug in his wallet and pulled out the fare and a modest tip.

Grabbing his things from the hotel, he hailed another cab and traveled to the airport, again paying with cash.

Aaron sighed as he saw the long security line. Glad he didn't have to check any luggage, he navigated the line. Handing over the documents, he was eyeing which X-ray line was moving the fastest.

"Sir, this ticket is no good," the checker said.

Aaron looked confused, "What do you mean?"

"I see that you had a flight on this date, but it is no longer valid. Did you make a change to your flight?" the attendant asked.

Aaron sighed, "My company may have."

"You'll have to get this straightened out at the airline ticket counter," the attendant handed Aaron's documents back and looked behind him, "Next!"

Aaron numbly walked out of line, staring at his useless ticket. He had no idea what to do other than see what he could accomplish at the ticket counter.

Walking back through the terminal, Aaron found the airline customer service counter. Explaining his situation, he handed his ticket across the desk.

"Yep, this ticket has been canceled, credited back to the company that purchased it. There is a seat on the five o'clock. It routes through Dallas Fort-Worth. Not exactly direct, but it will get you home," the attendant said.

Aaron handed over his corporate card. The attendant ran it and looked, "I'm sorry, the card was declined. Its code was 'inactive'. Do you have a newer one?"

"No," Aaron shook his head, frowning. Digging in his wallet, he pulled out his personal debit card, having no idea how much was in their account. "How much is it?"

"One thousand, three hundred and forty dollars and thirty-six cents," the attendant replied.

He knew they didn't have that much in their account. Aaron thanked her and pulled back from the counter. His mind reeled.

Pulling out his cellphone that had been converted to the corporate plan and dialed Cara to see if he could see if they had enough for a train ticket or whatever transportation he could find.

Not hearing the dial tone, he glanced down at his phone, it read "Network Unavailable". He tried texting her, but met with the same error code. Closing his eyes and taking in a deep sigh, he slid his useless phone into his pocket and looked around, trying to conjure a game plan for a next step.

Pulling out his wallet, he leafed through his cash. He was grateful that he pulled money out for the trip as a just-in-case fund. He snapped his fingers, remembering the bonus he received.

Hustling to an ATM, he slid his card in. Selecting the balance button, his heart sunk when he saw how little was available. "They already pulled the bonus," he mumbled to himself. "Well, they work efficiently, I'll give them that."

Relenting that he had to go on whatever cash he had, returned to wandering for inspiration. Seeing the rental car sign, he decided to see what he could come up with. Waiting in line at the rental counter, he finally got up to the attendant. Asking for the rates, he calculated how much he had and roughly how much gas he would need. With the cheapest car, he figured that he would be stranded a state away.

"Do you have anything cheaper?" Aaron asked.

The attendant frowned and wrinkled their nose, "Our sister company is "Rent-A-Wreck. It is off property, a mile south of the airport."

"Any chance there is a shuttle?"

"Not for Rent-A-Wreck. Sorry," the attendant shook her head.

"No worries. Thank you. Merry Christmas!"

"Merry Christmas, sir."

With at least somewhat of a plan, no matter how feeble, Aaron headed out of the car rental wing and walked outside into the chaotic O'Hare traffic. Plotting a path that took him across the departure lanes, through a series of parking garages and then along the drive into the airport.

The wind was blowing from the northwest, cutting through Aaron's overcoat. He was glad that he had packed light for the short trip. The total trek covered a little over three miles. Following a crude map drawn on a rental envelope, Aaron ultimately found his way to the Rent-A-Wreck lot.

"Wow, this place lives up to its name," Aaron said to himself.

Looking around the lot, were an erratic sampling of slightly dented newer cars to surprisingly older vehicles that had clearly seen substantial use.

With his calculations, saving for gas, he pulled his available cash out of his wallet. "What can this get me for a few days?"

"Returning when?" the clerk started tapping into a computer that appeared to be in similar shape as some of the cars in the lot.

"Uh...huh. Good question. Do you have one-way rental?" Aaron asked.

The clerk eyed Aaron, "No."

Aaron looked perplexed, tapping his fingers on the counter.

"I have an idea, but no guarantee, literally."

"I am up for just about anything, at this point," Aaron admitted.

"We have this eye-sore out back. Last I checked, it ran. I was going to send it off to one of those donation places. For what you have in your wallet, it's yours. About all we would have gotten in write-off anyways. Come on. I'll take you to it," the attendant said, digging for a set of keys in a drawer.

Following the attendant behind the shop, they stopped in front of a tiny little car with rust under door sills. "What is it?" Aaron asked.

The attendant shrugged, "A Geo? Something or other. A ninety eight-three...eighty-four, something like that. Not even sure where it came from. It just showed up one day. I think a customer rented something else and left this. Anyway, give it a crank."

Aaron opened the door and was instantly met with a blast of musty air that was anything other than a new car smell. The seats were torn and stained. Half of the knobs and buttons were missing. Giving it a shot, he put the key in the ignition, pushing in the clutch, he turned the key.

The dash lights pulsed, and a whirring noise emanated from the engine bay. Pumping the gas as he turned the key, the car sprang to life with a clatter and a puff of exhaust smoke. The check engine light blinked, but the car was running.

"I guess I'll take it," Aaron said, with a tinge of question in his voice.

"Told you she runs. Look, even has half a tank of gas," the attendant pointed. "Hand me the registration from the glove box, and I'll write up the bill of sale, get you on your way."

Aaron had to laugh as he leaned forward, wiping the inside of the window with his sleeve to free his view from the fog. He had the HVAC cranked, using a little piece of protruding metal where the knob used to be. A far cry from the European luxury car that his company had provided for him.

Still, he was on a freeway, traveling in the slow lane since any faster than the speed limit made the little car shake violently. He was indeed heading away from the city of Chicago. He was pretty sure third gear was gone, but the tall fifth gear at least afforded him good gas mileage, a commodity to covet on this trip.

He knew he had taken a gamble, as the little car was clearly on death's door and could meet its end at any given mile marker. Regardless, it felt good to be moving and heading in the direction of home.

Forty Nine

Cara was frustrated and concerned that she hadn't heard from Aaron. He was expected home, and yet, as she stood on the porch of the cottage, there were no sounds of engines or lights ascending the hill.

She oscillated between anger and worry. Angry for the job, the move, missing family time, for not calling. She imagined Aaron being caught up in a meeting with elegant people at some trendy five-star restaurant. Black SUVs with drivers chauffeuring them around. Doing his job and doing it well, but getting lost in the frenzy and the atmosphere.

Yet, she was worried and wondering. Aaron was always faithful about calling and texting, whether sharing a quick note, an "I love you' or an update on his travels. With the new job, she didn't even know who to call.

Folding her arms and shivering against the cold, she relented to going back inside. Pressing the door closed with her back, she sighed. She just wanted her family together and whole, again.

Aaron gripped the wheel until his knuckles were white. The little car struggled mightily against the winter blasted roads. The engine was challenged with highway speeds and any change in elevation, demanding frequent gear changing. The tires and chassis lacked grip and stability, forcing Aaron to steer constantly, even on straight stretched of road.

What frustrated Aaron the most was the defroster was insufficient, and the tattered wipers did a poor job of sweeping away new-fallen snow. Despite the nuances of the car, he was happy to be moving along in the right direction, humming Christmas carols to himself since the radio didn't work.

Stopping for gas, each time, he counted the remaining bills in his wallet with renewed anxiety. Affording himself only gas station coffee to remain alert and nutrition bars from an undetermined shelf date, he pressed on, a laughable far cry from the posh restaurants and hotels provided by Jans and Barnett.

On the road again, he wiped the windshield with his sleeve, fought the clutch to find the right gear and mashed the throttle for all that it was worth.

Hal could tell that Cara was anxious without word from Aaron. He had hoped that inviting her and the kids over for dinner and games would help take her mind off of her concerns. If he was honest with himself, he wanted the company himself.

"Hi guys," he said as heard the rap on the door. "Come on."

"Thanks for inviting us. I wasn't sure what we were going to do for dinner tonight. What can I do to help?" Cara asked.

"Hmm. A sous chef, that might work," Hal smiled. Hesitating to ask, but the question bore the necessity, "Any word from Aaron?"

Cara shook her head, "Not yet. I have my cell phone with me."

"Well, let's manage what we can control, and that, right now, is dinner. You guys like spaghetti?" Hal asked, leading them to the kitchen. "Sous chef, would you do me the honor of preparing the garlic bread?"

"You know, I think I like making spaghetti dinner just so that I get to make garlic bread," Cara smiled.

Hal eyed the children hovering, not knowing what they should be doing. "Would you two mind setting the table? I have plates over there, silverware is in this drawer, and if your Mom is okay with it, once you set those glasses out, I have soda in the fridge."

Cara nodded, "That's fine."

The motivation worked wonders as the kids divvied up the chores and completed them to soda fulfilling efficiency.

As Cara slit the loaf of bread and slathered it with butter and garlic, she asked, "So any more busy days to brace for?"

Hal had an unusually long pause before answering. "I...I have been thinking that maybe it is time to shut it down. Fewer families have been coming out. I think the bell has rung."

"I thought we were going to finish out the season," Cara inquired.

"I just don't know anymore. You can focus on the family and Aaron on his new job. I need to start thinking about the next phase for the farm. Come January, the offers will roll in, I have come to terms with it, I'm good," Hal shared.

"We don't mind helping. In fact, we have thoroughly enjoyed being a part of your season this year," Cara expressed.

Hal pulled back, "I didn't mean...you guys are welcome to stay as long as I have the farm."

"Thank you. I just meant I...we wanted to give you a great season," Cara said.

"It has been a great season. It will continue to be so with the Shepherds here for Christmas, whether the farm is open or not," Hal said. "Enough talk, we don't need to decide anything tonight. Let's eat!"

Fifty

Aaron was horrified as he ascended the hills straddling the state lines. The little car, jammed into second gear, couldn't get enough power to jump to third. The oil pressure and temperature gauges were maxing out, and he was being passed by eighteen-wheelers going up the hill.

Pushing the car too hard, its engine finally blew, just as he crested the peak of the highest pass en route to Maple Valley. Fluid shot out in a blast of steam. He thought of pulling over, but knew there was a rest stop at the bottom of the hill. Riding the momentum, he allowed gravity to roll the car to the bottom. With no resistance, and no power anything, Aaron white-knuckled a terrifying ride, actually passing cars as he hit the highest speeds he had on the entire trip.

At the bottom of the hill, the rest stop was still a mile away, Aaron hoped the momentum would carry him all the way. Losing speed quickly, he steered into the emergency lane and leaned forward as if that would have some impact on encouraging the car to roll farther.

To Aaron's great fortune, the little car did make it to the rest stop. He quickly discovered another issue in the busy rest stop parking lot. Without power brakes or power steering, the car was exceptionally difficult to maneuver. He dodged cars and semis as he navigated to an out of the way spot where he could wrench on the wheel and ultimately use the hand brake to slide to a very unconventional stop.

His heart racing, he sat in the deceased car while he collected himself. Taking a deep breath, he knew his next task was an obvious one. He had to find a ride home or at least that direction.

A truck driver saw him exit the car and head towards the restroom. "Did you just pass me in neutral?"

"Uhm, yeah."

"Everything okay?"

"Not really. I think the uphill, where you passed me, killed it, and I used the downhill to, well, get here." Aaron admitted.

"Hmm. Not the best idea, but I've been in situations on a haul before myself," the man said. "Look, we're a long ways... anywhere that you can get that car fixed."

"Oh, it won't be fixed. I'll call a recycler to come and pick it up," Aaron said.

"Where are you headed? I can take you as far as the interstate eighty-four split," the driver offered.

"That would be fantastic. I'm only about thirty minutes from there, should be able to get the rest of the way," Aaron agreed.

Cara checked her phone for what she felt must have been the thousandth time. She kept expectantly looking for headlights sweeping up the drive. Putting the kids to bed, she kept up a calm persona, but as they fell asleep, she let her guard down as she stared out of the window. She dialed his phone, and it once again returned as an inactive number.

Collapsing on the sofa with a blanket, she faced the door, hopeful that at any moment, her husband would be strolling through the door. Leaning against the couch, she pulled her knees in close, tightening herself into a ball.

She had no intention of closing her eyes, but an hour into her vigil, her weary body and mind gave way to fatigue.

When Cara awoke the next morning, she found herself still on the couch, still wrapped into a ball. Shaking herself awake, she quickly scanned the room, seeing no signs of Aaron.

Putting on her slippers, she shuffled to the very edge of the porch, but did not see the black sedan in the driveway. Her phone had no messages, no calls.

As she returned to the house, she found Annie and Chase waiting for her at the bottom of the loft stairs.

"Is Daddy coming home today?" Chase asked.

"Yeah, I think so," Cara nodded. "He's been really busy with his new job, and I think something is wrong with his phone."

"I hope he comes home. I miss him," Annie said.

"I do too," Cara. Not wanting the kids to get a sense of her concern, she clapped her hands together. "I am going to whip up some pancakes, then what do you say we build the best snowman ever?"

"Yay!" the kids cried as they bellied up to the kitchen table.

The truck driver pulled to a stop outside of the Maple Valley Community Center. "Wish I could take you all the way," he said.

"You've been more than kind to take me as far as you have," Aaron said. "Merry Christmas!"

Giving a wave, Aaron headed into the center, hoping that there was an event taking place. He hadn't taken stock of how disheveled he appeared and lightly smelled.

Seeing that a bazaar was taking place, he had a hop in his step for the first time in several

thousand miles. Entering the bustling building,
Christmas carols filled the air. The aisles
overflowed with local art, crafts, and food.
Shoppers filled most of the corridors.

"Shepherd!" Aaron turned to see John
grinning at him. "Is Cara and the kids here?"

Aaron shot him a look that suggested there
was a story to tell. Giving the quick spin version of
his adventure, Aaron shared his experience. John
placed his hand on his shoulder. "I'll let Janice
know, and I'll run you up the hill."

"That would be great," Aaron admitted.

John pulled his car into the farm drive.

Aaron felt good to be back at the farm. He
felt as though he had been away for a long time.
"Thanks again, for driving me, you're a lifesaver."

"Hey, I hate to ask, but the youth
Christmas…"

Aaron nodded and smiled, "Just let me know
when."

"Deal. I'll send you an email later," John
said.

"Get back to your family. I am overdue to be
with mine," Aaron said, giving John wave.

Stepping away from the car, Aaron looked
towards the house. In between the main house and
the cottage, he was treated to see his family
diligently working on a snowman. They looked

over when they heard the car come up the driveway. They rose and watched as Aaron got out.

Aaron couldn't stifle his grin, picking up his pace, wanting to be with them. Chase threw down the shovel he was using and sprinted towards his dad. Aaron dropped to a knee, disregarding the snow and threw his arms wide to receive his son.

"I missed you, Chase," Aaron said.

"I missed you too, Daddy," Chase leaned into the hug.

Pulling Annie in, she and Cara caught up to the boys. Giving his kids a firm squeeze, he stood up and faced Cara. Her joy in seeing him was evident, despite that, her first reaction was to hit him on the shoulder. "I was so worried about you!"

"I know," Aaron looked sheepish. "The company cut off my phone, the truck driver's phone didn't' work…"

"Truck driver?" Cara gasped.

Aaron put his arm around his wife, "It has been quite the crazy last couple of days."

"Well, come on inside and tell me all about it," Cara said. Looking around the driveway, she asked, "Where is your car?"

"All part of the story," Aaron grinned. Glancing over at the family's handy work, he added, "Nice snowman!"

"We are almost done," Chase said.

"I have a few finishing touches in mind," Annie said.

"Why don't you guys finish and then come inside. I'll put some cocoa on," Cara suggested to the kids.

"Ok, come on, Chase," Annie agreed.

With arms linked, Aaron and Cara entered the cottage. Aaron dropped his bags next to the door.

"So," Cara leaned against the counter. "What happened to you?"

"Well, I was giving my pitch and the way that the board wanted me to leverage clients, partners, and competitors in the field, it just didn't sit right to me. I couldn't help but think about Hal. If a big farm pressured him to make a decision that affected all that he and his family had worked for, it's not fair. It's not right," Aaron shared.

"And...," Cara pressed.

"And I quit. Right then and there," Aaron said. "By the time I left the building, they killed my phone, froze my credit card, discontinued the car service, and canceled my ticket to fly home."

"Oh my gosh, how did you get here?" Cara gasped.

"Well, it turns out, they reversed the hiring bonus as well, so I am pretty sure our account is overdrawn," Aaron informed his wife. "I used what little cash I had taken out for the trip and bought a car."

"You bought a car?" Cara exclaimed.

Aaron wrinkled his nose, "Well, sort of a car. Cost a couple hundred bucks. A thousand or so miles and a gas station coffee later, it died at the pass. A nice truck driver, that was the truck driver part, brought me to Maple Valley. I found John at the community center, and I figured, I had gotten this far without a phone call, another thirty minutes was not going to change a whole lot. That's about it. Here I am."

"I can't believe you quit!" Cara shook her head. "I'm glad you quit, I mean, we clearly need the money, but that company, Chicago…they weren't the right fit for our family."

"I'm glad you see it that way," Aaron confided.

Cara looked confused and placed her hand on her husband's chest, "See it that way? How else would I see it?"

"We needed me to get a job with a proper salary," Aaron said.

Cara squared her eyes with Aaron's, "Not at the costs that were so high. Not with you not being with the family or moving to Chicago or pulling us apart. Not with having to pull away from our community and let those that we have made commitments to. And not if they wanted you to go against what you know to be right."

"I had to do something, and on paper, it hit all the marks," Aaron shrugged.

"Yes, but this is a 'we' problem. Not one that you had to solve yourself, I think you took it all on your shoulders. I could have worked more hours, but you were concerned that the kids needed me, but the fact is, they need us," Cara said. "I need you."

Cara stood on her tiptoes and kissed her husband. Aaron grabbed her gently by the shoulders and pulled her close.

Annie and Chase burst into the cottage and saw their parents kissing. "Ewwww!"

"We finished our snowman!" Chase grinned.

"He is rather handsome, I must say," Annie giggled.

"Well, let's go check out our new friend," Aaron said.

Chase craned his neck around his parents, searching in the kitchen.

"What?" Cara asked.

Chase pursed his lips, "I thought you said you came in to make cocoa."

"I did say that, didn't I? Well, your dad was catching me up on his adventure, and I guess I lost track. Let's check out the snowman, and then I will make cocoa," Cara offered.

"Ok," Chase shrugged.

Back outside, the Shepherds trudged through the snow. Aaron and Cara walked arm in arm while the kids frolicked ahead of them. Aaron felt a great warmth despite the winter chill. He was glad to be with his family, delighted to be home.

Aaron chuckled silently to himself. They had literally less than zero dollars in the bank, yet he somehow felt richer now than he had when he left for Chicago.

Fifty One

As the kids were tucked into bed, Aaron and Cara snuggled by the woodstove. Aaron had made tea for them, and they held warm cups nestled in their hands.

"I'm glad you're home," Cara said softly.

"Me too. I wasn't sure how it was going to happen. I'm grateful."

"I was scared. I didn't know if anything had happened to you," Cara said. "I don't know what I would have done.'

"Sorry. It was a crazy trip, that is for sure."

Cara suddenly turned towards him, "What happened to your company car?"

Aaron laughed, "GPS tracker, found it at the airport, and hauled it away."

"Wow, they work fast," Cara said.

"Yeah, they do. We have a hole to dig out of again," Aaron admitted.

"We will. I have been praying."

"Me too," Aaron said.

Cara pivoted her body to look at Aaron more squarely, "Hal and I had a discussion while you were gone."

"Oh?"

"He is thinking he is going to sell the farm. He appreciated the run and us being here," Cara said.

Aaron looked grim, "Aww, Hal. He loves this place. He needed a strong season. I let him down."

"Hal said it was a slow season with or without you. It wasn't your fault," Cara shared. "He admitted if he had the best season in a decade, it wouldn't have been enough. The family trip to the farm just doesn't bring in the numbers that it used to."

"I don't understand…"

Cara smiled, "I think he just wanted to keep us excited in the prospect of helping to run the farm."

Aaron shook his head, "Wow." He looked distant and then frowned. "No."

"No?" Cara was confused about what her husband was saying 'no' to.

"We're here. We might as well go out swinging! No one is giving up on Hal's legacy until Christmas day itself is here," Aaron said defiantly.

Cara stared at her husband, absorbing his words. Nodding, she agreed, "I'm in."

Aaron had to admit to himself, it felt pretty good to trade his business suit for a henley cloaked in flannel and a pair of jeans. Lacing up his boots, he left the cottage. Seeing the rack of split wood low, he decided that was as good a spot to start the day.

Grabbing a piece of a log, he set it upright on the stump near the woodpile and hoisted the heavy axe overhead, bringing it down, splitting the log in two. Setting another in its place, he repeated the action until he had a pile growing.

Hal wandered out and started stacking logs as Aaron continued to split them.

"I gotta say, this feels good after spending the last few days traveling and in uptight conference rooms," Aaron said in between swings.

"It is good work out here on the farm, isn't it?" Hal grinned, setting two logs carefully in the stack.

"So, what's the plan?" Aaron asked.

Hal shuffled a bit, "Well, it's no secret that business isn't what it used to be."

"I suppose not," Aaron admitted. "In a perfect world, would you sell?"

Hal looked square at Aaron, "No, not in a perfect world. But, this place has run its course. Without the ability to hire staff…there's no real benefit to pushing."

"There's still time," Aaron pressed.

"Look, unless we turned around a decades-long streak of declining business, with the two strongest weeks of the season at our backs, it's done," Hal said.

"I know. Cara told me," Aaron admitted.

Hal looked a little confused.

Aaron grinned, "It's Christmas. The season for miracles."

"It would take one to make this thing work," Hal said.

"What's the harm? We're here. Might as well not turn away the families that do find their way out here," Aaron suggested.

Hal stooped stacking wood, looking thoughtful. "Yeah, alright," he nodded.

"Great, Maple Hill Tree Farm will remain open for business," Aaron grinned.

"For one last season," Hal was dubious. "What about you? What happened to your job in Chicago?"

"I realized that our principles weren't on par with one another. I quit and they unraveled every bit of what they had provided. By the time I reached the sidewalk, it all went away, including my way home," Aaron shared.

"Cara was very worried," Hal levied.

"I know. The company killed my cellphone. But here I am," Aaron said, his arms wide, the axe still in one hand.

"Back to the job search?"

Aaron grinned, "In January. For now, I have a job. Right here on this farm."

Hal cocked his head at Aaron.

"I'm penniless, I do not know what my future holds, but I am here with my family. I made an amazing friend who was kind enough to give us a place to live for the season...I am blessed," Aaron said.

Hal studied Aaron carefully, "I believe you are."

In between caring for the handful of families that came up to the farm, Aaron had his laptop and phone working in a frenzy. He was a successful marketing and sales director, he put his talents and experience to work on behalf of the farm.

He started a social marketing campaign, sent press releases to the local media outlets with his spin on the classic Christmas tree farm experience. He even reached out to churches and his business contacts.

Encouraging Cara and the kids to keep the store open. Reaching out to the neighboring farms and the vendors from the Christmas bazaars that assumed their seasons were over, to use the farm as their storefront. They could stay and work their tables, or they could mark their items and Cara would keep a log of their sales.

Soon, the shelves were stocked deeper than the start of the season, and shoppers who regretted

passing on an item at a bazaar could come out to
the farm for a second chance.

Aaron kept the fire pit roaring, and Cara
kept the coffee and cocoa warm. Seeing the
beginnings of his plan take action, he started to craft
a second phase, adding to what had already started
to take shape.

Fifty Two

The Shepherds were hard at work. Visitors to the farm had taken a sharp increase, Cara and the kids were serving joyously while Aaron buzzed around in between tree prepping duties.

The farm was more energetic than Hal could recall. Hal watched, completely charmed by the Shepherds, their hearts, and their effort. He himself played the gracious host, just as he remembered his father and grandfather doing.

Aaron spent his free time finding more vendors that would attract more visitors and more visitors to support the vendors. The local apple orchard arrived with their cider and apple cider donuts. The pumpkin farm brought pies and pastries, just as they did for their harvest festivals in the fall.

The school choir and band took shifts playing music, which naturally brought out their families. Groups of carolers filled open slots.

Churches and other non-profits were encouraged to donate for trees to be delivered to families who were struggling. The Ladies Auxiliary moved their operation to the farm and made wreaths and other crafts from items found at the farm.

Seeing all of the activity, Hal was beside himself. He had not recalled a season as busy as this one had become.

Aaron shifted gears from traditional consumers of trees and began working with his commercial contacts. Encouraging local businesses to make tree decorating part of their holiday party festivities. He highlighted a selection of immature trees at a discount, perfect for employee cubicles.

He contacted senior care homes, bringing busloads out to the farm for Christmas shopping and nostalgic tree farm experience. Aaron would take requests and run out to the field with Chase, loading the tractor and trailer with trees matching their preference. Placing tags on them, Aaron promised to deliver them that evening right to their rooms.

Once he exhausted his local contacts, Aaron started hitting the surrounding counties, all within an easy driving distance.

Chase suggested a sledding hill for the children in the valley who didn't' have snow.

Liking the idea, Aaron marked out a sledding area with rope staked at either end to serve as a handrail for the hike back up the hill.

Annie suggested a snowman competition. Aaron liked her idea and took it one step further. Instead, he invited families to make a snowman and commemorate their family with it for the remainder of the season. Annie loved the idea and put herself in charge of welcoming families on their snowman expedition and handing them family name tags that they could place around their snowman's neck.

In a brief moment amidst the tremendous activity, Aaron took a break on the main house porch overlooking the farm. Hal joined him, holding out a cup of coffee, "Here."

"Thanks," Aaron accepted the cup and took a sip.

"I...have never seen the farm this busy. This is exceptional," Hal said.

"I don't know that it will be enough, but I wanted the town to experience this. I wanted them to remember the relevance of Maple Hill Tree Farm. Of taking the family out among the trees to find that one that is special for their home. Getting out of their hectic in-town lives and spending time outside, slowing things down and enjoying themselves," Aaron said.

Hal just stared at him, "I don't know that I could have made a more impassioned statement, and I am third-generation farmhand."

The Tree Farm   290

"I have had the humbling, enriching experience of being reminded about the importance of being present with family," Aaron replied.

"You Shepherds are special people," Hal said.

"I don't know about that. You invited our destitute family to squat on your property."

"One, the Shepherds might be the richest family in town, even if your bank balance disagrees. Second, you squatters are welcome. You have brought life to this farm, and I am eternally grateful," Hal said.

Aaron patted him on the back, "It is such a pleasure to share this season with you and build our friendship."

"Likewise," Hal nodded.

Fifty Three

With a solid day on the farm under their belts, the Shepherds piled into their SUV and headed into town. Admittedly, an evening at home in front of the fire after working all day sounded appealing, but after being checked out for a bit, consumed by the new job, they were joyfully compelled to participate in the church event.

Arriving at the church, they greeted their friends and scrubbed their hands before entering the kitchen. The kids were filed into an assembly line while their parents manned the cutting boards and stoves.

Before long, soup was being poured into disposable bowls. The kids would place them in a paper bag, layering in a spoon, napkin, and a cookie. Closing the bag shut, they would staple a Christmas card to it and set it next to a pair of gloves that another assembly line of older kids wrapped.

Caravanning downtown, they followed a series of maps to specific locations. Maple Valley didn't have a large homeless population, but they were made aware of displaced individuals and families living in cars or other challenging situations.

The Shepherds and carloads of other families embarked on a tour of visiting seniors who lived alone in their homes. Instead of gloves, they gave out blankets. Wreaths that Hal donated were hung on their doors. Most importantly, they weren't rushed in their deliveries, but gave their time. They paused to visit, talking about Christmas, the blessing of Christ on mankind, and family memories around the holidays.

In one house, they stayed to watch a half-hour Christmas special. In another, they hung a star that hadn't been able to be placed on the top of a tree all season. In yet another, they sang Christmas carols while their host played on their piano.

As they wrapped up their evening, a weary Chase yawned, "It was like visiting relatives. It was fun."

"Can we visit them again?" Annie asked.

Cara grinned, pulling her kids in for a hug as they made it to their SUV, "Of course we can."

Fifty Four

Aaron had gotten up early and was busy tapping on his laptop when Cara shuffled out for her first cup of coffee. Noticing the familiar green background and gridline of a spreadsheet, she frowned, "What are you working on?"

Looking up, Aaron grinned sheepishly, "A business plan."

"A business plan for what?"

"To see how close we can get Hal to what he needs to hire the help next year so that he can keep the farm," he answered.

"And you are making a spreadsheet?"

"Yeah. I know roughly what he needs, I can enter in what we have brought in so far, what the bump has been since returning from Chicago, and given how many days are left to Christmas, how much more work we need to do," Aaron replied.

"Don't show Hal that, you'll scare him," Cara teased. "So how much more work do we need to do?"

Aaron winced, "Quite a bit, especially given that the likelihood of someone buying a tree between here and Christmas goes down each day."

"Wouldn't it be better just to enjoy the experience and go out swinging knowing that we did everything we could?" Cara asked.

Aaron grinned, "I have a plan. The spreadsheet and the numbers are just the litmus." Switching screens, "I have ideas and corresponding timelines to meet the goal, or try to, at least."

Cara laughed, charmed by her enthusiastic husband, "You are something else. What can I do to help?"

"I'm glad you asked," Aaron said. "You know how I told the board at Jans and Barnett that you can't force people's hand to get their business, well you can, but it's not the right way to do business. I told them that you needed to be a beacon and draw people willingly to your platform."

"Like the events the farm has been hosting, giving people a reason to be here, if not buying a tree, shopping at the store," Cara nodded.

"Yes," Aaron said and then, with a mischievous grin, added, "Now it's time to amp that up!"

Aaron recalled the boxes of lights that he had seen in the loft of the barn when he borrowed light strands for their Christmas tree. Sliding them all out into a row, he grinned. There were a ton of lights that he could use for his project, assuming they all worked.

Behind the boxes of lights, another row of containers and items caught his eye. The containers were full old signs and décor. Sifting through them, he found a stack of photos. Holding them up to the light streaming in from the open barn door, he saw that they were black and white pictures of the farm. Taking note of his discovery, he put them away and focused on his task at hand.

Recruiting Chase and Annie, Aaron filled them in on his idea. They clapped, excited to help their father. Pulling each strand of lights out of the boxes, they made sure they worked, setting those that didn't aside.

The functional sets were placed in the large trailer attached to the tractor. Next to the lights, Aaron loaded a ladder and a generator with a tank of fuel. Firing up the tractor, with their load intact, they traveled along the trails. Chase and Annie snuggled close to their dad as they drove to the top of the ridgeline.

Aaron hauled the ladder out of the trailer and leaned it against one of the tall evergreens atop the ridge. Grabbing a strand of lights from the trailer, he climbed the ladder. Getting to the top of the tree, he attached the strand as high up as he dared. Releasing the other end, he let it fall towards the ground. Connecting a second string, he climbed down and moved the ladder to another tree.

"Alright, guys, you get the fun part. Have you ever heard of a maypole?" Aaron asked.

Annie and Chase looked at each other and shook their heads.

"A maypole is an old dance where people would hold onto a ribbon and swing around the pole, making a swirl with the ribbon, like a candy cane," Aaron replied. "Think you guys can make a candy cane with lights around the tree?"

"We can do it," Annie assured.

Aaron handed over the string of lights and tackled the next tree. While Annie and Chase danced around the first. They repeated the exercise until they were out of lights. Hooking them together and connecting them to the generator. They headed back down the hill.

"I can't wait to see them!" Chase said.

"Me too," Aaron said. "Soon enough."

Aaron had two more ideas to employ. The first would require some advice from Hal, the second, a little time at his laptop.

Parking the tractor in front of the barn, Aaron sent the kids to the store to help their mom with whatever customers came through and to work with the vendors. Looking around the farm, he went to find Hal.

The buzz of the Gator could be heard coming from the western fields. He was carting an older couple who had selected a tree and was toting it back with the gator and small trailer.

Helping them with their tree while they went around the vendors and into the store, Aaron nudged Hal away. "I was hoping you could help me on a project," Aaron requested.

"Sure, what do you have in mind?" Hal asked.

"Let's go for a ride," Aaron suggested mischievously.

Nodding, Hal started towards the Gator. Aaron jumped in the driver's seat and led them to a field that didn't have as many families in it. Parking amid some average-sized trees, he asked, "If I were to pull a tree out for transplanting somewhere else and keep it healthy all the way, how would I do that?"

"What are you up to, Shepherd?" Hal eyed him suspiciously.

"I am upping our game with a unique offering, if we can pull it off, that is," Aaron said.

"Well, fall and winter is the right time to attempt it. We would want to dig around the root ball. I can give you a formula relative to the trunk size. I have a shovel attachment for the tractor. Dig out the roots, wrap it in wet burlap and try to get it replanted as soon as possible," Hal instructed. "No guarantees on survivability, however."

"What if we gave a guarantee?" Aaron asked.

"We could, but if I sell the farm, that guarantee wouldn't be worth very much," Hal warned.

"Put the money in savings account until the time when you were reasonably confident with survival, or better, make the guarantee part of your sales agreement if you have to," Aaron suggested.

Hal nodded, "That might work. Do you really think there will be enough buyers interested to go to all that trouble? We are weeks away from Christmas. Most people have their trees."

Aaron grinned, "I have an idea."

"Of course you do," Hal laughed.

"One more thing, as I was looking for Christmas lights…for our tree, I uncovered some old photos and trinkets from seasons on the farm long ago. Can I borrow some of them?" Aaron asked.

"Sure, why not," Hal grinned, overwhelmed by Aaron's enthusiasm and relentless angles to ramp up activity for the farm.

Fifty Five

With a tree, an old wagon, some décor from the farm's nostalgic glory days, and the old photos, Aaron borrowed Hal's classic farm truck and headed into town. Stopping at the Maple Valley City Hall, he walked into the building.

City Hall was buzzing with activity. Aaron realized that he was entering their holiday party. "Hi, Aaron!" Sam, the mayor's assistant, called as she saw him enter.

"Hi Sam, I'm sorry, I didn't realize this was your holiday party tonight," Aaron started to back out.

"It's okay. We are always here to serve, well, between the hours of nine and five, at least," Sam said. "Come on in. What can we do for you?"

"Well, you might now that I've been working up at Maple Hill Tree Farm. Hal, the farmer, is struggling to manage the place on his own, and his only chance to save the farm is to make enough this season so that he can hire help for next year," Aaron explained.

"I love that place. We used to go up there all the time. I heard you were doing some great things there," Sam said.

"Yes, it's been fun. There is still more to do," Aaron admitted.

"So, what would you like from your servants at City Hall?"

"I found a bunch of things hidden away at the farm, old photos, some farm implements, old fashioned Christmas décor...," Aaron shared. "I was hoping that I could set a display up in the shadowbox window. An in-town reminder of the century-old fixture of Maple Valley, a reflection of the long-standing tradition that families have enjoyed for years."

"You know what? I think we can do that. In fact, we had discussed putting together a historic display there, but no one has carried it out. We got as far as stringing the Christmas lights," Sam agreed.

"Really? That would be great!" Aaron smiled. "I will go and get prints made of the photos I found, and I'll set it up!"

"I'll do you one better. We have a poster printer. If we get to keep the prints, I'll do them for you," Sam offered.

Aaron snapped his fingers, "That would be wonderful."

"Go grab your stuff, I'll get the printer warmed up," Sam said.

Aaron rushed out to the truck and started carry boxes into City Hall. Adding the Christmas tree and the old farm tools to the assortment, he found a small crowd had emerged from the holiday party.

"They liked the idea and wanted to help," Sam shrugged.

Aaron looked at everyone who had gathered and nodded earnestly, "I'll take it. I am not sure I have the decorator's touch in my household. Thank you."

Sam sorted the photos of the tree farm and selected a few that helped tell the story of the farm and the families from town that visited. Heading off for the printer, Aaron helped line up the items that he thought would be interesting. A small group sorted through the farm tools and décor. Another group tackled the tree and decided on a classic decorating theme.

Aaron was impressed by how they came together to help him. The conversations carried a consistent theme – people loved the farm. They all had a memory of visiting the farm with their families to pick out their Christmas tree, but hadn't been up themselves in years.

As Sam returned with the posters for the window, "I thought of the theme, 'Remember When, Christmas Traditions of Maple Valley'. What do you think?"

"I think it is perfect. You are all awesome," Aaron acknowledged.

"Is there anything else we can do? While my family hasn't been out there in years, I would hate to see it go," a woman asked.

Aaron perked up, "Share that exact sentiment. Everyone loves the farm, but this year might be it's last, at least as we know it. Let them know about the season-long bazaar, the carolers, the food, and, most importantly, the trees."

"We will," they nodded, nearly in unison.

The mayor walked out to see where his revelers had disappeared to. Frowning, he asked, "I love the idea of helping out the farm and helping the community reflect on it, but haven't most people already gotten their tree this year?"

"Hi, Mayor Johnson. Most have," Aaron admitted. "But this year, we are selling living commemorative trees, with a guarantee of successful replanting. Families in Maple Valley can forever have a reminder of the farm, but an enduring family memory as well. And, the hardware store from Junction City is selling outdoor ornaments, and the farm will deliver the tree to your house."

"That is an interesting plan," Mayor Johnson said. "You know what, City Hall will be your first customer. I would love a...say twenty footer for the center of the turn-around upfront."

"I'll have it ready for delivery tomorrow," Aaron grinned.

Aaron returned to the farm, just as the sun was going down. Gathering the kids, he left Cara and Hal with mouths agape as they walked out without a word.

Hurrying to the Gator, they piled in and sped up the trail towards the ridgeline. Stopping at the top, they hopped out, just as evening had turned to dusk. Aaron fired up the generator. As it sputtered and then roared to life, Aaron looked at Annie and Chase with anticipation. They grinned at their father.

Flipping the switch, the trees shone to radiant brilliance. Up close, they were blindingly bright. The entire ridge radiated in artificial daylight. "What do you think?"

"I bet they can see it at the store!" Chase's eyes went wide.

"I hope so," Aaron said.

"I bet they can see it in town," Annie added.

Aaron smiled, "That is the idea. Let's get back to the store and see what they think."

Climbing into the Gator, they headed back down the hill, as much aided by the light of the trees as they were by the headlights on the ATV.

Sliding to a stop outside the store, they saw a crowd looking up at the ridge.

Cara and Hal stepped out of the crowd. Hal had his hands on his hips, "You three responsible for that?"

Annie and Chase looked up at their dad.

"We are," Aaron admitted.

"That, is amazing!" Hal smiled. "Holy cow."

Aaron grinned at his wife and held his hands towards the ridge, "Eh?"

Cara shook her head. Turning her attention to Annie and Chase, she asked, "You two helped?"

The two children nodded vigorously.

"Not at the top, I hope," Cara questioned.

"Nope, that was Daddy!" Chase grinned.

"Of course it was," Cara nodded.

"We circled the trees to make candy canes with the lights," Annie said.

"That sounds like fun. You did a great job. That is so beautiful," Cara admired.

Aaron put his arm around her and looked up at the lights on the hill. "It is," he admitted.

Fifty Six

The phone began ringing almost as soon as they had opened the store for the day. The town was utterly viral over the ridgeline tree lights. Aaron and Cara used the opportunity to pitch all of the activity at the farm.

In between calls, Aaron ignited a social media campaign regarding the family commemorative tree idea. He had Hal make a wooden placard from an old piece of barn wood, commemorating the time span to present that Maple Hill Tree Farm had been a part of the Maple Valley community. Despite the farm needing the money, he decided to give the tree away to City Hall for the people of the town to enjoy.

Heading out to the tree that Hal had personally selected, the farmer showed Aaron how to dig around the tree to carefully free the root ball. Wrapping the ball in wet burlap, they loaded it in the back of the trailer and filled in the hole that was left.

Arranging to meet with city workers at the turn-around island, Hal and Aaron loaded the tree into the back of the classic farm truck. Waving goodbye to the family who were already hard at work greeting people visiting the farm and helping the army of vendors that had assembled, Aaron and Hal headed into town to plant the tree.

They were surprised to see a crowd gathered around the island. A construction crew had already dug a hole to match Hal's specifications. Members of the media were capturing the event with their cameras. Aaron and Hal felt awkward from the attention, but Aaron knew it could be perfect for the farm.

Hal took over the transplant guidance, helping the city crew make the tree comfortable in its new home. Aaron informed Mayor Johnson about the decision to donate the tree.

"I love the idea. We will absolutely place the placard there. That way, generations will know where it came from and how special the connection is to the town," Mayor Johnson rationalized. As reporters gathered and dropped in on their conversation, he added, "I think we should decorate it. Just have to figure out what to use."

"I have an idea," Aaron suggested. "It is the town tree. Let's allow the community to decorate it. We can string it with lights and then let families bring an ornament of their choice, like we are all celebrating together."

"That is a great idea. I would say we should send out a notice, but I think we just did," Mayor Johnson noted, nodding toward the press pool.

The reporters gathered around the mayor, asking his thoughts about the tree, the farm, and the balance of town evolving yet, maintaining its roots, a clear attempt at a pun by a reporter.

Turning to Aaron, they asked about his experience this season at the farm. He relished the opportunity to explain how special the farm was, the uncertainty of its future and how families can order a commemorative family forever tree they pick out and have delivered and transplanted at their homes.

As the finishing touches of the island landscape were finessed, Aaron, Hal, and the mayor stepped back to admire their handiwork. "It is a beautiful tree," Mayor Johnson said.

When Aaron and Hal returned to the farm, they were surprised by how many cars were there. Hal had to park behind the barn as there was no room in the parking area.

"I can't believe this," Hal remarked.

"The farm is amazing, people just needed to be reminded about it," Aaron said.

Checking in on the family and ensuring no one needed help loading a tree, Aaron added the "Family Forever Tree" option to the Maple Hill Tree

Farm website and the social media campaign he had been managing for Hal since he returned from Chicago.

Hitting "send" on his communications and marketing broadcasts, Aaron left the cottage to see how he could help. Stepping off of the porch and towards the store, he froze in place. He paused to witness the crowd and abundance of activity that the farm welcomed.

As he resumed his trek into service, his phone started buzzing. Pulling it out, he found dozens of messages coming in regarding orders for the "Forever Trees". Some had requests for him and Hal to use their best judgment and select one on their behalf. Others asked how they could come to the farm and pick out their own tree.

Waving to Hal, he suggested Hal personally select the trees. Aaron showed him how he could mark them on his phone's GPS after he tagged them and send a report to Aaron's phone to go back and harvest.

"I guess this is where technology and good old-fashioned farming can come together, huh?" the farmer grinned at Aaron.

"As they come in, I'll send the requests to you, and then we can work together with the families who come out to select their own tree," Aaron suggested.

"It's a good thing the bazaar vendors have been pitching in. I think we are getting busier than we can handle," Hal said.

"That is a good problem for us to grapple with," Aaron said. "I'll take on that challenge any day."

Aaron was excited to see the vendors benefitting from the farm bazaar as much as Hal was. His goal of getting the community excited about one of its forgotten icons was coming to fruition.

Walking through, he said hello to the vendors and guests alike, asking if he could help anyone of them. With the bazaar running well and most tree duties ringing in as Forever Tree orders, he got the fire going in the firepit before checking on his family in the store.

Cara was just loading Annie and Chase up with trays of cocoas for the vendors. "Got time to help?" Cara asked, holding out another platter.

"You bet," Aaron grinned, grabbing the tray and following his children.

"You two have been terrific," he said to the kids as they walked out to the vendors. "This is not likely the most common way for kids to spend Christmas break."

"There is Christmas all around us, every day. This is awesome," Annie replied.

"I like the trees. And the cocoa. And we get way more snow here than my friends," Chase added.

To his amazement, more and more families were streaming in. Among them, a quintet of Dicken's era carolers. As he passed out cocoa to the vendors, one of them shared that families admitted they had largely forgotten about the farm, but the nostalgia display downtown and the bazaar was a good reminder of a family tradition that they should re-instill.

As Aaron handed out his last cocoa, he saw Hal waving him over to the main house porch, where a crowd of cameras gathered around him. Two news vans with their towers raised were parked near the barn.

"This…this fine young man and his family are the masterminds behind this season's resurgence. He has inspired the whole community and me to open their hearts and their lives to celebrating Christmas serving others. Delivering hope, cheer, and love as far as they could reach in so many ways," Hal said, circling his arm to bring Aaron in front of the reporters. "Aaron Shepherd, say a few words for these folks."

Aaron hesitated for a long moment before speaking, "Hal, and the generations of his family before him, have been part of the fabric of Maple Valley and the surrounding communities since, nearly the town's inception.

The farm, the experience that families have enjoyed pulling a sled through the fields, searching for that special tree that would become part of their family for the season is something so special. I get that things change, I do. But there are some things worth holding onto. Slowing life down a bit, taking the time to put the electronics and chaos away, if just for a bit, to spend time with the family, as a family. Maple Hill Tree Farm provides that, if just once a year."

One of the reporters noted, "You have a lot of passion for this farm."

"Sure, I love the farm. But what is truly amazing is the people and the farm's effect on them. The impact that Hal and his family have had on all of us. I remember how kind and welcoming they were. It has been etched in my head since I was a child. It is wanting to share that experience with all of you, the community, and their families," Aaron replied.

"There is a trickle-down effect. So far, City Hall reports over 700 families have brought an ornament to the downtown tree. We have footage of an impromptu caroling that started about an hour before we came up here," a reporter shared.

Another reporter spoke up, "And the lights. Was that you too?"

"Well, the kids helped, and they are Hal's lights. I told an overzealous corporate board recently, that you don't want to twist people or force them into action. You want to be a beacon that draws them in and welcomes them to your door. I guess those amazing pines up the ridge just inspired me to create an actual beacon for Maple Hill Tree Farm," Aaron admitted.

"Reports from three surrounding towns commented on the lights from last night. It is an impressive display, to say the least. Shops in Maple

Valley report benefiting from the interest drawn to our area," the reporter shared.

"My family and I have been blessed by the experience, to get to know Hal and to serve his guests. Hal, his father, and his grandfather have shouldered the weight of creating this experience from the literal ground up," Aaron concluded. "Merry Christmas, everyone!"

Aaron walked away from the reporters and joined a huddle of his family and Hal. They rejoiced in the attention that the farm had received and the success that they were bringing to the community and the Hal.

Fifty Six

The families, couples, and busloads of seniors coming up to enjoy the farm continued to grow. Hal still personally oversaw selections for those who placed an order over the phone or online.

Aaron helped the families that came up to select their own. He set hay bales in the trailer for families to ride on as he carted them towards the species that they requested. A few wanted to take the tree home and transplant it themselves as a family project. For those families, Aaron would swing the hydraulic shovel and dig up the root ball and load the tree right then before helping them get the tree in the bed of their trucks.

Others placed a special tag on the tree for delivery later that day or the next. The Forever Tree sales were so strong that Hal called up a larger truck and hired a driver that toted a small tractor along with the trees to help families transplant the tree if they wanted help.

Taking a break late in the day, Hal and Aaron stood on the main house porch soaking in all of the activity. "This has turned into the busiest Christmas ever, and nearly all of it well past the two biggest selling days of the season," Hal said.

"I'm glad. It's great to see so many families fall in love with this farm either for the first time or being reacquainted with it. I'm also glad it has been successful," Aaron replied. Turning to Hal, he asked, "Successful enough?"

Hal looked directly at Aaron. Nodding, he confided, "After the past two days…yes. It looks that way."

Aaron beamed, patting Hal on the back, "Yes! That is great news, Hal!"

"It bears repeating, I could not have done this without you, and your family."

"It's been a pleasure, Hal. A genuine pleasure," Aaron said.

The two leaned against the porch rail for a minute, taking a last deep breath, enjoying the farm full of revelers.

Their attention was diverted by heavy-duty flatbed truck steaming up the driveway. With the number of cars and traffic, it did not have an easy time negotiating the drive. Getting to the widest part of the lot, the driver had to execute a sixteen-point turn. Each shift into reverse released the loud back-up signal, giving way to first gear only to sound again as reverse was re-engaged.

"Another tree delivery?" Aaron asked.

"None that I'm aware of," Hal shrugged.

As the driver finally positioned the truck so that the cab was facing down the driveway, the driver seemed to scan the parking lot. Hopping down from the cab step that he was using as a vantage point, he appeared to stride towards his target.

"Why is he…that's our car," Aaron noted, not comprehending was happening or about to happen.

Aaron and Hal watched as the driver peered into the Shepherd's SUV and try the door handle. Aaron hopped off of the porch and made a beeline for the driver.

"Can I help you?" Aaron asked.

The driver looked up, little affect showing on the man's face. "You the owner?"

"I am," Aaron nodded.

"Sorry, pal, got an order to haul it away. Here's a copy of the order for you," the man said. "Nothing personal, just doing my job."

Aaron slapped himself on the forehead. "When the company pulled my bonus, the catch-up payments didn't go through," he cursed to himself. He realized there was no argument to be made. "I understand. I tell you what, I'll get you the keys, be easier for you to move it."

"Thanks man, I was trying to figure out how I was going to angle the truck to get it hooked and dragged," the driver admitted.

Aaron ran off to get the keys and tossed them to the man. "Merry Christmas," he muttered.

The man started the SUV and wheeled it behind his truck. Hopping out, he tilted the bed, hooked the Shepherd's family SUV up, and dragged it on to the flatbed. Without another word, he climbed into the cab and drove down the driveway and turned onto the highway.

Hal caught up to Aaron, who was intent on focusing on work, "Everything alright?"

Looking up at Hal, Aaron shrugged, "Yeah, it's okay. We'll figure things out." His short response and tone told Hal everything he needed to hear. He could tell that Aaron was embarrassed and distracted by this event. Letting him go, he knew how he would respond if something like that happened to him, especially in view of half of the community that he lived in.

Aaron, for his part, just hit stride right back into his work, trying to force a smile and not let on his frustration. He couldn't hide from Chase, who tugged on his dad's jacket. "Why did that man take our car?"

"Well," Aaron said sheepishly, "We are returning it."

"Why?"

"Uhm, because it was too expensive," Aaron replied.

"Aren't we going to need a car?" Chase pressed.

The question hit Aaron hard. He was overwhelmed with the public display of his shortcoming. He hadn't begun to think about the practical implication of the event. Being out on the farm, they had no way of getting to town – to go to church, get the kids to school, Cara to work...

Since he had returned from Chicago, he hadn't thought much of their financial problems and job loss. Thoughts of affording food, gas, their car payment, where they were going to live after the holidays, had all but completely melted away to his focus on the farm, Hal, his family, and the community.

Aaron sighed. It was a problem he was not going to be able to solve right then. He might as well focus his attention on what he could control – helping the community that he helped to invite out to the farm. Shaking off his thoughts, he looked at the families enjoying their tree farm experience and smiled a genuine, happy smile.

"Merry Christmas," he said to a family that drove up past the flatbed. Handing out candy canes to two children, he asked. "How can we help you today?"

"We are hoping to pick out our Forever Family Tree," the husband said. "Any recommendations?"

"The Spruces are hearty. Come on, I'll take you up on the tractor," Aaron called, waving them

towards the waiting tractor and trailer adorned
with hay bale seats.

As the record-shattering day at the farm
came to a close, the lights on the ridge ablaze, a
brilliant sentinel for the farm, the community, and
the spirit of Christmas, Hal, and the Shepherds
were the last remaining to help finish with the clean
up.

"What a day," Hal said. "We have had more
forever tree requests than we sold trees the day
after Thanksgiving."

"We equaled that in U-cuts," Aaron tallied.

"The bazaar vendors asked if we were going
to do this next year, they had better luck all the way
out here than they had at the Community Center,"
Cara added.

"I can see why that firm in Chicago wanted
you," Hal said.

Aaron grinned, "They didn't deserve me."

"No. No, probably not," Hal nodded,
shutting off the lights in the store.

Closing up for the night, they sauntered
toward their perspective homes.

As the Shepherds made their way through
the empty parking lot, a weary Cara frowned,
"Where did you park the car?"

Aaron closed his eyes and froze. "Yeah,
about our car..."

"We gave it back!" Chase blurted.

Wrinkling his nose, Aaron corrected, "More like they took it back."

"The catchup payment!" Cara exclaimed.

"Bounced when the bonus was reversed," Aaron acknowledged.

"What are we going to do?" Cara asked.

Aaron's calm and confident smile inspired Cara to smile with him. Together, they grinned, "We'll figure it out, we always do."

Fifty Seven

Before the bustle of the day, when it was just Hal and Aaron out on the farm, Hal pulled Aaron aside. A hand on his shoulder, he prodded, "Come on, I want to show you something."

They walked past the barn and along the twisting drive that went beyond the cottage. "You doing alright?" Hal asked as they walked.

"Yeah, I'm good," Aaron nodded. Sensing Hal was referring to the repo of the Shepherd family SUV and them spending time on the farm instead of other more lucrative ventures through the season.

"Look, I don't regret my decisions. I had to give Jans and Barnett a shot and find out for myself that they were not the right fit for me. I have loved every minute of working on the farm, side by side with my family and you, Hal," Aaron confided.

"I know this has been a tough season for you," Hal conceded. "You have been a blessing on my farm and me."

Stopping outside of an outbuilding that Aaron hadn't been in before, Hal began pulling away the overgrowth and scraping away the snow that had piled up, impeding the doors from opening.

When they had sufficiently cleared enough out of the way, Hal grabbed the handle and pulled the large door open. "Let's see if we can clear enough of this away to see what we came here for," the farmer said, moving plywood and containers out of the way.

Aaron lent a hand and started setting things aside. With enough items cleared, Hal's intent was revealed. "There she is," Hal exclaimed. "This little beauty was my favorite back in the day. Got me up the hill when the snowplows couldn't make it. I'm not gonna lie, I put her through her paces."

Smoothing his hands over the hood, Aaron looked up, "International Scout?"

"Yep. Great part of American automotive history. Jeep, Ford Bronco, International. All those SUVs out there today, this was one of the originals," Hal shared. "She's not much to look at, but I think we can get her running again. If we can, she's yours."

Aaron looked at the farmer and protested, "Hal, you don't have to do that. We'll get by, figure something out."

"I don't have to, that's true," Hal said. "You didn't have to come back to the farm, which by the way, would have been shuttered without your help. I appreciate all you have done. I know times are tough, I've been there myself.

This tree farm, it was started by accident. On a Christmas like this, my grandfather hunted on this land. His business was failing during the holidays. He noticed the fir trees in the woods and thought that they would make pretty good Christmas trees. He started selecting the best, cut, and hauled them to town. He sold enough to get through the holidays.

The next year, he scraped together enough to buy the place. The rest is history, our family history intermingled with the town's history. You helped revive that story. I am grateful."

"I didn't know that about the farm," Aaron admitted.

"That's the story. And now you are a part of it," Hal said. Returning the conversation to the Scout, "This thing isn't doing anybody any good in here. It would be nice to see her used again. As much as I love this SUV, she doesn't rank against the farm truck. Come on. We've got a little bit before we are inundated with the crowds that you helped wrangle. Let's see if we can clear enough space to do a little work."

While Aaron continued stacking things out of the way, Hal was circling the Scout, making notes. The more Aaron pulled away from the vehicle, the more he admired its muscular lines, two-tone paint with a faded blue body and white top.

"Are you sure about this? This truck is cool. Sixty…"

"Nineteen sixty-seven 800 series, an inline-six under the hood," Hal informed Aaron.

"Wow. I have to warn you, I'm not all that handy," Aaron said.

"You didn't know anything about Christmas trees a couple of months ago…"

Aaron moved a pallet away from the rear quarter panel, "True!"

"I remember why it was parked and put on blocks, the part actually came in for it, but we were knee-deep in fixing up the old Ford truck, so it stayed in mothballs. Glad she'll be going to a good home," Hal said.

Glancing at his watch, Aaron noticed, "As much as I want to explore more of the Scout, we had better head down to the store and make sure the bazaar vendors have what they need. I have the new list of Forever Tree requests that came in overnight, too."

"Go ahead and hand that to me. I'll manage the Forever Trees today," Hal offered. "Go on ahead. I'll head out in a minute." The farmer remained focused on the International Harvester SUV and his notes.

Aaron handed Hal the list of tree requests and hustled to the vendor area, where a couple of early risers were already setting up. "Can I get you guys some coffee?" Aaron asked.

One of the vendors lifted their heads and called, "That would be great! Thanks again for setting this up."

Waving, Aaron headed into the store to start the coffee and turn on the lights. Flipping the switch on the stereo, carols began to fill the air. Beginning on Thanksgiving and carrying all the way through to New Year's, he never tired of listening to Christmas music.

The door swung open, and he was greeted by Cara and the kids. "Good morning, guys!"

"Hi Daddy," Annie walked straight into him with open arms for a hug. "Who wants to help me deliver coffee to the vendors? Come on, Chase."

The day at the farm was the busiest yet. Hal's hired drivers had a constant flow of orders to fill. Hal himself, handpicked some orders to run himself in the farm truck. Hal enjoyed meeting the families and getting a chance to help them plant a tree that they could watch grow and decorate over the years.

When he was finished with his last run of the day, he stopped by the automotive parts store. Purchasing four new tires, new belts, each type of fluid, fuses and spark plugs – all the most likely to need replacement.

Stopping by City Hall, he got out and walked to the window display that Aaron had brought into town. Memories flooded Hal's brain, from life on the farm as a child with his grandfather, and then his father and then he and Laura. He was grateful that the Shepherds provided him a chance to make his future with the farm his choice and not be forced into a decision.

He admired the Maple Valley's new Forever Tree. He walked around the tree, studying the ornaments. Most had family names and dates on them. Some had messages and family photos. He had never seen one of his trees look so beautiful and have such a community impact.

As he drove through town, he started seeing trees in the front yards of homes, decorated with love. What was setting up to be a sad, disappointing, and perhaps final season for the farm had turned out to be alone of the most amazing, emotionally fulfilling years ever.

Hal and the Shepherds enjoyed dinner together in the main house. When he was in town, he bought gingerbread ingredients for the kids. Cara agreed to do the baking, and Hal set the kids up at the kitchen island with a wide assortment of candy for decoration and a little eating along the way.

"What do you say we work on that project?" Hal suggested.

"If you're up for it, I am," Aaron said, acknowledging they had just completed another in a string of long hard days.

"Let's go," Hal said, slipping his thick jacket on.

Aaron kissed Cara and asked the kids, "What should I expect? A castle? Santa's village? I can't wait to see it. I'll be back in a bit."

Hal had backed the truck up to the Gator's trailer. "Do you mind moving the tires and the battery over? I'll grab the rest of the stuff."

"Wow, you went shopping. I didn't mean for you to have to go to a lot of trouble or spend money on this," Aaron said.

"You didn't ask, besides, you have done a whole lot more for the farm than acted as a simple farm laborer. You have been my marketing department, spokesman, city liaison, social media coordinator. You name it. Plus, your entire family has pitched in. This is nothing compared to what you have done for me. Consider it a Christmas bonus," Hal said.

Firing up the Gator, Hal and Aaron drove up to the small barn that housed the classic SUV. Using a bank of work lights attached to the Gator's roll cage and hooked up to a spare battery, they got to work.

Aaron hauled the tires into the barn while Hal, gathered the rest of the supplies. "Where do you want to start?" Aaron asked.

"Go ahead and loosen the lug nuts on the wheels, we'll swap the tires and get this thing back on all fours and ready to roll, then we'll worry about getting her running again," Hal instructed.

Aaron began working the wheels with a lug wrench. Then using a farm jack, they lifted the SUV one side at a time. As Aaron hauled the wheels and tires around, Hal started up the compressor and made the swaps before Aaron remounted them, and they moved to the other side.

"Looks good to see her with proper tires again. I chose mud and snow tires, I figured as long as you are here, might as well be able to go wherever you need. She can handle just about anything," Hal said.

"They look good," Aaron agreed. "What's next?"

"Just sitting here, I know that all the fluids and rubber parts will be junk. We'll flush and restring before we move to electrical and try to get her started," Hal said.

Systematically, Hal maneuvered around the car, replacing parts that he assumed would be bad from time and elements. He then showed Aaron how to drain, flush and refill every fluid system on the truck.

Talking about farm life, families, and vehicles, the men lost track of time. Lost in their work and in their company. Aaron's cell phone ringing brought them back to the present.

"Hi Cara, is it getting late?" Aaron called sheepishly into the phone.

"It is, and I have two architects and designers that would like to show off their dream homes to you and Hal before they shuffle off to bed," Cara sang.

"I got it, we'll finish up and be right down," Aaron said.

Hearing the conversation, Hal piped in, "We did good work tonight. This is a perfect time to shut down for the night."

Shutting down the light and the tools, Aaron and Hal packed up for the night. Climbing back into the Gator, they made their way to the main house.

The sweet and spicy aroma of gingerbread met them the instant they entered the farmhouse. "That is a warm smell of Christmas. Add pine tree, and we've got plenty of those, wow!" Aaron called as they followed the scent to the kitchen.

"Whoa, what is all this?" Hal exclaimed as they saw the kitchen table turned winter wonderland of cookie and candy.

"Daddy, Hal! Look at what we made!" Annie called.

A sleepy Chase nibbled on a piece of gingerbread as he sat up on his knees so that he could lord over the table. "It's...," Chase started between bites before his sister cut him off.

"Let them figure it out," Annie snapped.

Aaron and Hal surveyed the scene. Four buildings of various sizes stood amidst an army of gingerbread trees and people.

"Wait a minute, is this…let's see. A store, a house, another house, and is this a barn?" Hal identified.

"There are a lot of trees…" Aaron added. His eyes widened, "Is that a farm truck with the tree in the back? That looks really good."

"Mommy added that one," Annie shared.

"You guys made the farm. It looks even better than the real thing. It's beautiful," Hal admired.

"Tastier looking too," Aaron winked.

"How about I get a picture of the artists with their creation. This is amazing," Hal said. "Aaron, the secretary desk in the parlor, I believe, is where I left my camera, could you grab it for me?"

"Sure thing," Aaron nodded and disappeared down the hallway to get the camera.

Finding the desk Hal mentioned in the parlor, he slid open the roll-top and grabbed the camera. About to turn around and head back, he paused.

A document on the desk caught his attention. It was a deed of sale for the Maple Hill Tree Farm. He realized he should not have been surprised, but seeing the paperwork was a stark bolt of reality. As gracious and generous as Hal had been, and regardless of the season's success, the Shepherd family's days at the farm were finite.

While a foregone certainty when they moved up there, the busyness of the season had distracted Aaron from its inevitability. All at once, Aaron was hit with the thoughts that they had no plans of where they would live, and he had no prospects for a job. Tasks that would dominate his mind and time following the holiday.

Aaron certainly couldn't blame Hal. As much as he loved the farm, the toll of decades of labor was evident. He was perhaps ready and undoubtedly deserving of retirement.

They certainly helped one another throughout the season in so many ways. This season on the farm was a fantastic chapter in their lives. They made a lifelong friend and grandfather-like figure for Annie and Chase.

The fact remained, the Shepherds would need to consider their next steps after the holiday, including a place to live. The truth was a looming black cloud seeping in over the family over an otherwise joyous time.

Aaron closed the desktop and pivoted to return to the kitchen. Taking a deep breath, he shook off the worries that he would have to tend to after the holiday. Hearing the giggles from his children down the hall was sufficient to snap back into joyous spirit.

Returned to the kitchen, Aaron handed Hal the camera. The farmer instantly launched into taking several photos of the kids.

Aaron hugged his wife and congratulated his children on their artwork.

Hal had the kids bookmark the display, each grinning for the camera, Chase stifling a yawn.

"We should probably get these kids home. Dishes are in the wash, the pans are clean and drying," Cara said. "Come one, guys!"

The kids gathered their coats. Annie stepped in front of Hal. Looking up at him, she gave him a big hug.

Having received thousands of them himself, Aaron knew the melting effect that the farmer was experiencing.

Bidding him goodnight, they headed home.

Fifty Eight

Three days before Christmas and the Maple Hill Tree Farm was remaining busy. The crowd that arrived was less about trees, but more about the experience.

Carolers, homemade treats, and snow zone play with sledding, a snowball fight arena and family snowmen crafted throughout the farm remained strong draws from not just Maple Valley, but from towns all around.

A camera crew with a drone captured the scene, flying over the entire expanse of the farm. Highlighting the families at play, the crowd at the bazaar, and the snow people dotting the farm by the hundreds.

U-cuts had all but stopped, but Forever Tree orders continued to come in. Hal ran that program, occasionally disappearing for swaths of time throughout the day.

Aaron focused on the main event area while cycling through the snow zone, making sure all of the vendors and guests had what they needed.

Cara had to place calls to local farms to restock their items, a welcome, though unheard-of event.

As evening began to fall, just before Aaron was due to turn on the generator, Hal flagged Aaron down, "Come on, let's go for a ride."

Jumping in the Gator, the farmer drove them up to the small barn. Rushing in, Hal grinned to Aaron. "Take that battery there, and connect the terminals, positive first and then the negative," Hal instructed.

"I did the fluids earlier, installed all new belts and most of the fuses. Even gassed up the tank," Hal declared. Tossing him a key attached to a keychain with the Maple Hill Tree Farm logo on it. "Go ahead, let's see what happens."

Aaron slid into the driver's seat. Pressing in the clutch, he turned the key, dash lights went on, and the starter began to churn, but it wouldn't quite turnover. "Hold on a second," Hal called from under the hood. A few moments later, he shouted, "Try again!"

Aaron turned the key a second time, and the SUV roared to life.

Hal slammed the hood and went to the driver's side window. "These old hands, I didn't quite get the distributor connections tight enough. You should be good to go."

"Let's go for a ride," Aaron suggested. "I was just about to turn on the Christmas lights, do you think this can make it up there?"

"Are you kidding me? This Scout will take you up and over the whole mountain if you want it to," Hal grinned. Circling to the passenger side, the farmer hopped in. "Let's go."

Aaron pushed the clutch, maneuvered the shifter into first gear, and let out the clutch. The older style gearbox launched the vehicle with a slight lurch, but the engine roared, and the SUV was on the move, cycling through the gears, Aaron built up speed until they reached the bottom of the hill.

Aaron paused to lock the hubs for four-wheel drive and pushed the vehicle to make the ascent up to the top of the ridge. "She runs great, Hal!"

Stopping to start the generator, Aaron hopped back in, and they made their way back down the hill.

"Stop at the small barn. I'll close things up there and grab the Gator," Hal said. "You go on down and give your family a ride. Be mindful, we'll have to get new plates for it tomorrow."

Aaron dropped the farmer off and joyfully went to find the rest of the Shepherd clan. Driving the nearly six decades-old vehicle was a visceral experience, the ride, the steering, the brakes, the response to the accelerator were direct and rough, nothing like modern cars. Aaron kind of liked the raw connection the Scout provided.

Pulling into the driveway, Aaron stopped next to the store. Cara was just shutting the store down and was leaving with the kids. Leaning over to roll down the hand-cranked window, Aaron called, "You guys want a ride?"

The kids ran to the SUV and opened to door. "Just tilt the seat forward and jump on in," Aaron said to the kids who were used to a four-door.

Cara slid in the front passenger seat, "What is this?"

"This is our new family car," Aaron grinned. "Hal and I started working on it after our car was hauled away. He gave it to us."

"It smells funny," Annie said. "But it is kind of cool."

"I like it!" Chase bounced in the backseat.

"We might want to add a few things like seatbelts," said as he wheeled the SUV back up towards the ridge to show off the vehicle to the family.

Fifty Nine

Christmas was two days away, and the farm was tremendously busy. The vendors were on their final day and worked largely on autopilot. Hal made or catered them lunch every day and invited their families up to play in the snow.

It seemed as though the entire town of Maple Valley was participating or a guest at the farm. It had become a winter wonderland for friends and families to gather.

Tree sales had quieted down, leaving Hal and Aaron to hover and help as they could. For Hal, it meant slowing down and being the front and center host, greeting as many guests personally that he could. Connecting with people and listening to their memories of farm visits from decades ago.

For Aaron, it meant working closely with his family. Taking snow zone breaks with Annie and Chase. Taking coffee breaks with Cara. They had always been a close family, the circumstances of this Christmas only served to bring them closer together at a crossroads that could have begun to separate them.

As Aaron had time to slow down, it was the first time that he paid attention to the wares that the vendors were selling. He had focused on serving them that he didn't take note of as to what was in their displays. Seeing the handcrafted toys, the bow and arrow sets, the dollhouses, the games, he reflected that he couldn't afford anything there for his kids.

Part of him felt guilty towards the vendors that he couldn't buy anything from them. He also saw adorable items that his family would cherish, but he just didn't have the resources to get anything.

They had been so busy, he hadn't taken the time to think about presents or Christmas dinner. He was grateful that they were together, had a safe and warm home, and were more certainly full of Christmas spirit.

Looking at the vendor booths and reflecting on working on projects with Hal, Aaron started to formulate some ideas. The more he conspired, a grin crossed his face.

Cara walked up and handed him a cup of coffee. Pulling her close, they observed the happy scene. The community had come together to support Hal and the farm, but also each other.

"Isn't this better than Chicago," she teased.

"Chicago was nice, but this is home," Aaron agreed.

Cara snuggled closer.

Hal pulled up in the farm truck and stopped next to them. "You want to give me a hand? The precut lots are closing down, and I usually pick up any stragglers that didn't find homes and recycle them."

"Oh, yeah, sure," Aaron said.

"How do you recycle them?" Cara noted.

"Run them through a chipper for mulch, make wood chips, sometimes the city wants them to support berms," Hal shrugged. "That's what the city does after Christmas with trees picked up at the curb or by the youth associations. This is just the first batch."

"Would it be okay if we found an in-between purpose for them?" Cara asked.

Hal shrugged, "Sure, if you've got one."

"Let me make a call," Cara ginned.

A cup of coffee later, Cara had a list of families and addresses that they had served in some way over the holidays. The entire Shepherd family piled into the cab of the farm truck, and they headed for the tree lots downtown to load up trees.

Following the list of families that were identified as likely without a Christmas, they donned their Santa hats and began knocking on doors. Aaron carried the trees while his family carried a strand of lights, a small box of ornaments, and cookies, all donated by the farm, church, or vendors.

Knocking on the first door, it took some time for someone to answer. A confused older woman scowled, "I didn't order a tree."

"We work with Maple Hill Tree Farms and volunteer for Hope Valley Church. We are delivering free trees for people who may want one but don't have one," Cara explained. "My name is Cara. This is my husband, Aaron, our daughter Annie and our son Chase."

"What am I going to do with a tree? I am an old woman who lives by herself," the woman.

"What's your name, ma'am?" Aaron asked.

The woman hesitated, taking stock of this quartet that landed on her doorstep. "Ruth Gaines."

"Ruth, it's nice to meet you," Aaron smiled. "Christmas is a celebration of the past, present, and future. When you see a tree, smell it, and the lights are strung, twinkling, they all come together. You might not think you need a tree this year, but this tree can bring back the past. It can reignite lost hope."

Ruth let out a slight gasp, "I appreciate the sentiment, but at this age…besides, I'll just have to figure out how to get rid of the thing when Christmas is over."

"That's no problem, we'll come by on New Year's Day and pick it up for you," Aaron said. "What would be the harm? If there is not Christmas magic with this tree, so be it. But if there is…"

"Fine, fine," the woman laughed. "You can bring it in. Can I make you some coffee or tea?"

"You know, tea would be nice," Cara nodded. "May I help you?"

"Oh no, I've got it," Ruth waved Cara off.

"Where would you like the tree?" Aaron asked. "How about in front of the window?"

Ruth stopped and smiled, "That would be nice. That way, it can shine for others too."

"That is a great thought, Ruth. We'll do that," Aaron nodded.

The Shepherds went to work, putting the tree together. Ruth came with a tray of tea and two cups of milk.

"Most of my visitors are over the age of eighty, I don't have cocoa, but I have milk. I noticed you brought cookies," Ruth offered.

"That's fantastic," Cara said. "Thank you."

"What do you think?" Aaron said, motioning towards the tree.

Ruth placed her hands over her heart, "It's beautiful! Thank you, I am glad you brought it. Can you stay and finish your tea?"

"Of course, we can," Cara said.

Aaron looked out at the truck laden with trees, but sat down and understood. Sometimes God's plan was to put you in a situation only to reveal the real impact that you were intended to make. This trip may not have been about mass distribution of trees, but time spent with a sweet lady who may have benefitted from visitors and a dose of holiday spirit.

An hour and a cup of tea later, the Shepherds had a new friend, and Hope Valley Church had a new RSVP for Christmas Eve service. As they gathered to leave and exchanged hugs with Ruth, she stopped them.

"There is someone else who might benefit from a tree and visit from you," Ruth confided. She went on to share that a family down the street was struggling through tough times.

By the end of the evening, the Shepherds had only delivered three trees and were left with six in the back of the truck that would need to be recycled. As Aaron drove his family back towards the farm, his heart was full of warmth. His family was amazing with each of the households they visited, the impact that their visits made was far more than he had imagined that they would be.

After visiting with Ruth, they met a family that had just moved to town and had very little as they were trying to make a new start. They had moved with just enough money to get into their rental, but didn't have enough for the luxury of a tree.

Their final stop was with a man named Marcus, who was struggling with PTSD. He was separated from his family as his challenges had made them incompatible. The Shepherds learned that his family had moved to Junction City. He wanted to be with them, but didn't know how to show he was making strides.

Aaron reasoned a Christmas tree most certainly couldn't hurt. He also offered to invite him to their church's men's group, where family challenges from a multitude of male perspectives were represented.

Making the turn to head out of town and up the hill, Aaron smiled to himself. This was, without a doubt, the poorest he had been at Christmas since he was a college student, yet it had absolutely turned out to be the most fulfilling.

Sixty

Christmas Eve began with one final event at the farm. Hal had arranged a pancake breakfast for the vendors. Not all of the vendors came back, some had last-minute items to pack up before heading home to spend the holiday with their own families. The breakfast was a great start to their chores for the day.

Others who couldn't make it had already been sent Christmas cakes Hal ordered from a neighboring farm. He was overwhelmed by the support that he had received and wanted to give back in whatever way he could.

The Shepherd family served alongside Hal, flipping pancakes, stirring scrambled eggs and frying bacon on a long outdoor griddle. Vendors who got to know each other over the season swapped gifts with one another and made lasting personal connections.

Hal observed the growth of this mini-community over the past few weeks, amazed at how this tree farm could make such a tremendous impact with so many people.

When all of his guests were served, and the last pancake was flipped into an aluminum pan resting on the warm but turned off griddle, the farmer leaned towards Aaron and said softly, "This was all you."

"What do you mean?" Aaron said.

"All of this, this whole season. The farm has never had the reach and impact that it has had this year. Ever," Hal shared.

Aaron shrugged, "Just sharing what the farm had to offer, being a vocal fan, if you will."

Hal laughed, "You are far too modest, Aaron. Don't get me wrong, the farm has always been a great place for families to launch into the Christmas spirit. A quiet respite for families to spend time together. You have made the farm, how did you put it, a beacon on the hill. Literally with the trees on the ridge."

"It's been pretty fun," Aaron admitted.

"With all of this activity winding down, I hardly know what's next," Hal said.

Aaron sighed, realizing that slowing down can sometimes reveal missing truths. His was Christmas was a day away, and he had nothing for his family to open for Christmas morning. Turning to Hal, he asked, "Would you mind if I slipped away for a bit? And borrowed some tools?"

"Sure, whatever you can find in the barn and outbuildings is yours. Let me know if you need some help," Hal grinned.

"I may just do that. You have seen my handyman skills after all," Aaron said.

Taking off his apron, Aaron snuck away from the festivities. Heading out towards the barn where Hal had revealed the Scout, Aaron decided that would serve as his creative workshop as well as any other.

Opening the doors to the small barn, Aaron walked into the center of the space. Spinning around slowly, he began to take stock of the items and raw materials available for his creative outlet.

His hands out in front of him, almost as an orchestra conductor preparing to lead his musicians or a sculptor sizing up a piece of granite, things began to take shape. Sorting through what he recalled from moving things to free the Scout, he snapped his fingers.

In the back corner of the barn, he saw the elegantly curved front of a sleigh. Different ideas began to assemble in Aaron's mind. Removing wood pieces and debris from the area to free the sleigh front, he realized it want just the front section, but the entire sleigh. It was beaten up, the seats were tattered, but the overall structure and rails seemed in good condition.

Scrapping his thought of using pieces, he yanked it free of its hold and moved it to the center of the barn. Walking around it, he made a mental list of what needed to be done and the tools and materials to make it happen.

Feeling good with the first idea, Aaron continued poking through the barn looking for other items. Spying a small riding lawnmower, he picked it over. Inspecting the tires and structure. Looking over the engine, while not his specialty, he determined it didn't look in too bad shape. They likely had used it at the farm until they upgraded the tractor implements that took over the small lawnmowers task.

With a second inspiration under his belt, he moved on. Taking another survey around the barn, he found an old, ornate mirror. With the wood, including a pile of spindles, he formulated his third idea.

Sifting through the wood, to ensure he had what he needed, he made another discovery. "What is this?" he muttered to himself. Sliding a large flat piece of wood free from the pile, he set it against the sleigh. Admiring what he saw, a warm grin crossed his face.

Happy with his treasures, he rushed to the main barn to gather the tools that he would need, along with a battery and inverter to power the necessary equipment.

For the rest of the afternoon, he sanded and hammered. He drilled and screwed and cut. He painted and oiled and buffed. One by one and working quickly, he created some, from his perspective, quite imperfect, yet impressive handmade or at least salvaged and refurbished gifts.

Only on one present did he call in Hal for assistance, and another to clarify that he was okay using it as a gift.

By the end of the day, Aaron had completed his task. Exhausted, sweaty, speckled in sawdust and paint, he was proud of what he had accomplished. Glancing at his watch, he knew he would just have time to shower before gathering the family and heading to Christmas Eve service.

As Hal completed the finishing touches on his requested part, Aaron hovered. "Come to Christmas Eve service with us?"

"Well, I uh...," Hal began wiping grease on his pants. Looking up at Aaron's eyes, he relented, nodding, "Yeah. I'll go."

"Great! I've done about all I am going to get accomplished in here. We should probably head back and wash up," Aaron suggested.

"I'm done too," Hal said. "I think I may have an idea for Cara's gift. I can call in a favor." He went on to explain his thought.

Sixty One

Aaron drove the Scout into town. Cara sat in the back with the kids, allowing Hal to ride upfront. Aaron stopped at the church and parked curbside at the front entrance. After Hal got out, he helped Cara and the kids. As they started to go in, Aaron paused, "Annie, you want to run a quick errand with me?"

Annie shrugged and hopped into the front seat. "We'll be right back!" Aaron called as he hopped in and drove away.

Not far from the church, they pulled up to a familiar apartment. Annie grinned, "I know what we are doing."

Knocking on the door, they waited. Moments later, Ruth opened the door. She looked at her visitors and let out a big smile.

Aaron held out his arm, "May we escort you to Christmas Eve service, Ruth?"

"I remember you said something about that. I got ready just in case. I wasn't sure if you were really going to come," she told them.

"I wouldn't tease about such a thing," Aaron said.

Ruth slipped her arm in Aaron's, and he guided her to the Scout. Opening the door, he helped her in. He and Annie scrambled to the driver's side, with Annie crawling in the back.

Before they pulled away, Aaron looked past Ruth to her apartment. "Your tree looks great from the road."

Ruth grinned wide, "It does, doesn't it?"

Aaron pulled up to the church. Getting out to open the door for Ruth and helping her out, an usher escorted her and Annie into the church.

Aaron parked and hurried into the church. Annie and Ruth found Cara, Hal, and Chase. "I see you all have met," he said as he walked up, checking his cuffs and pulling at the lapel of his jacket, ensuring that he was put together properly after rushing.

"Hal, you clean up well, my friend," Aaron declared.

"It's been a while I wore anything different than coveralls or dungarees," the farmer admitted.

"Look, there is the family we visited!" Chase said, pointing at a wide-eyed family that walked through the door.

Knowing that church, as open and a welcoming place as it may be, could be intimidating to the uninitiated, he quickly waved them over.

"I'm glad you made it!" Cara cooed as they joined the Shepherd's growing circle.

As the church worship band started playing carols, they knew it was time to gather in the sanctuary. Following Aaron, they were handed candles and a program.

Finding seats, they stood and sang carols until Pastor Barber stood on the stage. Wishing the crowd a Merry Christmas, he began his sermon.

"There in the field, were shepherds. The lowest of the blue-collar workers for the time. A class of people that had little respect, little credibility in the days when Joseph led Mary to Bethlehem, to report to the census as members of the house of David.

Think about it. Of all the people, Jesus didn't come into our world as men in a temple with religious leaders of the time. He didn't start his walk with man in the mighty kingdom. He could have incarnated in any fashion, anywhere. Instead, he chose the least of average. Simple men abiding by their flock at night. They were the first to receive the word of God through angels.

These average men were terrified. Terrified. 'Do not be afraid, for we bring you tidings of great joy. Great joy!

Jesus chose to walk in the most average of our shoes. He chose to experience life as the most common among us. Us. What he showed with this act of being born to a simple mother and earthly father in Mary and Joseph. In a feed trough for livestock of all things. That had to be the least kingly way to make an entrance for the King of kings. And yet, there he was, lying in a manger.

Beautiful. Amazing. Powerful. He lived with us. He died for us. He walked the life showing how the most common of us, could do great things when done so on God's behalf.

Tonight, I invite you as we celebrate the birth of the Messiah, to embrace your missional life, regardless of what walk of life you find yourself in, the walk with God, allowing the Holy Spirit to guide you, living our earthly lives as Jesus would have us live them, we can do great things," the pastor paused, allowing his words to sink in.

"Now, one of my favorite things as a pastor, allowing the house lights to dim, we will light our candles and sing "Silent Night". As the ushers come by your row, tilt your candle into theirs and repeat down the line, keeping the lit candle upright, allowing the new candle to tilt in its favor, that way none of you go home with a souvenir of wax on your shoes."

The ushers approached the stage and lit their candles from the large ones in the décor. As the sanctuary went dark, and as each row lit their candles, they began to sing along with the pastor and worship band. Soon, the entire auditorium was singing acapella.

When the song was over, they sat in silence, candles flickering. Finally, Pastor Barber suggested the congregation could extinguish their candles. The worship band launched into a final song before they were dismissed.

On their way out, in the back row, Aaron saw Marcus, the man that they visited the night prior. He sat silent, holding his candle out in front of him. Aaron nodded to Cara that he would catch up with the family in the lobby.

"I'm glad you made it," Aaron said.

"Didn't think I was going to. I just kind of...felt I was supposed to," Marcus admitted. "Maybe it's because of the Christmas service, the candles, Silent Night…I haven't felt this calm in years."

"I know what you mean. I haven't experienced what you have. I just know when I am up against it, being here refreshes me. Sets me straight. The longer I am here, the better I manage throughout the course of the week," Aaron said.

"I don't know what the answer is. I don't know what I am supposed to do," Marcus said.

Aaron sat quietly before he replied, "Take a step. See where that one takes you and take another. Pray, if you don't want to do that or aren't ready for that, be silent before you act. Before you speak. It will serve you well. When you are at wits end, find a quiet place. Come here to this sanctuary. Find a peaceful place so that you can find peace."

"Sounds simple enough," Marcus admitted. As if in wary epiphany, he turned to Aaron, "Would you pray for me…and my family?"

"Of course," Aaron nodded. With a hand on Marcus' shoulder, he bent his head and prayed.

Aaron and Marcus met up with Cara and their new friends in the lobby. Aaron suggested that he should take Ruth home.

Marcus stepped up, "I can take her. The apartments along Sixth? I pass right past there."

"You are all welcome at the farm tomorrow. We would love to have you up for Christmas dinner," Hal offered.

"That is very gracious," Ruth said, "But the Bennet's and I are going to get together."

"That's wonderful," Cara said. "How about you, Marcus?"

Marcus grinned, "My wife is inviting me to come over and spend Christmas with her and the kids."

"Nice," Aaron nodded. "If you need anything, here is my number."

"Thank you," Marcus accepted the card, "Merry Christmas."

"Merry Christmas."

Sixty Two

Just as the Shepherds and Hal were making their way out of the church, Mayor Johnson stopped them. "I thought I would see you tonight. I need you to come with me, all of you," the mayor said.

"You need us to come with you, for what?" Aaron asked.

The mayor grinned, "You'll see."

Curious, they followed the mayor out of the church and out to the sidewalk and down the street towards the town's Forever Tree. As they got closer, they could see that a large crowd had gathered. As they got closer still, the heard the sound of a thousand voices growing in a single tribute to the tree, to the season, to Santa Clause and the miracle baby that had come to save all mankind.

"This is all because of you all. The work you have done up on the farm and around town. In all my years, I have not seen the community such a single spirit. It is nothing short of a miracle," the mayor informed them as they closed in.

Wary, the focal point shy farmer, asked, "What exactly are we supposed to do? I ain't making a speech."

The mayor laughed, "It is so much more simple and special than that. I just wanted you to join them. Sing. Hear their rejoicing. Feel the heartbeat of our city wrapped around that Christmas tree."

Gathering near the mayor as he found his own family, they became part of the citywide choir. Aaron held his wife's hand while Annie and Chase squeezed in next to him. Hal stood next to Aaron, looking at his friend, he smiled, shrugged and began singing alongside their fellow townspeople.

Looking around as they sang, Aaron recognized friends from church, the staff from City Hall, former fellow employees, vendors, families he served in volunteering runs and vendors. Behind them, the Bennett family arrived with Ruth. Pastor Barber and his wife filled in immediately behind them.

Aaron whispered to the mayor, "Was there like a memo or something?"

"No," the mayor conferred, "It just started organically, families placing their ornaments on the tree and enjoying it all lit up. I got a text while we were in the Christmas Eve service. Can you believe this? It's amazing."

Aaron continued to take in the crowd, nodding, waving, and smiling as he made eye contact with people he knew as they sang. The mayor's words danced through Aaron's mind. It was an amazing experience with so many families from the town that they knew or had touched in some manner. Aaron was especially impacted by how many were new connections since he started working at the farm.

Together, they sang in earnest. A joyous, united, gathering of a town that needed and found holiday cheer.

Pulling back up at the farm, the Shepherds and Hal were still singing carols, right up to the point where they stood outside of the main house porch, where Aaron and family would split off towards the cottage.

Hal turned to address them. "Thank you for inviting me to church. I am glad the mayor found us. To see the impact of what we, what you have done in this community is life-changing."

"It's been a team effort," Aaron shrugged off the praise.

"There have been a number of people who have participated and been involved, to be sure. But it has been your drive, passion, and leadership that has encouraged all of those people to get involved, to do things differently this holiday season, that is no easy task.

Think about all of those people in the center of town tonight. Maybe you didn't wrangle them all there directly. But it was your idea with the tree and your idea of what to do with the tree.

To watch what you and your family have endured, and yet, you keep forging ahead. They keep working right alongside you. You are all blessed and are all such a blessing," Hal continued.

"We feel the same, Hal, blessed to have spent this season with you," Cara said.

"You have given a lonely old man…a family again," Hal choked back a rare display of emotion.

Cara hugged him, "You have become family to us, too, Hal. Please know that."

Annie and Chase followed suit, hugging the farmer with their mother. Reluctantly, Aaron piled in.

"Okay, okay, stop it now. I think I made my point. I look forward to you all coming to the main house for Christmas dinner tomorrow. Now go home. I believe there is a visitor due tonight who tends to shy away when children are still up and not in their beds," Hal grinned. "Goodnight, all."

Hal started to turn to go into his house. Annie stepped forward, "I love you, Hal."

The farmer was emotionally stricken. Kneeling, he smiled, "I love you, too, sweetheart."

"Goodnight, Hal," Aaron nodded, "He's right, time to get you guys to bed. Put up your stockings."

Annie and Chase ran to get ready for bed while Cara found their stockings. Aaron stoked the woodstove and put hot water on to boil.

As the children returned in pajamas and brushed teeth, they gathered together on the couch. "This has been the best Christmas ever!" Annie declared.

"Yeah?" Aaron squeezed her tight in his arms, "How so?"

"Everything. The singing, the trees, the snow!" Annie shared thoughtfully.

"I like the snow!" Chase chimed.

"It has been spectacular, hasn't it?" Aaron confirmed.

Cara set out the cookies for Santa, as well as a few carrots for the reindeer.

"You have eight of them, right, Mom?" Annie ensured.

"Cookies or carrots?"

"Carrots. Eight tiny reindeer," Annie confirmed.

"Right," Cara nodded. "I'll get two more."

"You think Santa can find us up here?" Chase asked nervously.

Aaron looked thoughtfully for a moment, "Sure, he will. Christmas spirit is the real magic of Christmas. It flows through us and follows us wherever we go."

"Like the Holy Spirit!" Annie suggested.

"Well, without the Holy Spirit, there is no Christmas spirit. There is a connection there, to be sure," Aaron nodded. "Santa Clause got his start by taking care of those who needed it the most. The spirit of giving, of love, and celebrating the birth of Christ is like the recipe for Christmas spirit."

Chase looked confused.

"Think of it like this, Chase," Annie shared. "Wherever family is, Santa Clause can find us because we have the Christmas spirit!"

"Oh, okay," Chase nodded.

Cara smiled as she poured tea for Aaron and herself. She admittedly liked listening to her husband skirt, the fine lines of deep discussions with the children.

Placing the remaining carrots on the plate for all eight reindeer, she joined her family on the couch.

Slipping a book out from under the sofa, she handed it to her husband. "I think it is time."

"Ah, the book," Aaron grinned, setting the book out where the children could view the illustrations while he read. "T'was the night before Christmas…"

Stockings hung, prayers prayed, tired children fast asleep in the loft, Aaron and Cara collapsed on the couch together.

"I love this part of Christmas Eve," Aaron said softly.

"The children in bed part?" Cara asked.

Aaron laughed, "No, the sweet silence. Especially with snow on the ground. The whole world seems to slow down, nearly to a stop. Even in town, it is quiet. Calm. For a moment in time, there are no worries, no concerns. Even the excitement of Christmas is quelled from anticipation to appreciating the beauty of the moment.

I find the moment Christmas Eve turns to Christmas is the most spiritual moment for me throughout the year. As much as I love Santa and trees and presents, that is the defining moment of the season for me. The living realization of Silent Night."

Cara looked up at her husband while wrapped in his arms. "You are delightfully cheesy, Mr. Shepherd. But in a good way. I get what you mean."

"Besides, it's nice to get away from the worries and whatever the future holds. Jobs, where we are going to live in the next couple of weeks...," Aaron started.

"What do you mean?" Cara asked.

"The night that you and the kids were making gingerbread houses, when Hal sent me to get his camera, I saw a deed of sale on the property. No real surprise as we knew it was going to happen at some point," Aaron said.

"But we did so well this season," Cara said.

"We did so well that we gave Hal the chance to make the right decision for him and not be forced one direction or the other. That is a great thing. Working with him, I could see how much he wanted to do, but his body just wouldn't let him. Even farmers need to retire," Aaron said.

"Yeah, I guess. I was just hoping we had time in the new year to find our path," Cara said.

"For Hal, selling while the farm is on such a high, it is an incredible opportunity for him. It's the right time. Who knows when the sale will be final," Aaron said. "I just keep thinking about how the events of this season, the company shutting down, the job in Chicago, the farm…we were led down a path. It has been pretty incredible."

Cara agreed, "It really has. Connecting with Hal, becoming like family with him. The work with the vendors and the community and the church have been spectacular. We have even grown closer as a family. Regardless of what happens after Christmas, the road to here has been amazing. You are right. We can worry about what's next after Christmas."

Grinning Aaron added, "Besides, we'll find a way, we always do."

Sixty Three

Aaron had gotten up early to bring in the gifts from the barn. Stepping out onto the porch, he paused to appreciate the morning. The sun cresting the horizon peeked through a thin layer of clouds, reflecting off of the fresh layer of snow that fell overnight.

In front of the door was a package that he had not expected. A quick inspection clued Aaron in that it was a collection of presents marked "For Annie" and "For Chase", each marked "Love Santa".

Aaron smiled, looking out towards the main house.

Pulling the package in, he quickly set the gifts under their tree and added a couple of smaller items to the already modestly filled stockings. Admiring the presentation, picturing the children waking and sticking their eager heads against the spindle rails of the loft peering down to their tree.

Hurrying off, Aaron went to fetch his own presents. Starting at the large barn, he fired up the tractor and the big trailer. Pulling out into the drive, he wheeled the tractor and throttled his way to the small barn.

Aligning the trailer to the door, Aaron hopped out and opened up the barn door. Starting with the sleigh, he used the harness around his own shoulders and dragged the sled across the floor and up onto the trailer, pulling it as far forward as he could. Next, he loaded the other gifts that he had so proudly assembled or fixed onto the trailer. Closing up the barn, he drove down to the cottage. Just offset of the window, so you would have to go outside to see them, he worked quickly to unload them, each with a giant red bow and tried to craft.

Hopping back on the tractor, he moved it onto the driveway. Taking his gift for Hal, he leaned it against the main house under the covered porch. Hustling, he returned to the cottage to find a little face peering down at his from the loft.

"Good morning, Chase!" Aaron whispered.

"There are presents!" Chase hissed.

"Yes, there are," Aaron replied.

"I got a book!" Chase lifted his first gift in the air.

"Good. Until Mommy and Annie are awake, you can read it. You can stay up there or come down with me," Aaron said.

"I want a hug!" Chase said, bolting from the loft rail and bounded down the steps, leaping into his dad's arms.

"Merry Christmas, Chase!"

"Merry Christmas, Daddy!" Chase said. Showing his dad the book up close, "See?"

"That looks awesome."

"I'm going to read it," Chase announced and plopped down on the couch. He was distracted, spying the gifts under the tree and poking out from under the stocking. Eventually, he relented to focusing on the book.

Aaron stoked the woodstove and warmed the coffee. As if on schedule, Cara and Annie met at the intersection from the hall to the loft steps.

"Good morning, ladies!" Aaron beamed. "Merry Christmas!"

Chase tossed his book down and sprinted over to his mother.

"Merry Christmas, baby," Cara ruffled his head and pulled Annie in for a hug.

"Sleep well, princess?" Aaron asked.

Annie nodded, "I did. I thought I heard the tractor this morning."

"Hmm. That's weird," Aaron shrugged, "You guys want some cocoa with candy canes?"

The kids nodded eagerly.

The Shepherds assembled in the living room, waking up with their hot beverages—the woodstove leaving the room cozy.

Starting with stockings, Annie and Chase found their little treasures. Candy and candy canes, scented pencils, tiny stuffed animals to clip on their school backpacks, and a new toothbrush were like finding gold to them.

Cara looked at Aaron as the kids found their gifts under the tree. Aaron shrugged and motioned his head towards the main house and Hal. Cara nodded in understanding.

"Santa found us!" they called.

"It looks like he did," Cara replied.

"Let's see what you got," Aaron said.

Chase ripped his open first, his eyes lit wide, "A train! I got a train set!"

Annie, opening her wrapping carefully not to tear any of the paper, revealed hers, "An easel and paper and pencils! Awesome!"

Opening their remaining presents from Santa, they found items that complemented their first gifts. Chase got unique train cars, including one that hauled Christmas trees. Annie got paints and a book on how to draw characters.

Cara looked at her husband, "I'm sorry we don't have much for each other."

Aaron grinned as he squeezed her. "Are you kidding me? This, right here, is all I could ever hope for."

"I made this for you," Cara said, producing a present from behind a couch cushion.

Opening it, Aaron revealed a calendar. Thumbing through it, he found that each month had one Friday of the month circled with a different activity planned for just the two of them.

"A night with you all to myself, all year long," Aaron acknowledged. "I love it."

He gave her a hug.

"Well, if you put your coats and boots on, I have something to show you," Aaron said.

His family looked at him, quizzically. "It is a beautiful Christmas morning," he grinned.

Leading the family outside, Aaron stepped aside, letting his family peer out to where he staged their presents that he worked on. The kids' eyes went wide and rushed down the steps.

Annie rushed to her present. A vanity made from the inspiration of the mirror that Aaron found in the barn. The spindles made the legs, a semi-circle piece of wood he found that came from half of a large industrial spool made the top with the mirror attached. He painted everything an enamel white with a trim board he painted lavender with her name spelled out in the center.

"Did you make this?" she asked.

Aaron wrinkled his nose, "I did. I'm not all that handy."

Annie grinned, "I love it!" Running to her father, she leaned with a deep hug. Cara looking on approved of her husband's gift.

Chase was sitting in the driver's seat of the lawnmower turned go-cart. Fitted with larger, knobby tires and widened track to prevent tipping, and of course, Monaco racing stripes made it complete.

Turning the wheel and making engine noises, Chase was already wheeling around the farm.

"We'll do a real driving session after lunch, what do you say?" Aaron asked. Chase nodded excitedly.

"What is this?" Cara asked, running her hands along the sleigh. It's fresh enamel paint gleaming in the sun reflecting off of the snow. Deep red and black tartan flannel covering the refreshed cushion seats.

"Hal said if I could make use out of things in the small barn, I could use them, including this."

Cara laughed, "You clearly did not make this."

"No, but I gave it some love. A fresh coat of paint, new seats, scraped off a few years of rust...," Aaron said. "I saw how much you liked the one in the store."

"It is beautiful," Cara admired. "I'm not sure what we'll do with it, especially once we move back into town."

Aaron shrugged, "We'll find a use for it. If nothing else, we'll have the coolest Christmas decoration in front of our house."

"I love it," Cara kissed her husband.

"Let's get Annie's vanity in and out of the snow. I think the day's surprises are not quite over yet."

Finding a little spot in the corner of the loft, they made a temporary home for the vanity.

Cara offered to make breakfast, Aaron and Chase took advantage of the time while Cara cooked and Annie organized her hairbrushes and bows on her new vanity to try his new present.

Strapping on Chase's bike helmet, Aaron gave his son some driving tips on steering, braking and throttling. Making parameters of staying in the relatively flat drive between the cottage and the small barn, Aaron cranked the engine and let him go. With a grin, Chase pressed the throttle and raced along the drive.

Hal had rigged several safety mechanisms to cap the speed and automatically cut off the engine using the lawn mower's original safety defaults. Aaron was consumed by Chase's broad grin as he enjoyed his new gift.

Braking to a stop at his dad's feet, he said, "Best. Christmas. Ever." With a press of the throttle, he was off again. Driving carefully as he got used to his new toy, the knobby tires eating up the snow with aplomb Chase looked as happy as a child should on Christmas.

A few laps around the circuit, Aaron and Chase were called in for breakfast. Chase took care to park his vehicle in front of the cottage.

Heading into the house, they were quickly met by Annie, who pulled her father up to the loft before he had a chance to wash up for breakfast. Holding out her hand in dramatic fashion, she pointed towards her vanity. She had laid out her hair items and lip glosses in strategic lines.

"Very nice," he said. "Ooh, I have an idea, I'll be right back."

Running down the steps and out to the farm truck, he reached in the back where the spare decorations were and grabbed a set of lights.

Returning to the cottage, he kicked off his boots and ran up the stairs. Winding the lights around the frame of the mirror, he plugged them in. "Now, what do you think?"

Annie grinned, "That is perfect, thank you, Daddy."

"Now, we should wash up for breakfast that your mom has worked hard to prepare for us," Aaron prodded.

Assembled at the kitchen table, they said grace and dished up Cara's Dutch babies and berries.

"This Christmas was amaaaazing," Chase said between bites.

"It has been," Annie agreed. "The whole season, today, the presents. Best Christmas ever!"

"I think you guys are right," Cara approved.

Aaron was contemplative, "It really has been. For a year that was a bit challenging, it turned out pretty fantastic."

"I don't ever remember being so active or working so hard, but I don't remember it ever being quite so fulfilling, either. I think we experience more of the true meaning of Christmas as we ever have," Cara added.

Aaron raised his coffee cup, "Merry Christmas! A toast to the Shepherd family."

"And to the Maple Hill Tree Farm," Cara added.

"And to Hal," said Annie.

"And to be baby Jesus!" Chase declared.

Aaron and Cara laughed, "Especially baby Jesus."

Sixty Four

When the Shepherds were just finishing breakfast, a knock at the door garnered their attention. Opening it, they found Hal standing there.

"Aaron, I found the missing part that you were looking for," the farmer said.

"Excellent. Cara, let's go for a walk," Aaron suggested. "Annie, you're in charge, we'll be back in a little bit."

Aaron led Cara with his arm in hers. Stepping off of the porch, the sleigh that Aaron had refurbished was connected to a draught horse.

"Oh my, where did you get a horse?" Cara asked.

"Hal has a farmer friend that has a team of them. He was kind enough to bring one by this morning," Aaron said.

Hal stood by the sleigh, waiting by the rear seat. "My lady…"

Aaron escorted her over where he and Hal helped her into the sleigh. Hal jumped in the front. Cara gave a curious look. Aaron laughed, "What, you want me to drive?"

Climbing in next to her, they snuggled close. Hal turned and handed them a gift bag. "For you. You might enjoy that during your ride."

Cara opened the bag. Inside was a plaid blanket handmade from one of the bazaar vendors. Spreading it out over their legs, they cuddled close to each other.

Smiling, Hal faced the horse, lifted the reins encouraging her forward. As they pulled, bells rang out from their harnesses.

Cara turned excitedly to Aaron, "Jingle bells!"

Hal guided the sleigh from the cottage to the main house. On the porch was the refurbished sign that Aaron cleaned up and repainted for Hal.

"Did you do that?" Cara asked.

Aaron nodded, "Found it tucked away behind a bunch of stuff in the small barn."

"It's nice, looks old," Cara noted.

"That sign is about as old as the farm truck. That was the sign that I came home to, every day after school. My grandfather made it. It's etched in my memories, and probably a photo or two, but otherwise, I forgot about it. It was a fantastic treat to wake up to this morning. Thank you."

"It looked special," Aaron admitted.

"It is. Great gift to spruce it up and bring it to me. Like a family portrait," Hal said.

Continuing, Hal led them through the snow-dusted evergreen trees to the far west field. Aaron and Cara cuddled under the blanket. A light snow flurry sent soft flakes dancing in the air around them.

Circling Laura's tree, he slowed the horse. "I still see Laura on the bench, under a blanket in the snow. Her moments with herself, with God. Amid the holiday rush, she would find a few minutes to reflect. Sometimes, she would get lost in the moment, and I would come out and find her here. She would invite me to join her."

Hal chuckled, "She wouldn't let me speak for at least five minutes. Providing me my own time for peace and to not just talk to God, but listen for once."

"Always a challenge for me as well," Aaron admitted.

Moving on, Hal completed the circle and headed back towards the cottage. Pausing out front, Hal suggested, "Why don't I go in, see if Chase would like help with the train set and admire what art Annie has produced so far."

"Thank you for doing that, and for the ride," Aaron said, standing up.

"The ride has just begun, but you two are going to have to come up here," Hal said.

Aaron looked confused, "What do you mean?"

"Gladys knows what to do. Just hold the reins soft. Pull up if you want her to slow down or stop. Give them a little jingle if you want her to move on. She knows the route," Hal grinned.

Aaron looked wary.

"Come on, come on. You two deserve your own ride without an old man blabbering on about memories," Hal insisted. "Here you go."

Aaron helped Cara from the rear seat to the driver's seat alongside him. Grabbing the reins, Aaron pressed, "You're sure about this?"

Hal grinned, "I'm sure."

With a slight wave, he gave Gladys the slightest tap, and the sleigh was off with Aaron holding the reins.

"I can't believe we are on a sleigh ride," Cara giggled.

"In your very own sleigh," Aaron added.

"With my very own, very handsome driver," Cara gave Aaron a squeeze.

Guiding Gladys and the sleigh or as it were, allowing Gladys to guide the sleigh, they headed up the hill to the high ridge. Gladys knew to make the circuit and stopped when Aaron held the reigns high.

Pulling the blanket higher as the wind on the ridge was more biting. Heavier snow began to fall over the scene. Aside from an occasional mutter from Gladys, the world had gone silent. The snowflakes made their impact around them without a sound.

"This is breathtaking," Cara said, her hand on her husband's chest.

"It is. I am going to miss it. I genuinely love it up here," Aaron said. "Without respect to my friends in Chicago, I am so glad I am not there."

"I am glad we are all here together, that is all that matters," Cara cooed.

"When we were dating, before we got married, you said you would stick with me even if we were living in a cardboard box," Aaron said.

Cara pulled away slightly, "I did. And I will, though I would rather not if we can help it."

Looking at one another, they smiled, "We'll figure something out, we always do!"

Settling back in the reupholstered seat of the sleigh, they enjoyed the view, the moment, and each other.

Gladys did just as she was supposed to, stopping gently in front of the cottage. Hal stepped out onto the porch and took hold of the reins.

"How did she do?" Hal asked.

"Gladys was an angel," Aaron replied.

Hal nodded, petting her neck, "She is a good girl. You mind if I take the kids for a ride before I let Pete know she can head back and spend the rest of Christmas day with her team?"

"I think that would be a great idea!" Cara agreed.

Annie and Chase rushed out and piled into the sleigh.

Hal leaned back, "You guys ready? Alright Gladys, let's show these kids what you can do!"

Once more, the jingle bells were announcing the sleigh's progress. The kids squealed in delight as they glided down the path.

Aaron and Cara watched them from the porch as they sailed along. "I don't think I could have dreamed a more perfect day," Cara said, leaning into her husband.

"This one would be tough to beat," Aaron agreed.

"Kids are happy. I'm happy," Cara added.

"What a year," Aaron sighed.

They watched the sleigh glide by for its ascent up to the ridge, waving at a pair of deliriously happy children as it passed.

Heading inside the cottage, they were greeted by a train, making a circuit around the tree. A car just ahead of the caboose, was diligently hauling Christmas trees.

Next to the window, which framed Chase's go-kart perfectly, was Annie's easel. Her first masterpiece was displayed. At the top of the paper was a sign that mimicked the Tree Farm sign by the road.

Underneath the sign was a scene of the farm. Starting with the lit trees on the ridge, swirling down to the cottage with a sleigh out front, she captured the farm. Moving down the sheet, she drew the barn with a giant wreath over the doors. Her favorite parts were Hal's home with the farmer on the porch and the store with the red farm truck with evergreen sticking out of the bed.

Amidst the structures and the ridge, were trees, lots of trees. Hidden in the scene were four family members. One was making a snow angel, another was building a snowman, another sledding down the hill, and the fourth one was painting the scene on her new Christmas easel.

Hearing jingle bells arrive from the distance, Aaron and Chase walked out onto the porch. Hal and Gladys brought the children home.

"That was so fun!" the kids cried.

Hal helped them out and let them pet Gladys. Clearly a highlight of Annie's day.

"Thanks again, Hal," Cara said.

"Don't mention it," Hal waved them off.

"For everything," Aaron pressed.

Hal laughed. "Seriously, don't mention it. You guys are like family now. Even if not, this is how we treat neighbors out here on the hill anyway," Hal said.

"I like that," Aaron nodded.

"So, I'll see you for dinner?" Hal asked.

"We'll come early to help you cook," Cara offered.

"I would argue, but I have learned that there is no point," Hal smiled.

Sixty Five

Following a busy Christmas day, the Shepherds cleaned up before heading to Hal's home for dinner. Dressing in their most Christmas worthy attire, they headed to the main house.

Knocking on the door, they were quickly met by Hal, who had holiday beverages in each Shepherd's hand by the time they had taken their jackets off. "I have games for the kids on the kitchen table so we can all be together when we cook. I have ham in the smoker out back and prime rib in the oven," Hal informed them as they joined him towards the kitchen.

"Sounds...and smells delicious," Aaron commented. "What can we help with?"

"It looks like you brought Christmas cookies..."

"And fudge!" Annie added.

"One of you want to work on the root vegetables, the other on green vegetables?" Hal asked.

"I've got the green vegetables. Brussel sprouts and bacon?" Aaron asked.

"I can hardly wait," Hal said.

Cara suggested, "If one of you strong men don't mind splitting the rutabaga, I'll get it and the potatoes going."

Rolling up their sleeves, Aaron, Cara and Hal worked to get dinner ready while Annie and Chase played games. When dinner was nearly ready, the children cleared the table, washed up, and started setting the table.

Finding their places, the kids waited as Hal brought out the meats, with Cara and Aaron in tow with the vegetables and starches. Gathered, they linked hands and bowed their heads. Hal indicated to Aaron if he wouldn't mind saying grace.

Aaron took a breath, "Dear Father, we are grateful to be together, celebrating the birth of your one and only son, the savior of the world. We are delighted to be able to have come together as a family and expand what family is to us, including Hal. To be able to live your message and your plan in the community in whatever way we can, whether large or small.

We are grateful to always find provision, even in bleak times, and when we rely on faith instead of our strength alone, things work out well, as you would have them.

Lord, we pray that you look after the families that travel this evening and keep them safe with hearts that are warmed with your grace.
Bless the food and those who have prepared it. Amen."

"Amen," Hal echoed. "Let's eat!"

Carving up the ham and the prime rib, serving the rutabaga and potatoes, piling on the Brussel sprouts cooked with bacon, Hal and the Shepherds enjoyed their Christmas feast.

"This is the best Christmas dinner I have had in years," Hal said.

"It is delicious," Aaron agreed.

"And your kids eat Brussel sprouts. I have to say, I wasn't sure, but you lured me in with the bacon and didn't disappoint. These are excellent," Hall added.

"Yeah, Dad tricked me with that, but I have liked them ever since," Chase said.

Hal laughed, "You have brought such a sense of family to the farm, to me. Neither have enjoyed that sense in a long time, since Laura."

"Oh, Hal, you are definitely part of our family," Cara assured.

"You're pretty good around this place, this was our best year....ever...by a vast margin," Hal informed.

"We were glad to pitch in," Aaron said modestly.

"It's more than that, seeing the way you care for each other. The way you care for this community, for me... You brought this farm back to life, so much more than it ever has been. You mean so much to this community. I, I would like you to have the farm," Hal said.

Aaron frowned and shook his head, "What? Hal, I know you want to sell the property. I saw the papers when I grabbed your camera. I'm sorry, I didn't open the document..."

Hal laughed, "I was afraid that you might blubber on about how you can't accept it. So, I had these papers drawn up. You get the land, the house, the trees, and to pay for it, you give me 10% of the net profits each year. Now, I would like you to put 10% of the proceeds into a charity of your choice, your church, you decide."

"Hal, you're right, we can't accept. I appreciate the idea, but..." Aaron protested.

Hal waved his hands in front of him, "Hear me out. I am ready for retirement. Even with the money to hire a crew, my old bones are ready for rest. As amazing as this season was, I certainly felt that the time has come. I realized how tired I was running this place, right before you came on. I just love it so much. I couldn't let it go. Seeing you all here and putting so much of your hearts into it, well, I realized all I really wanted was to see it into good hands."

"Maybe you can hire me on, as your right hand," Aaron suggested.

"No. I think that may have crossed my mind at one point, but I think I was overestimating what I could still do here. What I need is to feel good about the farm's legacy, not see it run over by a big commercial operation," Hal countered. "What do you say? Will you help an old man into retirement?"

Aaron and Cara exchanged glances, their eyes confirming what the other was thinking. "That would be amazing, we have fallen in love with the farm, but..."

"Don't worry about me. I have been sitting on some stock for decades now. I never looked into it, but my accountant keeps telling me I am rather wealthy, well, wealthy enough."

Aaron and Cara's minds reeled.

"Please, don't make me ask you again."

Aaron looked at Annie and Chase, "What do you guys think?"

"Yes!" the kids exclaimed, jumping out of their seats and hugging their parents. Aaron and Cara urged Hal to join the family hug.

"Good. Now that that is settled, I'd like to note a few provisions. If it would be alright, I would like to move into the cottage. I would like to be here through next season. Work with you all the way through, and then, I will determine my next step. Thinking maybe one of those all-inclusive places somewhere warm," Hal raised his eyebrows.

"You will always have a home here with us, you're family, after all," Cara grinned.

Sixty Six

Annie and Chase collapsed asleep, exhausted from a long, fun-filled day. Aaron and Cara bundled up, stepping out onto the porch. Wrapping his arms around his wife, Aaron gazed out upon the farm.

"What do you think?" he asked.

"It's all so hard to believe, to take in," Cara shrugged.

"It is. Wonderful to wake up to every day. This place has been good for our family," Aaron said.

"It has. According to Hal, we've been good for the farm, too," Cara offered.

"I hope so. I just don't want Hal caught up in the romance of the season and have second thoughts," Aaron said.

Cara turned to look at her husband, "I don't see Hal as one to mince words or waiver."

"Yeah, I suppose that's true," Aaron acknowledged. He sighed as he watched snowflakes fall, twinkling off of the Christmas lights as they settled over the tree farm.

"This place is…amazing," Aaron said. "The kids love it here, too."

"A Christmas prayer answered," Cara nodded.

"My Christmas prayer was answered the day I came back from Chicago to you and the kids," Aaron admitted.

"Merry Christmas, Aaron."

"Merry Christmas, Cara."